THE TRUTH ABOUT
Triangles

ALSO BY MICHAEL LEALI

The Civil War of Amos Abernathy

Matteo

THE TRUTH ABOUT
Triangles

MICHAEL LEALI

HARPER

An Imprint of HarperCollinsPublishers

Library of Congress Control Number: 2023943360
ISBN 978-0-06-333736-7

Typography by Corina Lupp
24 25 26 27 28 LBC 5 4 3 2 1
First Edition

For my grandparents

Chapter 1

Most kids go home after school. Not me and my twin siblings, Nina and Elio.

We book it to Mamma Gianna's, the pizzeria Ma's family has owned for three generations. When Nonna Zaza retired and moved to Florida two years ago, Ma and Pop took over, which means me, Nina, and Elio did too.

Our beloved redbrick pizzeria is a one-mile hike from Riverfront Junior High; Eagle View Elementary is the midpoint between the two. So every weekday, I pick up the twins, who are in fourth grade, and shepherd them to Mamma Gianna's thumb-smudged door with the broken bell. Today is no exception. I shove my sibs out of the cold January wind into the warm, garlic-infused air. Mamma mia, it smells like heaven.

"Ma, we're here!" I shout.

Our mother's brunette blowout, gold hoop earrings, and signature red lips burst through the kitchen doorway. Not a hair is out of place, but from the way her nostrils flare, I can tell she's in a mood. *Madone. Here we go.*

"You're late," she says. "We open in thirty, I don't have any cutlery rolled 'cause the dishwasher broke down, we've got a party of seventeen blue hairs coming in right at five, which is the most business we've seen all week and we desperately need it, and your father's nowhere in sight." She grumbles something about Pop under her breath that I can't make out, and then she rampages on. "You're all going straight to work. No lip, you hear! Nina, Elio, grab the napkins and the bin of clean forks and knives from Cesar and get rolling. Luca, I need you on dough. Your father was supposed to start a batch more than an hour ago, but—"

I raise my hands in surrender. "Ma! I'm on it, I'm on it!"

"Grazie, Luca." She looks like I handed her a gallon of water after taking a day trip through the Sahara. Then her face snaps to my little brother. Her right hand shakes at him, fingers pressed together, thumb and forefinger pinched into a perfect O. We call this . . . *the Ciao.* A one-handed *ciao* is fine, but two means business. "Elio, what's with the fac?"

Fac is Italian American slang for face. The *c* makes a "ch" sound that bites the air.

Elio's pouted lip and thick, scowling eyebrows don't let up. "I'm supposed to hang with Eddie. He got a puppy just like the one I want. Can't you hire people to work here, like a normal restaurant?"

Ma takes a single step through the doorway. Her hands hit her hips. "*You* the owner of this joint? *You* gonna pay someone, Elio? Maybe we take it out of your allowance, huh?"

Since Ma and Pop nixed the puppy idea from ever happening, Elio's been saving for a hermit crab for months. He's obsessed with getting a pet, but the kid can barely take care of *himself.*

His jaw drops. "NO, no. I got it, I got it."

"Then hang up your backpack and roll." Ma claps her hands and disappears into the kitchen shouting, "Andiamo! Let's go!"

Elio groans. "Why can't we have a normal life?"

Nina slides past him, snickering in his ear. "Normal's for kids who don't snore like a forty-year-old man."

"I do *not* snore!" He shoves her shoulder.

Lord, give me patience.

In a single fluid motion, I wedge myself between them and smack 'em both upside the head. They wince in unison, cradling their skulls like I bludgeoned them with a frying pan even though I hit them with all the force of a duckling swishing its tail feathers.

"Basta!" I say. "Save it for later. We've got less than thirty minutes before doors open. How about we make it a competition? First one to roll the most utensils decides what we're eating for dinner."

3

"Oo! I want tacos!" Elio hurls his backpack at the wall hook behind the register. Then he launches into the kitchen, shouting to our single employee. "Cesar, can I get the forks and knives?"

"Hello to you too," Cesar says. He's about forty, Mexican American, and has the best laugh. He's worked at Mamma Gianna's for as long as I can remember.

"Hi, Cesar!" Nina bolts after our brother. "Elio! We had tacos last night."

Elio's voice blares. "You can never have enough tacos!"

Madonna mia. A sharp pain tingles behind my right temple. I massage it with my index and middle finger. I hang up my backpack, mentally prepping pizza dough in my head while simultaneously trying to predict where Pop is and how to smooth over whatever's going on between him and Ma. The stress of the restaurant has really been wearing them down. On top of all this, I try not to think about the gobs of math and English homework looming like the Leaning Tower of Pisa, waiting to topple me when I finally get home tonight.

Elio and Nina slide past me through the kitchen doorway, a bundle of fresh napkins and a bin of cutlery between them. She bosses him and he pouts, but I ignore their bickering since they're getting the job done.

I catch Ma quick before she has a chance to lose herself in the spreadsheets open on her laptop. "So, uh, did you taste the pizza I left you?"

Her nose wrinkles. She mutters something about electric bills, eyes bouncing between the numbers locked in little white rectangles.

"Ma?" I nudge. "Did you try the tortellini pizza I made? I know it's a little weird, but I think it could be a hit if we added it to the menu—"

"What? Oh, sorry, hon. I didn't have a chance," she says, the words drawn out, like she's only using fifty percent of her brain to answer me. Which makes sense, since she's still death-glaring the spreadsheet. (Her budget *and* her arch nemesis.)

I press a little further. "A new menu item could boost sales if—"

Now she looks at me. "Luca, what did I say? Stick to what we know. Okay? Now, the dough. Please?" Her chin sinks into her palms, and she's nose deep in her computer again.

My lips twist to the side of my face. I sniff. I nod. I know Ma well enough that this conversation is over.

Someday she'll hear me. Someday she'll actually try *my* pizzas and get that I'm trying to help her. My pizzas are good. No—they're freaking *great*. But I worry she'll never know.

With a sigh, I grab a clean apron and a hairnet. When I put them on, I feel like a superhero dressing in his mask and cape. The kitchen is my metropolis for the rescuing, and pizza prep is my superpower.

Before I start more dough, I check the rise on the batch we'll use for tonight's orders. I pop the top of a container holding the golden dough balls. Yeasty goodness fills my nose. My stomach gurgles. I love that bready smell. I press my finger into a plastic-wrapped sphere. A shadowy crater appears. Wrinkles like a nonna's smile fill the space. Then the sticky, spongy substance springs back.

Satisfied, I grab the flour, sugar, yeast, salt, olive oil, and potatoes. Yeah, you heard me right. Potatoes are the ingredient that makes our dough so special. My great-grandma, the famous Mamma Gianna, learned to add potatoes to the recipe from *her* great-grandma. I can't explain why it works so well, but it does. Our dough is light and fluffy, and the crust bubbles a little at the edges, especially when we brush it with garlic butter.

As I peel potatoes to get them boiling, I imagine Travis Parker—my celebrity crush and host of my favorite streaming series, *Pizza Perfect*—narrating my actions.

"Watch how Luca Salvatore expertly shaves the russet potato, leaving the bulk of the vegetable for use. Next, he'll boil them so he can blend the starch into the dough, just before he adds the yeast."

Man, I'd give my left freaking lung to meet Travis Parker. To be on his show. For him to eat *my* pizza. *Pizza Perfect* has been showcasing pizza joints all over the United States for six seasons now. When a pizzeria is featured, it blows up big. But that's not all—every episode he does this bit called the "Pizza Perfect Challenge." The pizzeria serves up their best pizza. He rates it on his trademarked *Pizza Perfect* scale, and depending on where it ranks, Travis Parker gives the pizzeria anything from a new stove to a kitchen makeover to a check for $10,000.

Ever since we took over, Mamma Gianna's has been struggling. A couple pizza chains moved in nearby, and Ma and Pop just can't agree on marketing or specials. Or *anything*. It would change everything if we were on his show. We'd have a chance at fame *and* some serious dough. Ma and Pop might actually chill out. Act like real parents again. But there's no way Travis Parker would ever come here—we're too small and clinging to the fringes of Chicago proper, which is home to a bajillion famous pizzerias.

If there's one thing I, Luca Salvatore, do not do, it's give up hope. Not on my family or my pizza. Someday people all around the world will know my name and my delicious pies, even the ones off menu. No—*especially* the ones off menu. And when that happens, Travis Parker will *have* to put Mamma Gianna's on his show.

I dump peeled potato chunks into a pot of boiling water. While ghostly curls of steam rise into the air, I measure out the flour, sugar, and salt. I get the dry ingredients mixing, the metal arm scraping against the silver bowl.

I'm forking a potato chunk to see if it's tender enough

to mash when a key clicks in the lock of the back door. The hinges squeak. Pop appears in his dirty jeans, his navy-blue winter coat, which is unzipped, revealing a stained graphic T-shirt. The few dark wisps left on his scalp are windblown. His normal five-o'clock shadow has overstayed its welcome by a day or two. If I'm being honest, it looks as bad as mold on a week-old pie, especially that neck beard. *Eek.* Ma hates when he doesn't keep it trimmed.

"Luca, hey," he says, nodding to the mixer. "You got the dough going?"

"Good to see you too." I want to ask him where he's been, but I don't. Too close to opening for casual conversation. "I could use some help."

"Gimme a minute, kiddo," he says. "I've been on the phone with the credit card company for the last two hours. Your mother spent—"

"Gio!" Ma appears out of nowhere. I swear she's got better snooping skills than the CIA. She shouts at Pop, hands flailing in a double *ciao.* (*Uh-oh.*) "What's the matter with you? We open in five. Nothing's ready!"

Pop hunkers down like a bull noticing a red cape. "I would've been here sooner if I wasn't cleaning up your mess, Christine. Maxing out a card after we talked—"

"How'd you expect us to pay for parts to fix the fridge?" she snaps. "And fill the pantry? *And* that last shipment of pizza boxes? "Are *you* gonna get a second job while I run this place? 'Cause I can't do more than the two I already got."

"Selling makeup on the side is hardly a second job," Pop scoffs.

While they bicker like contestants on a reality cooking show that is our actual LIFE, I strain the potatoes, dump them into the mixer, and turn it on full blast. *Whir-CLANK-scrape! Whir-CLANK-scrape!* They fought before we took over Mamma Gianna's, but owning a restaurant has turned up the volume on their fighting to a deafening level. Even louder than this ancient, obnoxious mixer apparently.

You'd think they'd take the hint, but they only shout louder over the machine's noise. My eyes track the second hand on the clock, the same ancient one Mamma Gianna got when she opened the place. It's six and half minutes fast, but no one's ever bothered to fix it. Nonna Zaza used to say it keeps us on our toes. But right now, it's telling me we've got seconds before a party of seventeen's gonna come pouring in.

I smash the off button on the mixer. The sudden silence prickles my skin. It does the trick for Ma and Pop too. They look at me like they just realized I'm standing here.

Now that I've got their attention, it's time for me to become the parent whisperer. A job I've gotten pretty good at in the past couple years.

"Guys, we've gotta open any second," I say calmly, but

with a firmness that makes me feel like I'm *their* parent. I stare down my dad. "Pop, you know we can't get by without a working fridge. Ma did what had to be done." Then my neck cranks to Ma. "And somebody's gotta figure out a plan with the credit card company. We all know money's tight. We've gotta stretch the dough where we can, am I right?"

Ma glares at the ceiling. Pop sniffs, scratches the side of his nose.

Their silence is a good thing. That means they're listening. Now for the kicker.

"We've got a big, *money-spending* party coming in," I say, stretching my arms wide, fingers reaching, like I'm trying to pull the two of them together with just my mind and my words. "We've gotta give them the best Salvatore-run Mamma Gianna's experience they could ask for. Let's earn big tips, bigger word-of-mouth advertising, and get our place back on the map. What do you say? Eh?"

The phone rings before either of them can answer. Ma presses the cordless to her ear. "Thank you for calling Mamma Gianna's world-famous pizzeria. This is Christine speaking. How can I help you?"

Ma only uses her trademark Dazzlingly Bright voice with customers. Never for me or the twins. Definitely not Pop. When she's got patrons in front of her, she transforms into this ultra-accommodating, soft-spoken alien.

Lips zipped, Pop and I watch Ma's cheery smile droop

as she listens to whoever's on the other end. The longer she doesn't say anything, the more worried I get.

Finally, she says, "Well, I hope we see you some other time. Thank you. Yes, you too. Thank you. Buh-bye now. Yes, uh-huh. Buh-bye." She hangs up.

"What was that?" I ask.

Ma pinches the bridge of her nose. "Our party of seventeen just canceled. Flu's going around the old folks' home. Too many sick for them to come." She curses in English, then Italian. "We really needed this! The week's been too slow. We're gonna be way under."

"Again," Pop says under his breath.

"Don't remind me, Gio!"

I shout over them. "Guys, hey!" The used tissue sticking out of Pop's jacket pocket gets me thinking. I step closer. "Ma, was it the head cold flu or the stomach flu?"

She fidgets with her left hoop earring. "I didn't ask."

"Well, call 'em back and see. If it's just sniffles and body chills, they still gotta eat, right?" I turn to my dad. "Pop can deliver. I'll go with and help carry the pizzas in. Who knows, maybe they'll order more for the workers since we're delivering?"

We used to have a delivery guy named John, but we had to let him go last month because things are too tight. We only seem to make enough to cover the basic bills. Ma and Pop have pretty much exhausted our savings to keep the restaurant going. Now they trade off driving around town, dropping off orders, but it gets tricky juggling us kids, managing the restaurant, and random stuff like when Elio gets a bloody nose or a circuit shorts. They only just started letting me babysit this year, but they know I'm good in the kitchen, so lots of the time we all end up here. We just don't have enough hands to manage it all.

"That's not a bad idea, Luca," Pop says. "What do you say, Christine?"

Ma nods. "Worth a shot." She marches out of the kitchen, phone in hand, shouting for the twins to stop rolling and start folding pizza boxes.

Instead of following Ma, Pop tells me the minivan's nearly on empty so he's gotta go fill up in case we gotta deliver tonight. He walks back out the door he came in. A clump of pale-yellow dough drops off the metal spatula in the mixing bowl when the door slams shut.

I turn it back on, grinning to myself. Once again, Luca Salvatore worked things out. Creamy potatoes churn into the dusty white flour, sugar, and salt. Humming, I drizzle in olive oil, then a bowl of warm water and yeast. A thick, earthy scent fills the kitchen. A few more spins, and the dough glows like sunlit amber. Pockets of air make circular indents as the dough pulls apart, comes together, and pulls apart again. I get sort of mesmerized by it.

When everything in my life is riding the hot-mess

express—Ma and Pop, Nina and Elio, Mamma Gianna's—making a pizza is the only thing that feels right. From dough to sauce to toppings, I'm in control. I can make it right.

Thing is, there's just too many things to make right. Saving Mamma Gianna's from going under. Keeping my parents from fighting. Getting them to parent Nina and Elio so I can get back to my one true passion: perfecting the pizza.

Sometimes it's overwhelming—all the have-tos, all the different things I've gotta fix—like a pizza stacked with too many toppings. The weight of it piles up on my chest. It gets hard to breathe.

But I hear Travis Parker's voice in my head: *"Pizzas are made one ingredient at a time. Slow it down, Luca. You got this."*

I flick the mixer off. "You're right, Travis," I say out loud. "One ingredient at a time. I'll make this pizza *perfect*."

Ma's head pokes through the kitchen doorway. "We got it, Luca. Giant order for the old folks' home, plus some for the workers. We're gonna be all right tonight. Good thinking, kiddo." At the sound of the front door creaking open, she disappears, off to greet whoever's decided Mamma Gianna's is on the menu.

And me? I keep doing what I do, and all is right in the world.

Chapter 2

The temperature drops like a sledgehammer. Pop and I bundle up in scarves, gloves, and jackets (fully zipped) to trek into the freezing, snowy night. We deliver seven large and two medium pizzas, a chopped salad, and two orders of garlic bread to Sunshine Retirement Home around six o'clock. I shiver as I hand off the bags of salad and garlic bread to the worker who greets us in scrubs and a surgical mask. She's so grateful that we were willing to deliver that she gives Pop and I a 40 percent tip. In CASH. That never happens. Most customers tip twenty percent, and a lot of customers never tip, which is rude as heck. (ALWAYS. TIP.)

When we get back in the car, Pop turns the key in the ignition, heat blasting in our faces, and then he hands me a twenty. "You deserve this," he says, "for your quick thinking today."

Most kids would grab the cash and dash, but I push it back at him. "It can go to the restaurant."

"Seriously," he says, shoving it back at me. "You've earned a little something for yourself. Twenty bucks isn't gonna change whether the lights stay on."

Travis Parker *does* have a new cookbook coming out in a month . . . but then I think about the argument Ma and Pop just had a few hours ago about the broken refrigerator. And I know our landlord for Mamma Gianna's, Mr. Cheeks, has been blowing up Ma's phone lately, which is never good. I suspect we're behind on rent. Again.

I shake my head. "Keep it. Every little bit helps."

I slide my phone out of my pocket and open Instagram as a hint that this conversation is over. Pop catches my drift. Wagging his head, he stuffs the cash into his coat pocket and shifts into reverse. The wheels crunch on salt and ice as he says, "You're one in a million, Luca Salvatore. Don't know what your mother and I did to deserve a kid like you."

I don't stop scrolling through my feed, but I say, "This's what family does. We take care of each other. It's no big thing."

"Still," Pop says, throwing on his turn signal.

My eye catches on a new video from one of my favorite *Pizza Perfect* fan accounts—PizzaPaulie07. He's a mega-fan like me. PizzaPaulie07's face—pale complexion, ruddy nose, and coiffed chestnut hair—fills the rectangle. Small silver hoops glint in his earlobes. There's something off about his expression, though. I can't tell if he looks happy or sad.

The text below the post has the red siren emojis and says, "BREAKING PP UPDATE!!!" I tap the video, sound on.

PizzaPaulie07's brash voice fills our car. "What's up, Pizza People? *Pizza Perfect*'s number one fan"—LIES. *I'm* the number one fan, but I'll forgive PizzaPaulie07 for the confusion . . . *this time*—"coming at you with an update about our show that's fresh out of the oven, and it's a DOOZY." He drags his hand down his face, pausing. I don't like that pause. "I can't believe I'm saying this, but after six pizza-tastic seasons—"

My stomach drops. I pause the video. My head whips to Pop, whose eyes are squinting at the road. "He's not gonna say what I think he's gonna say, is he?"

Pop snort laughs. "I'm no psychic, but, uh, yeah, I think I know where this is headed."

"Mamma mia. Please let us be wrong."

I tap the video. PizzaPaulie07's face reanimates saying, "*Pizza Perfect* . . . is coming to an end. Now, don't get me wrong. We haven't seen an *official* announcement of the show's cancellation yet, but my source—my very *reliable* source—says we should hear something in the next few days. Sorry, pizza people. Today's a sad day for all pizza-dom. I'll be back with more details as they come out. Until then, Pizza Paulie out!"

The video ends, a shaded filter darkens his face, and a replay button appears. I let my screen fade to black. The headlights of oncoming traffic are much brighter all of a sudden.

"You okay, Luca?" Pop asks, turning onto Jefferson Avenue. The windshield wipers swish away a dusting of snowflakes.

"I just—" My fingers squeeze around my phone case. I stare at the dark screen, hoping a notification will appear to tell me it's a practical joke. But it stays dark. "You don't expect your favorite things to end, you know?"

"I mean, it might just be a rumor," Pop says.

"Maybe, but PizzaPaulie07 usually knows what's up. I think he's friends with one of the crew or something." Oh, man. It would SUCK if *Pizza Perfect* ended. I look forward to a new season every year. I have my whole life. And it's not just that—my dream of being on the show would be obliterated.

I shake my head. "It's stupid . . . but I really thought we'd be on it someday." The words sound ridiculous out loud. It's impossible that our tiny hole-in-the-wall restaurant would catch Travis Parker's eye, but still. Embarrassment gets the better of me. I suck my lips inside my mouth and turn my face to the window.

Pop adjusts in his seat, squirming a little taller against the headrest. His gloved hands grip the steering wheel tighter. "Maybe there's something better headed your way." He clears his throat. "Sometimes things have gotta come to an end, you know? Even good things."

I stare out the passenger window. My breath fogs the glass. The lights of the passing businesses blur. "Good things shouldn't end."

"Maybe not, but sometimes endings can be beginnings too," Pop says, articulating each word like he really means it. He sniffs. "But hey, until Travis Parker announces something, I don't think you should worry about it."

I shrug. "Maybe."

We drive in silence the rest of the way, but my mind spins out on the idea of *Pizza Perfect* getting canceled. I only sort of come out of it when Dad pulls into his usual spot in front of Mamma Gianna's and says, "Thanks, Saint Anthony."

It's a thing he does, thanking or asking saints for things. Saint Anthony is the patron saint of parking spots, I guess. Technically my family is Catholic, but we only go to Mass on Easter and Christmas, especially now that we run the pizzeria. Ma and I aren't all that up on church stuff, but Pop is pretty religious. Just one more thing he and Ma can't seem to agree on.

When Pop puts the car in park, he turns to me and says, "You don't have to pretend to be okay, Luca. Upsetting things can be upsetting."

For a moment, I almost buckle. As we drove, I realized it wasn't just the *Pizza Perfect* rumor that was bothering me.

It was Ma ignoring me. Not tasting my tortellini pizza. The idea that if I can't even get a pizza on my family's restaurant's menu, what chance do I—*did* I—really have of getting on Travis Parker's show?

For some reason, it's easier talking to Pop than it is to Ma, but he's usually so wound up in his own garbage that he doesn't ever *really* hear me, even when he asks me what's up. So I lie. "I'm fine."

"You sure?" he says.

"Yeah." I open the car door and hop out before I have to say anything else. Bitter wind bites my nose. My eyes water. I hustle to the front door and bust inside without waiting for Pop. I just need to get back to my pizza, and everything will be all right.

Chapter 3

Look, I get that you can't believe everything on the internet, but PizzaPaulie07 isn't some rando. His rumor about *Pizza Perfect* getting canceled doesn't sit well with me all night. My stomach cramps like I ate spoiled red sauce. Around five in the morning, I can't stand lying in bed thinking about all I'll miss out on if *Pizza Perfect* no longer exists. No pizza fame. No meeting Travis Parker. I mean, the show is the ultimate test of a pizza chef. If it's gone, I don't stand a chance of joining the pizza greats!

I tiptoe downstairs and my stomach sours even more when I find Pop asleep on the couch, a half-full beer bottle next to him on the coffee table. He's zonked out, his face ostriched into the cushions. One of our ratty old comforters covers everything but his socked feet. I creep past him, making for the kitchen (my favorite room, *obviously*). This happens sometimes. Ma makes Pop sleep on the couch after they've had a fight. But it's weird—I don't remember them getting into it more than they usually do last night.

Mamma mia. It's always something.

The tile floor in the kitchen is ice-cold. After I quietly open the blinds to look out into the purple snowy morning, I plop down on the heater vent, pulling my oversized pajama shirt over my knees. Warm air billows between my legs and makes my body tingle, but in a good way. I pull out my phone, turn the volume to a whisper, and open a random episode of *Pizza Perfect.*

Every episode is set up the same way. The first segment is always about the literal and metaphorical dough of the joint. Travis Parker talks with the owners about their foundation, their history. How they came to be. From there, he gets into the mucky, saucy middle: the savory ups and downs of the business. The final segment tops off (Get it? Like *toppings?*) the show by talking about the future of the restaurant. Their dreams. Their hopes. The final moment of the show, however, is the Pizza Perfect Challenge, where the restaurant serves up their most winning slice and Travis Parker decides just how Pizza Perfect it is.

Pop gorilla-trudges into the kitchen as I'm getting to the saucy section of an episode about a pizzeria in Tucson, Arizona. He yelps mid-yawn when he sees me huddled on the floor.

"Luca! What're you doing?"

"Couldn't sleep." I close my video app. "What were you doing on the couch?"

He shakes his head, reaching for the cabinet with the

coffee. "Don't worry about it."

Um. Does he even know me? Worry is my freaking middle name. (Just kidding. It's Massimo, after Pop's dad, but that's not the point.) I hug my knees closer to my chest. "You sure? I thought—"

Pop yawns again, spooning charcoal-colored grinds into the coffee maker. "Luc, I'm barely conscious. Too many words."

I never do get my answer as to why Pop was on the couch. When the twins and Ma wake up, we roll into our usual morning chaos of microwave breakfast, hasty showers, backpack filling, and tornado-ing out the door. But I'm still feeling off by the time I get to school, and now it's not just the threat of *Pizza Perfect* getting canceled that's bugging me—it's whatever's going on with Ma and Pop too.

"My dreams of pizza stardom might officially be over," I groan to June Mason, my best friend since kindergarten, on our way to our favorite class: Culinary Arts. Second semester of the class started last week when we came back from winter break. This semester we get to start *advanced* recipes.

June looks up from her phone. She's pretty with a long, pale oval face and blueberry-blue eyes. This past summer, she grew like a tomato plant on Uncle Tony's special fertilizer. At five foot three, she beats me by a whole inch. A strand of blond hair falls past her ear as she asks, "What now?"

She emphasizes "now" like I'm some living, breathing natural disaster. Which I'm not. Natural disasters are just attracted to me. Like mosquitoes. (*Also* a natural disaster, if you ask me.) It's not my fault there's more drama in my life than in an Italian opera.

I sigh, fidgeting with my backpack straps. "It's almost too awful to say out loud."

June's cell phone falls to her hip. Her voice drops. "Did something happen? Is it the twins? Your parents?"

When is it *not* my parents? But I don't want to get into *them* right now. My hands drag down the sides of my face like that creepy *The Scream* painting Mr. Dawdle showed us in Art last year. "Worse. Last night, I heard—oh, man, I can't even say it." I take a deep breath and hold it. June rolls her eyes and starts to look back at her phone. I cave and come out with it. "There's a rumor that, after six absolutely unbelievably amazing seasons, *Pizza Perfect* . . . is ending." I fling myself at her shoulder and heave a sob. (The tears might be fake, but the feels are legit.)

She pries me off, snorting. "Omg. *Tragic.*"

My head snaps up. "Sarcasm so not appreciated right now. If the rumor's true, I'm going into MOURNING."

June holds open the door to our culinary classroom. "And I thought *I* was the drama queen. It's just a show, Luca. It's not like Travis Parker *died.*"

"Bite your tongue!" I breeze past her. "This might mean

my life will forever be incomplete, that I'll never achieve my dream of being on *Pizza Perfect*."

"You could start your own YouTube channel," she says, dropping her seriously unsympathetic attitude. "Or, like, post cooking videos online? Maybe that would catch someone's attention. You could start a new series! Once I get a little better, that's what I'm going to do with my singing. I can see it now: a casting director will see me, marvel at my talent, and fly me out to audition for a Broadway show."

"I don't think that's how it works," I say, pausing for dramatic emphasis. "But you might be onto something." I *fwump* into my seat at our workstation at the front of the room.

The period bell rings. Mrs. Ochoa, our Culinary Arts teacher, flaps her hands at us to quiet down. She's short with straight black hair that falls past her shoulders. Her skin is rich brown, and she's got a mole on the left side of her nose. She's wearing a white apron over her "Riverfront ROCKS" T-shirt. Mrs. Ochoa gets super into school spirit. Lots of teachers are all business, wearing dresses or dress shirts and ties on the daily, but Mrs. O legit only wears Riverfront Junior High gear. I don't know what I'd do if I saw her in something other than burgundy and silver.

"Before we jump into making crème brûlée," she says, "I want to introduce a new member of our class. Everyone, this is Wilbur White."

I was so hung up on my pizza woes that I missed the boy standing next to her, but now that I see him, I do an actual double take. Wilbur White is . . . very nice looking.

Which makes me drop my red notebook with all my recipe ideas onto the floor. I fumble picking it up and drop it again. *Mamma mia, Luca.* SO AWKWARD. I'm pretty sure everyone is watching me flail like a T. rex on a balance beam. I focus my eyes on the stained linoleum, but they keep bubbling up to look at the new kid.

Wilbur's shorter than me, with ivory skin and dark brown almond-shaped eyes. He looks like he might be Asian, but I'm not sure. He's got pristine black hair that's salon-quality combed and parted. Seriously. It's shiny and thick as a model's in a Pantene commercial.

Madonna mia, he's . . . very nice looking.

Behind me, Anya Morrison chuckles. "*Wilbur.* Like the pig from *Charlotte's Web.*"

A few kids laugh, but not me. Who cares what his name is? Look at that hair! That chin. Those cheeks, which are turning red. It doesn't seem like Mrs. Ochoa heard Anya's stupid joke, but I want to feed her and the rest of the gigglers a knuckle sandwich.

It's clear Wilbur knows the giggling's about him. He says, "It's Will, actually."

So confident. So *cool.*

"Oh, okay." Mrs. Ochoa scribbles something on her

clipboard. "Will. Got it. Well, we're thrilled you're here, *Will*. We just formed new cooking groups at semester start last week, so you got here just in time. Let's see. I'll have you join . . ." Her finger trails down her clipboard.

I bite my lip. My knee jiggles. Part of me hopes she says my name, and part of me doesn't.

At last, she says, "How about June and Luca? Right over there. Wave to Will, kids!"

Omg. Can Mrs. Ochoa read minds?

June waves like a Miss America contestant. My fingers wiggle like squid tentacles. My hand shakes as I wave the new kid over. Our eyes lock for a second, and it's like getting struck by lightning. *Did he feel that too?* Then I feel so self-conscious about shaking that my ears heat up. That only makes me more embarrassed, so I end up sitting on my hands and staring at the desk by the time Will gets to our station. All of this happens in a matter of seconds, but it feels like an eternity.

"Hi," Will says. His voice hasn't dropped yet.

Before I can say anything, June extends her hand with a flourish. *Always* the star. "I'm June Mason. This is Luca Salvatore. I love your hair."

Slow-motion movie magic seizes the moment as Will White chuckles, runs his fingers through his hair, and it falls in ripples of ebony silk. I have a sudden and ridiculous urge to run my fingers through it too, but of course I don't

26

because that would be WEIRD. WHY WOULD I DO THAT? WHY WOULD I *WANT* TO DO THAT? WHAT THE WHAT IS HAPPENING TO ME? I breathe. *Cool it, Luca. Even your thoughts are embarrassed by you.*

"Uh, thanks," Will says. "But it's just, like, my hair, you know? Ha ha."

"I like hair," I say. The words are out before I can stop myself. *Oh God.*

Will gives me a weird look. "Cool?" He laughs awkwardly.

Then I laugh awkwardly.

And then it's just . . . awkward. Someone sous vide me already.

June swoops in to save the day. "Like I said, *great* hair. I'm, like, a little jealous. Mine never looks that shiny, not even when I use the expensive conditioner."

"What can I say?" Will laughs. "Good genes."

The rest of the period, I'm a total mess. I whisk the eggs like I've never beaten a yolk in my life, splattering yellow goo all over the place. I've gotta measure the sugar three times because I keep forgetting how many scoops I put in the bowl. And I can barely stack three coherent words together. Every time I talk, it's a nonsensical word salad. (*I like hair. GAH!*) Meanwhile, June's becoming Will's new best friend. And he keeps smiling at her. A lot.

That deflates my soufflé a little.

I've been out to my family and a few friends, like June, since sixth grade. Ma and Pop were a little surprised when I told them I'm gay ("So you're just friends with June?"), but they were (and *are*) so busy and distracted all the time with Mamma Gianna's that me liking boys was headline news for all of thirty seconds. They moved on. Or forgot. I honestly can't tell which.

One of the hardest things about being gay and having a super pretty best friend who's a girl is that anytime I think a boy might think I'm cute, he's *always* actually interested in her. And June gets a lot of attention. She didn't just get taller this past summer—she looks like more of a *woman* now, if you know what I mean. Sometimes she likes the attention, but most of the time she hates it. She's so not interested in dating or boys or any of that stuff. But with Will, she seems to like the attention. A lot. Which is weird.

Honestly, I don't even *want* to like-like anyone right now. I wouldn't even know what to do if I *did* like someone. But it would be nice to be noticed.

When class is over and Will leaves the room, June grabs my arm and whispers, "He's really nice."

My intestines twist like cold spaghetti. "I mean, I guess so?"

"He should definitely be our friend," she says. Then she seems to second-guess herself. "Right? Since he's new?" She chews her lip. "I wonder if I have any other classes with him."

"June, we barely know him," I say. "Let's see what he's like a little longer before we invite him into the BFC."

The Best Friends Club has always had two members: me and June. We briefly experimented with the idea of letting Brianna Graham into the BFC in fourth grade, but then she moved to San Francisco and no one since has lived up to her excellent braids or her mom's homemade brownies.

But the truth is . . . I totally want Will to be our friend too. Maybe it's time we reconsider our membership enrollment. He's cool. And funny. I'm only downplaying my excitement because hearing her talk about him like he's a pop star—it's annoying.

"Fine," she says. She turns right at the end of the hall to head to her honors math class, while I keep straight to my regular math class where we're studying triangles.

While Ms. Homer, my math teacher, is talking about scalene triangles and acute angles and varying degrees, all I can think about is Will White and June. Her saying nice things about his hair, his shoes, his teeth. Him saying nice things about her hair, her shoes, her teeth. Me rubbing egg goop off my shirt.

Then Ms. Homer shows a model of an isosceles triangle, and it looks so much like a pizza slice that my mind shifts entirely to daydreaming about being on *Pizza Perfect* and meeting Travis Parker.

While I'm supposed to be taking notes, I dream up new pizza recipes that might make my pizza idol's mouth water.

A waffle-inspired crust topped with fried chicken and a drizzle of savory maple syrup reduction. A white pizza with ribbons of salami, prosciutto, pepperoni, and dollops of creamy burrata. A mozzarella stuffed–crust pan pizza with hot giardiniera and Italian beef dripping in juice. Each idea gets me more excited than the last. Ma and Pop like to stick to the traditional recipes, but I like to dream big. The possibilities are endless. If only they'd let me try some of my ideas on our menu, I bet I could revolutionize our business.

And suddenly the bell is ringing while I'm in the middle of a pizza creation that involves hard-boiled eggs. (*Rude.*) It's like someone snapped their fingers. Whatever hypnotic spell I'd been under breaks.

I might not have any clue how to do the math problem on the board, but I have big ideas. And someday, television show or not, Travis Parker is gonna hear all about them.

Mark my words.

Chapter 4

"Hey, uh, can I sit here?"

I look up from hunting *Pizza Perfect* rumors on my phone Friday, surprised to see Will White standing next to me in the cafeteria. *How had I not noticed all week that we were in the same lunch period?* He's wearing a white oversized Harry Styles T-shirt and skinny jeans. A pearl necklace hangs loose around his neck. He looks just as cool as the pop icon screen-printed on his chest.

I'm so caught off guard that I dribble spaghetti sauce on my shirt. I dab it quickly with a napkin and say, "Yeah, yeah. Of course. Sit!"

Usually other kids only come around to talk to June, but she's not here yet. Which means: Will White wants to sit with *me. Why?* He plops his tray down: cheeseburger, carrot sticks, chocolate milk. "Whatcha looking at?" he asks, pointing at my phone.

I click it off, nervous he's gonna think I'm a giant nerd. "Oh, just some stuff for a show I like."

He chomps into a carrot stick. "Which one?"

"Uh, *Pizza Perfect*? It's this cooking show about pizzerias around the country. The host, Travis Parker, he's like a big—"

Will laughs. "Dude, I know what *Pizza Perfect* is. My mom and I watch it sometimes. We like cooking stuff. I mean, *obviously*. I'm in Culinary Arts, ha ha."

"Right," I say. Now I feel like an idiot for acting like he wouldn't know *Pizza Perfect*. "So, uh, how're you liking Riverfront?"

He shrugs. "It's fine. Kinda miss my old friends, though."

"Yeah, that's gotta be hard."

"It is what it is." He unfolds the foil wrapper on his burger. "You're pretty impressive in cooking class. Seems like you know a lot."

OMG. He totally knows I'm a nerd. I twirl my cold leftover spaghetti. "Uh, thanks, ha ha. I cook. A lot."

"That's cool." He bites into his burger, and I melt a little. *He thinks I'm cool.* He goes on. "I like when people know how to do stuff. Make food, play music. Like, I've got my guitar and—"

"Will! What are you doing here?" June sits down across from us, bursting the bubble around this moment between me and him that I hadn't realized was a *moment* until now. Whenever June arrives, it's all lights on her. That's just how it goes. I don't usually mind, but this time . . . it's different. *Will* is different.

She rambles for a while about musicals and theater and this vampire show she's watching, and all of a sudden it's the end of lunch. As we leave the cafeteria, I'm sure Will has totally forgotten he sort of said I was cool, but he stops me after June waves goodbye and puts something in my hand. A torn corner of notebook paper. "My number," he says. "Text me?"

His NUMBER. OMG. What does this MEAN? "Oh. Uh, yeah. I will."

"Cool," he says, smiling. And then he walks off, leaving me with that paper triangle burning in my hand. I stuff it in my pocket and power walk down the hallway, certain my heart is gonna alien-burst right out of my rib cage.

I can't bring myself to text him until I get to Mamma Gianna's that afternoon, but then when I do, Will doesn't respond. I wait and wait, but nothing.

Ugh. Maybe he changed his mind. Maybe he doesn't want to be my friend after all. I mean, who knows who else he gave his number to? Someone cooler? Someone . . . better looking? If he's even like that. Gay, I mean.

But he said I was *cool*. And *he* gave *me* his number. That's gotta mean *something*, even if it just means he wants to be friends. And I don't think he gave June his number, which makes me feel sort of proud, like I'm finally worth someone's attention all on my own.

Now, if he'd just text me back.

* * *

Friday night suddenly becomes Sunday night, and I'm cross-legged in the chair at my desk with my Chromebook open to an episode of *Pizza Perfect* while I have a staring contest with my math homework. So. Many. Triangles. The more I look at them, the more I just want to make a pizza.

My eyes wander to Travis Parker on my screen. It's been a minute since PizzaPaulie07's rumor posted, but I haven't seen squat from Travis Parker or the official *Pizza Perfect* account. (And I've been refreshing like a fiend.) Maybe Pop's right. Maybe it is just a rumor.

On the screen, Travis Parker jams a wedge of crusty, brown-spotted cheesy goodness into his mouth. A string of mozzarella gets stuck in his goatee. He makes a bunch of indistinguishable moans of foodie bliss, pulls the cheese from his chin, licks it off his fingers, and *mmm-mmm-MMMMs*. He compliments the chef, this little old Black woman from a pizzeria in New Jersey, and makes his signature chef's kiss hand gesture saying, "Now, *that's* a pizza perfect." But he says it in a way that makes it almost sound like he's saying "Now, *that's* a piece of perfect."

I love that. That's what pizza is to me too. A triangle of absolute perfection.

I'm daydreaming about Travis Parker saying his catchphrase to me, and *really* meaning it, when my phone buzzes. I look at the screen.

I gulp and pause *Pizza Perfect*.

It's Will White.

Will: hey

Will: srry I didn't text you back

He texted!!! OMG. My fingers hover over the keyboard on my phone. I type fast so I don't lose my nerve.

Me: Hey! It's okay!

I hit send and immediately regret the capital letters and the exclamations. Will sent me an understated, super chill "hey" and now I've sent him a "Hey!" which might as well include a confetti cannon and a marching band. *C'mon, Luca.*

I worry he's not going to text me back because I got so extra, but three little dots appear to tell me he's typing. *Phew.* Thank you to whoever is the saint of texting that I didn't scare him off with my ridiculous energy.

And then the dots disappear.

My head falls into my hands. *Total FAIL. Way to go, Luca.* This is why you don't have any guy friends. You have no friggin' clue how to be chill. And Will—he's the essence of chill.

But then my phone buzzes. My eyes pop open.

Will: what r u up to

Okay, Luca. Be COOL.

Me: not much. doing some homework. you?

Will: texting you Lol

I grin. My shoulders loosen a bit. I'm typing a reply

when another Will text appears.

Will: can i ask you a question

A question? He wants to ask me a question. Seven billion possibilities flood my brain, but I manage to keep it chill, matching his energy.

Me: sure

Will: I know you like to cook a lot

Will: and that pizza takes up a lot of your time

Will: but do you like video games

I legit laugh out loud. What a weird question. My fingers slide over the screen.

Me: I do more than just make and eat pizza. Yeah, I
like video games. Y?

As I hit send, someone knocks at my door. I flip my phone facedown under my thigh. "What?"

Pop's head pokes through the doorway. "Hey, can I come in?"

I kick my chin at my bed. "Yeah, we're open for business."

Pop nods, comes in, closes the door behind him, and sits on my bed, hands clasped. I know that tight-lipped, jaw-locked expression. I know those hiked-up shoulders and that Frankenstein's monster grunt. He's here for one of his classic vent sessions.

"How're you doing, kid?" he asks.

I spin around, so I'm fully facing him. This is how it

always starts, him asking me how I am. He doesn't actually want to know how I am, though. That's just his warm-up question. It's like a play we've rehearsed a million times. I know my lines by heart.

I say: I'm fine.

He says: Oh good.

There's never any follow-up question about me. And if I ever said anything other than "I'm fine," I don't think Pop would know what to do with that. We've never run those lines, and he's not so good at improv.

"Did you see those boxes on the stoop today?" Pop asks. He leans over his knees conspiratorially. "How many were there? Five? Six?"

Ah. I should've known. This happens every time Ma gets a shipment of the makeup and skin care products she sells. Time for damage control. "I counted five boxes, but I think she's stocking up for the spring sale in March."

"Five boxes?" Pop shakes his head. "We don't have room for more of that crap, let alone a budget for her to keep adding to her hoard. That other junk she was supposed to move over the holidays is still piled up in the living room."

He's right. There are three boxes of stocking-stuffer lip balms, Christmas elf–shaped makeup compacts, and candy cane–scented hand sanitizers. Product Ma said she'd already lined up for specific customers. But the holidays are long gone, and now we're stuck with clearance items no one's gonna want until next November, if we're lucky. But Pop getting ticked about Ma's failed plans isn't gonna help anything.

So I say, "You know how the holidays went. Ma got overwhelmed at the pizzeria. The twins got sick with the flu. There was a lot going on. I'm sure she'll come up with a way to get rid of it all *and* sell the spring items."

"Maybe," Pop says, "but that doesn't change the fact that she's getting us in more debt. That product's gotta be purchased outright first. She only makes commission if she sells it all. Those three boxes gathering cobwebs in the corner are wasted money. Money we need."

While Pop goes on, my phone vibrates under my thigh. Not once, not twice. Three times. It's gotta be Will. I don't want to ignore him, but if I don't talk Pop down from entering the Coliseum with Ma over her makeup overstock, our house'll be a shouting match in minutes.

"Maybe she can make winter/spring bundles. Ultra-clearance. A BOGO deal?" I say. But I'm off my game. Who wants a reindeer lip balm with their springtime lavender-lemon hand sanitizer? No one. But I can't focus with Will buzzing me.

"Maybe," Pop scoffs. "But you know I can't say anything to her about it. It's *her* business, just like Mamma Gianna's. What *she* says goes. God forbid I have an opinion."

Oh, so that's what he wants. Pop's an expert at asking me to do things without using an actual question. When he says he can't talk to Ma about it, he means he wants *me* to talk to her. Mostly because she won't blow up at me.

"I can talk to her," I say, trying to cut this session short. My phone has buzzed two more times. It's killing me not knowing what Will's saying.

"Nah, kid," he says. "I don't want to put that on your plate."

More lines we've rehearsed a billion times. Just like always, I say, "No big. I'll let you know how it goes."

Pop stands. His bear paw clamps the top of my head, squeezing gently. I like to think of it as a scalp hug. That's kind of the most physical Pop gets. Never real hugs. Just one-handed pats and squeezes. "You're a good son, Luca," he says. "Thanks."

Then he slips out, closing the door quietly behind him. Not because it disturbs me but because he doesn't want to tip Ma off that he was in here.

Soon as the door's closed, it's back to me time, something I'm getting less and less of.

I pull my phone from under my thigh.

Will: oh cool. just wondering.

Will: actually that's not true

Will: would you wanna hang out sometime?

Will: I have lots of games we could play

Will: hello?

Will: u there?

AHH! I can't believe I missed all these messages. Will

thinks I'm ignoring him, and he wants to HANG OUT. With *me*. Guys never want to hang out with me. I'm just not a guy-friend kind of guy. Sports aren't my thing, and that's like ninety percent of what most boys my age seem to be made up of. So I guess I'm not all that interested in *them* either. But the weird thing is, I want to be friends with Will. And he's different. In a good way. A really good way.

My fingers fly over the screen.

Me: HI! Sorry. My dad was talking to me.

Me: Yeah, I'd totally like to hang out.

I wait. I really hope Will doesn't ghost because I didn't respond faster.

Three dots appear. I sit up straighter.

Then they vanish. My fingers squeeze my phone. *Did I say the wrong thing? Maybe I sounded too excited. Maybe I shouldn't have said "totally." Maybe he's regretting asking me.* Oh man, now I'm totally spiraling.

Dots blink again.

Will: can you hang out this week?

My whole body fills with the same rush I get when I pull a perfectly timed pizza from the oven, the mahogany spots of caramelized cheese, the uniform curls of the pepperoni ridges lifting in the heat. Molto bene.

Part of me wonders if I should ask if June can come too . . . but I don't. June is my best friend, the other half of the BFC, but I kind of like the idea of just me and Will hanging out. Having another friend who's just mine. She's so outgoing and she's got all her drama club friends. Maybe I could have someone all my own too. Especially if it's Will White.

Me: I have to ask my parents. I'm at the restaurant helping most nights, but I can figure something out.

Will: cool

Will: let me know

Will doesn't send anything after that, so I hit play on *Pizza Perfect* and sort of get back to my freaking awful math homework. Instead of doing the actual problems, I get lost in the shapes of triangles. Tracing them with my finger, point to point to point. *One. Two. Three.*

One.

Two.

Three.

Gramma Salvatore, Pop's mom, says the best things come in threes. Her top three are Jesus, God, and the Holy Spirit, but I get to thinking about my trios. Crust, sauce, and cheese. Me, Ma, and Pop. Me, Elio, and Nina. And now—me, June, and Will. I'm connected to all these different people.

I make triangles.

That feels true. That feels good.

Maybe this math homework isn't all that bad.

Chapter 5

June and I are holed up in a booth with our homework at Mamma Gianna's on Tuesday, a couple nights after Will and I were texting. I've squared it away with Ma and Pop for us to hang out tomorrow, but I'm feeling a little guilty because I haven't looped in one very important person.

Okay. Not a *little* guilty. A *lot* guilty.

"I need to tell you something," I say.

June looks up from her math homework. "Uh-oh. I don't like that face."

"Look, I know I said I could . . . but I can't go with you to musical auditions tomorrow." I go into apologetic overdrive. "I'm sosososo sorry. I know you really wanted me there. I just—" UGH. I can't stand myself for lying, but a boy's gotta do what a boy's gotta do. "Ma and Pop need me at the restaurant."

Her pencil falls to her paper. "But you *promised*. This is important. You're my emotional support friend!"

The guilt. THE GUILT. It burns in my throat, but I can't give in. "You don't need me there. You'll be great. I'll do whatever you want tonight to help you prepare."

She starts to slide out of the booth. "I bet I can convince your mom—"

"NO!" I yelp. "I mean, *no*." I lean in to whisper, and this time . . . I don't have to lie. "Things aren't so good with my parents right now. I need to help."

"Oh." She slides back in. "I guess—I guess I'll be okay, then." She tucks her hair behind her ear. "What's up with your parents? Are *you* okay?"

I swallow. I don't want to talk about my parents, and I feel slimy for using their marital problems to lie to my best friend. *Should I just come clean? Should I tell her the truth about Will?* I mean, June's my best friend. Maybe she *would* understand.

"It's not . . . I mean—" I say, but then I chicken out, thinking about all the ways it could go wrong. *What if she decides to skip auditions and invites herself to hang out with us? What if she comes and Will decides he likes her more than me? What if this is my one chance to have a guy friend?* So I shake my head and smile. "No, yeah. I'm fine."

Her eyebrows furrow. "You're sure?"

"Yeah."

My shoulder muscles relax with relief, but I feel kinda gross. Situations like this *never* happen to me—I literally

43

don't have friends other than June. But I want to hang out with Will, just the two of us. Get some guy time, which I've never had before. (And if I'm being honest, the back of my brain wonders if this cute boy might think I'm cute too . . . but there's just, like, NO WAY, right? Will is *so* cool, and I . . . smell like pizza.) But if I tell June any of that, she won't get it because she's not at the center of it. And because she's my only friend, I always do what makes her feel good instead of me. Maybe it's okay to put me first this time?

Sometimes I hate the way my brain works. Turning over the same ideas and questions again and again. When I worry, I worry about worrying so much. It loops in this endless circle I can't escape. And the ambiance in the restaurant tonight isn't helping.

The dining room is quiet. *Again.* We've only got two tables of customers. An older Black couple in a booth near us and a Latinx family across the way—a mom and dad with two kids and a baby in a high chair. The little guy keeps throwing his fork on the floor and dying laughing. It's pretty adorable, but his parents aren't so amused after the seventh time he does it.

"Are you sure you're okay, Luca?" June asks, yanking me out of my doom spiral. "Do you want to talk about your parents?"

Guess I'm not doing a great job hiding my feelings. "No, no. They'll be fine. It's, uh, just these equations." I say, "I can't seem to balance them."

June grins. "Want me to take a look?"

"If I can't get it soon, yeah, I'll take some help." I slurp my Sprite, clear my throat, and add, "Do you wanna run through your *Into the Woods* audition?"

She bites her lip. "I think I'm okay? I rehearsed Cinderella's song all weekend. Mom says I sound great, but she *has* to say that." She leans over the table, eyes narrowed. "I heard Anya's trying out for the role too. She might be annoying, but she's talented. Devon said that she told her that Anya's been taking voice lessons since she was *six years old*." June slumps into the booth. "How am I supposed to compete with *that*?"

I lean in, whispering out of the side of my mouth, "If Anya needs lessons, doesn't that mean she isn't very good?"

"Total opposite." She slams her pencil down. "Voice lessons are for *serious* singers. Anya is serious. What chance do I have against a trained singer? My only teachers have been videos online."

I wag my finger at her. "Don't knock the internet. I've learned some impressive baking tips on there."

She folds her hands over her notebook. "Sure, but it's not the same. I don't have a teacher who can hear me or tell me how to do better."

"If you want someone to tell you you're awesome"—I grin—"I've got that covered."

June rolls her eyes. "No offense," she says, hiding a smirk, "but I don't think I should take singing advice from *you*."

Just as I'm about to take offense (though she's not entirely wrong—my singing voice is like a parakeet being strangled underwater), Ma storms over with Elio and Nina, one hand on each of their shoulders. Elio's got something red in his hair above his left eyebrow. Nina's fists are balled at her hips.

June gasps, staring at my little brother's forehead. "Is that blood?"

Elio sticks his finger in the red stuff, grimaces, and then licks it off. "Pizza sauce."

June relaxes. "Oh, thank God."

"These two were trying to have a food fight in back," Ma says.

Nina tilts her chin up at Ma, whining, "Elio wouldn't let me use the iPad."

"She already played with it for half an hour," Elio says.

"After *you* had it for an hour!" Nina almost shouts.

The few patrons we've got turn their heads at the noise. Ma flashes her Dazzlingly Bright smile at them. They shrug and go back to eating their za.

"That's enough," Ma says, squeezing the twins' shoulders. "Luca, can I speak with you in the kitchen? But you two"—she shoves Elio and Nina into the seat I just vacated—"you stay put. Why don't you video chat Nonna

Zaza? June, hon, you don't mind watching them while I talk to Luca, do you?"

June eyes my siblings warily. "As long as they don't throw food at me."

Ma shakes a finger at Elio, then Nina. "They won't. Or they'll owe you their allowance."

Nina and Elio sit up straight as breadsticks. They promise to be good. June hands Elio a stack of napkins to wipe the sauce from his head, and I follow Ma into the back. I got a feeling I know what's coming.

Soon as the kitchen door swings shut, Ma says, "Have you heard from your father? I texted and called him, but he's not answering. He was supposed to be back from—" She catches herself, like she was gonna spill a secret. "He was supposed to be back."

"I can text him." Not that he'll get back to me any faster. That's just how he is. Pop never moves fast enough for Ma, and she's a machine. I don't think it's in his DNA to do anything quickly.

Ma groans. "He's always doing this. Losing track of time. He doesn't understand that time is money. And when he's gallivanting around town, I'm holding down the fort. I've got Elio and Nina acting like wild animals on top of trying to run the restaurant. Madone. I haven't sat down for five minutes today. My feet are killing me. And you got me all worried about that makeup at home. I still need to get my spring e-blast out tonight, and—" She massages her forehead. "You'd—you'd just think your father could find it in him to let me rest long enough to eat a meal."

"June and I can watch the twins," I say, wedging myself into the space it takes for her to breathe. Though I'm not sure how we'll get any homework done with those two arguing over everything. (Chatting with Nonna Zaza usually helps—the twins miss her as much as I do.) But the better mood I can get Ma in before Pop gets here, the smoother things'll be tonight. So I add, "I'll keep an eye on the register too. Take a break. Eat something. I got this."

"I hate asking you to do more than you already do, Luca," she says. "But I just can't do it all today." She groans again. "I hate that your father makes me this way. Angry. Frustrated. It gives me agita."

"I'll get the Rolaids." I pat her arm. "We'll get through it. I'm sure Pop'll be here soon."

Ma pulls me in for a hug. "What would I do without you? Seriously, Luca. You keep me sane."

I hug her back. "I got you. Luca's here to save the day." I laugh to show her I'm okay, but I'm tired and worried too. I don't want to let her down though, so I can't tell her that. It would just stress her out more.

She lets go and gently pushes me to the door. "You better get back out there. Make sure the twins aren't pouring Parmesan on each other."

When I return to the dining area, the phone by the register rings. Nina and Elio are talking at the iPad (I assume to Nonna Zaza) and they seem to be behaving, so I answer it to give Ma a chance to breathe. It's an order for pickup: two sixteen-inch pizzas with extra cheese, artichokes, and garlic. I jot down the order and push the ticket through the window to Cesar, along with the bottle of Rolaids for Ma. Then the older couple want their bill, so I ring them up. And *then* I top off drinks for the family with the fork-throwing baby. By the time I get back to June and the twins, the few moments of peace between them are starting to decay.

"Give me the iPad," Nina hisses. "I want to tell Nonna about floor hockey."

"I'm almost done." Elio twists away from her, holding the tablet out of reach. "Nonna, did you know hermit crabs shouldn't be called hermit crabs? 'Hermit' means you stay in and you don't like people, but hermit crabs actually love other hermit crabs. They're very social—"

"That's enough, Eliooo," Nina groans, reaching around him. "Nonna doesn't *care*."

I scoot in beside June and say, "Guys, cool it. We have *customers*."

Elio flips the iPad around to me. "Say hi to Nonna, Luca!"

The screen is filled with Nonna Zaza's nose, lips, and purple glasses. She's never understood how to hold the camera. "Luca, bambino!" she says. "How's my sweetie pie?"

49

At the sound of her voice, the feeling of missing her avalanches inside me. I gulp back the sudden emotion. "Hi, Nonna. I'm . . . okay. How're you?"

"Blessed. Florida sun does old bones good," she laughs. "But I miss my grandbabies. You keeping my legacy going?"

I nod, lying. "Mamma Gianna's is good. Better than ever. We—"

Nina cuts me off, stretching over Elio for the device. Her fingers graze the glass. "Elio! Give. It. To. ME! It's my turn with Nonna!"

Elio turns the iPad back around, shouting back at her. Nonna Zaza tells the twins to settle down at the same time I do. June curls silently into the corner of the booth like she's trying to hide from the Salvatore storm. The family at the other table looks at us like *we've* got a fork-throwing baby now. And not just one. Nervous sweat rises on the back of my neck. "Cut it out," I whisper-shout. "Last thing we need is another bad review. Elio, let Nina talk to Nonna."

But they ignore me. Nina gets her fingers on the edge of the iPad. She giggles like she thinks she's won, dragging it to her, but then Elio groans and tears it from her grasp. There's just one problem: he does it too forcefully. When he yanks back, the tablet flings free from his hand. June, Nina, Elio, and I watch Nonna's face pinwheel in slow motion across the dining room.

It crashes onto the other family's table, smack dab in the

center of their half-eaten deep-dish. The screen goes black. Red sauce spurts on their shirts. One of their kids yelps in shock, spilling a plastic cup of Coke in the process. The mom shouts. The fork-thrower wails.

Oh crap.

Hot-cold tingles slither down my back. This is my fault. I let this happen. I leap out of the booth, an apology halfway out my mouth, when the kitchen door flies open. Ma and Pop (*when did he get back?*) bust through, heads swiveling like *Star Wars* droids.

It takes all of two seconds for them to see the mess at our only customer's table, the iPad sticking out of the deep-dish like a sad birthday candle. I know exactly what they're thinking. We're gonna have to give them their meal for free in addition to making them a new pizza to replace the one topped with an iPad. Buh-bye, money!

Ma and Pop share a furious glance. Some silent understanding passes between them. Then Ma plasters on her brightest smile and marches toward the family, while Pop stomps to our booth. He glares at Nina and Elio, who've gone whiter than fresh mozzarella, and says to them in a crisp whisper, "Kitchen. NOW."

I try to explain what happened, to say I'm sorry, but Pop cuts me off, his index finger jabbing the table in front of me. "You were supposed to be watching them, Luca."

My insides curdle. My voice cracks. "I was! I—"

His head shakes. "Not. Now."

"But—"

Pop doesn't give me a second chance to explain. He shoves Nina (stomping) and Elio (sniffling) through the swinging door and out of sight.

I'm so embarrassed, I can't even look at June. She's seen my parents angry before (it's sort of their natural state), but she's never witnessed a full-on Salvatore explosion. I want to melt and ooze out of sight.

But June scoots closer. Puts a hand on my wrist. She whispers, "It was an accident. That wasn't your fault."

She's wrong. I know she's wrong.

Wrong, wrong, wrong.

But I don't have words. I just shake my head.

There shouldn't have been an accident. I was supposed to be in charge.

And I failed.

Chapter 6

I put on a brave face but I'm a wreck as the USS *Salvatore* goes down in a pizza sauce ocean. Elio's upper lip is all snot because he won't stop crying. Nina is silent and fuming. Ma and Pop snipe at each other. I bounce from twins to parents, trying to keep us afloat. Nothing helps. June calls her mom to pick her up. I don't blame her, but I wish she'd stay. I need someone on my team. As she's walking out, she tells me it'll be okay, but I know that's not true.

Case in point, Ma and Pop call Gramma Salvatore, Pop's mom, who shouldn't be driving at night because her eyes are bad, to pick up the twins and watch them until we get home. When she picks them up, her gray hair is wind-blown and she's scowling. She hates Mamma Gianna's, and she hates it even more when it interferes with her Tuesday night police procedurals. (She's like the only person I know who watches *actual* television.) As soon as Nina, Elio, and Gramma Salvatore are out the door, I find myself in a lifeboat, inhaling fully for the first time in a minute. I want to apologize for letting them down, but I'm worried that talking will only make it worse. Instead, we work. Make pizzas. Wipe tables. Count the register. Turn off lights. Set the alarm.

The awkward tension doesn't end when we get home. Instead of Ma or Pop coming to my room for a rant session, they drop by my bedroom *together* as I'm about ready to get in bed. Their expressions tell me I'm about to get an earful. Ma's face is drawn, lips wiped clean of red and pinched tight. Pop looks like someone took a lawnmower to his herb garden.

"Hey, kid," Pop says. "We—we've gotta talk to you."

I've learned from movies and TV shows that any conversation starting with a phrase that resembles "we've gotta talk" is never good. I shy away from them, perching on the edge of my bed. "I know. It's all my fault. I should have stopped Nina and Elio. I'm really sorry—"

Ma closes the door, shaking her head. "Oh, hon. No, that's not— We just—we need to talk to you about something. Something important."

That's only a little relief. But then my brain trampolines from one possibility to the next, trying to figure out what is *so* important that they've both got to talk to me. It *can't* be good. "Did something happen to Nonna Zaza?"

"No, your nonna is fine." Pop sits on the bed next to me, but Ma doesn't come any closer. Pop puts his hand on my knee. "Kiddo, your mother and I have made a big decision.

Something we've been talking about for a while now. We think it's best to tell you before we tell the twins."

My gut sinks. "What is it? Are you selling Mamma Gianna's?"

Ma sputters an unhumorous laugh. "That's never happening. It's our family legacy. No, your father and I—" She pauses, like she tastes something bitter. "We've decided to separate."

SQUUUUEEEEE! Pump the breaks. There's a car accident in my brain. Glass shattering everywhere. Full airbag explosion. Did she just say "separate"? As in, that thing parents do before they . . . *divorce*? For the first time in my life, I really, truly don't have words.

Pop quickly adds, "It's a temporary separation. Your mother and I, we need time to sort some things out. Independently."

Ma says, "Your father's moving into an apartment nearby this weekend. We wanted to wait as long as we could before we had to tell you. But don't worry. Your father will be here anytime you need him. Isn't that right, Gio?"

Pop says, "That's right. You call, I come running. And I'll still be at the restaurant. You'll hardly notice a change."

I still can't drag my tongue and lips off the pavement. I can't believe they kept this from me. That I didn't know. They tell me *everything*. But maybe I should have seen this coming. More fights than usual. Pop sleeping on the couch even when they *weren't* fighting. And now that I know, I should have the words to fix this, but I don't. This isn't a regular problem, though—it's a freaking disaster.

And it means I failed. All the good I thought I was doing to help my parents clearly wasn't good enough. What happened tonight with Nina and Elio proves that. I pull my knees up to my chin. *Madonna mia, I'm gonna be sick.*

Pop squeezes my foot. "Kid, say something. Tell us what's going on in there."

"I—" We're supposed to be a family. Me, the twins, and our parents. My eyes flit to the scattered math homework on my desk. A few words slip out. "But we're a triangle." I know it doesn't make sense, but it's the only thing I can think to say. The only thing that feels true. "I mean, we're a family. We make each other whole. We aren't—we're not a shape without all of us here."

Ma finally steps closer. "Oh, hon. We're still a family. No matter what happens between your father and me, we're always going to be a family."

I nod. Their faces are etched with concerned wrinkles in the shapes of minus and plus signs. I can't make more problems for them. They already have too many to fix. They need to see that I'm okay, but I'm so *not* okay.

"Right." I dress my face in a smile. "Always a family."

"We wanted you to know before your brother and sister," Pop says. "We're telling them tomorrow night. It might hit harder since they're younger. You're such a good big brother. They're going to look to you for support. But keep this between us until then. Can you do that?"

Nina. Elio. I don't want to *lie* to them, but I guess this is what being a big brother means sometimes. Holding on to ugly secrets. I pinch my thumbnail against my index finger. I say, "Yeah. I'll look after them."

"Do you wanna ask us anything?" Ma says.

I have a million questions. A universe full of them. *How could you do this? I thought family came before anything else? What* things *do you have to work out? Why can't I help you?* But I see my parents' faces. Their exhaustion. The weight they're carrying just telling me about the separation. Questions will only make them feel worse. I need to be okay so something in their life is all right. I can be one less problem to solve.

"No," I say. "I'm fine."

"You're fine?" Pop says, like he doesn't believe me.

"I am. Really." I flash an all-teeth smile this time.

"We love you, Luca," Ma says. "So much. We promise this is for the best. If you decide you wanna talk tonight, I'll be in my room."

"And I'll be on the couch," says Pop. "Love you, Luc."

"Love you too." The words pass through my lips as solid sound, but they feel hollow.

What is love without the people who gave it shape?

Chapter 7

I can't sleep. Ma and Pop telling me about their separation plays on repeat every time I close my eyes. So I stare at the ceiling. Yellow streetlight seeps through the blinds. Bands of pale gold stain the white paint. *Separate.* Lines of light so close together but never touching. *Separate.* When the heat kicks on, the glowing bars shake, but they don't cross. *Separate.* I stare at those parallel lines until I can't stand it any longer.

My phone is supposed to stay off at night, but what else am I supposed to do? I need a distraction. I flop to my side and open Instagram.

The first thing I see is a new video post from Travis Parker. He looks like he always does—pristine olive complexion, black goatee, and styled inky hair. The text below the post says, "MAJOR PP ANNOUNCEMENT!!!"

Oh snap. The rumor from PizzaPaulie07's post rushes to the front of my brain. I bend my pillow in half and prop myself up, even more awake than I was before. I tap the video, sound on low. I hold the phone inches from my face.

"What's up, pizza people? *Pizza Perfect*'s Travis Parker coming at you with an update." My goateed icon takes a deep breath. So do I. "There've been a lot of rumors going around the past few days. Figured it was time I put a cap on that sauce." He scratches his goatee, pausing. I do not like that pause.

"For six incredible seasons, the crew and I have eaten at the finest pizzerias the United States has to offer. From New York to Chicago to Detroit to Portland, Oregon, we've been wowed by the tastiest pies to ever grace this planet. We're so grateful to our viewers for tuning in episode after episode to celebrate the joy of the greatest food to ever exist. Unfortunately, it's time for our little production to hang up its apron. The seventh season of *Pizza Perfect*, which begins filming in just a couple months, will be our last. We know that's a disappointment to a lot of you, but I promise, we're gonna give you the best episodes to date. And we've got plans to make it extra special. Watch this space tomorrow for another major announcement about our final season. Until then, stay cheesy."

The video ends with his big, stupid grin. Like he's freaking happy he's taking my joy away. I can't believe it's true. I never thought I'd be ticked at Travis Parker. But lots of things I never thought would happen are happening . . .

so what the bunk do I know?

I let my screen fade to black. I put it back on my night-stand.

I stare at my ceiling, at all those separate yellow lines.

Pop is already gone when I drag myself out of bed Wednesday morning. I guess this is what our new separated life will look like. Nina and Elio ask where he is since he's usually the one who makes breakfast. Ma says he had an errand to run. Like it's no big thing. The twins buy the lie like it's a half-priced Italian beef sandwich. Makes me sick. I can't believe how easily Ma lies to them. I can't even eat my cereal. No Pop, all these lies, and no more *Pizza Perfect*. It's hurl central.

I feel super guilty walking to school with Nina and Elio, knowing what I know. The two of them blissfully bicker like normal, totally unaware that their lives are gonna implode tonight. The idea of telling them about the separation takes over every part of my brain. So much so that I forget that I'm supposed to hang out with Will until I see him. My gut says to cancel, that this is all too much. But Will is my chance to get away from this mess. He makes me feel good. Like I matter. Like I'm special. He chose *me* to be his friend. He thinks I'm *cool*. I don't want to give up the chance to see if we can be friends. I just wish I didn't feel so guilty about hanging out with him.

Plus, there was a lot of coordinating to make it happen. Not only did I have to lie to my best friend, but I also had to okay it with Ma and Pop and then arrange for Gramma Salvatore to pick up Nina and Elio from school. ("I guess I can cancel cards with the girls . . . *again*.") Then I had to be sneaky around June *alllll* day and find ways to keep Will from accidentally spilling the beans. I feel the way anchovies smell.

Maybe I'm doing the wrong thing. Maybe this isn't the best time to be thinking about what I want. Now more than ever, Ma and Pop need me. *Madone.*

After debating with myself all day long, as soon as the last bell rings, I decide I can't take the guilt anymore. I pull out my phone and open my texts with Will.

Me: I'm sorry. I can't hang out. My family needs me.

The message comes out quickly, but my thumb hovers over the blue send arrow. *Send it, Luca. Hit. Send. Your family needs you.*

But I can't.

Because I don't *want* to send it.

I want to hang out with Will. I imagine us laughing together. Doing whatever guys do when they hang out. My heart flutters. And suddenly, all my guilt turns into anger. I'm not just sad—I'm *mad* at Ma and Pop for separating. I'm mad that they're making me lie to Elio and Nina. I'm mad that I'm always the one who's gotta help and babysit and be the big brother. *I* don't get a big brother. *I* don't get to rely on anyone else. Sometimes I wish I were an only child, like June. She does her own thing. She always comes first. I never do. Nina and Elio do. Even Ma and Pop put themselves first. (Or the restaurant.)

Everyone else gets something they want.

So. Why. Not. Me?

Adrenaline searing through my veins, I backspace the message one letter at a time. I slide the phone into my pocket. Then I meet Will at his locker.

Ignoring the cottage cheese chunks sloshing in my stomach, Will and I walk in the opposite direction of Mamma Gianna's, to the apartment where he lives with his mom. It's a sunny, crisp afternoon. When I look at the clumped, glazed snow, white spots make it hard to see. Will talks the entire time, which is good, because I'm distracted by my emotions and feeling weirdly nervous. I'm not sure what boys talk about when they're together, which makes me feel stupid because I *am* a boy. I should know what to do. But I don't, and I *always* know what to do to make things work. I don't like not knowing.

But that's the thing about Will. He's an untested recipe, which is a little exciting and a lot scary.

Fortunately, he doesn't seem to have the same problem as me, which makes me wonder if he's a better boy than I am. If he "gets it" in a way I don't. In a way I never will.

He goes on and on about his new guitar teacher, how he's learning some Fleetwood Mac songs (note to self: google Fleetwood Mac later), how his fingers have finally callused enough that it doesn't hurt when he plays, how he's saving up for a new electric guitar. I'm his human bobblehead, nodding along as he talks. When we reach his apartment building, his cheeks are cotton-candy pink from the cold, and I'm sure mine are too. His turn a shade darker when he says, "Oh God, I just realized I talked, like, the whole time. Sorry. I, uh, do that when I get nervous."

My right eyebrow hitches almost to my forehead. *He's* nervous? Guess I read him all wrong. "You don't have to apologize," I say. "What are you nervous about?"

He shrugs, pulling a key from his pocket. "You're like one of my only, uh, friends here. I don't want to mess it up." He fumbles with the key in the lock. Then he looks at me like he said the wrong thing. "Is it okay I said 'friends'? We are friends, right?"

I laugh, mostly because I'm so relieved he's just as much of a weirdo as I am. "Yeah, we're friends." But a tiny part of me deflates. I want to be friends, but I also have these . . . *more-than-friends* feelings for Will. And I feel like he's saying we're *just* friends.

FRIENDS. FRIENDS. FRIENDS.

I should be happy. I have a friend who is a boy.

A boy . . . friend.

63

But I'm not happy. At least, not as happy as I hoped.

He *phew*s, turns the key, and opens the door. He holds out his hand to welcome me in. "Well then after you, Friend Luca."

I shake off my disappointment best I can, bow a little, and say in a British accent, "Thank you very much, Friend Will."

Then we're both laughing. I breathe again. This is okay. Maybe *this* is what boys do. Act like weirdos. I can do that. I'm a total weirdo.

I follow Will up a flight of stairs to apartment 2A. A mat outside the door says, "Friends Welcome," which seems like an unfortunate sign from the universe. *Will is just a friend.* He takes out a second key and lets us in. A warm wave of vanilla and sugar washes over us. I breathe in the smell as we walk inside. The walls are dark gray. The floors are wide, dark wood slats. A mirror and key hook hang on the wall to our right. Will kicks off his shoes, and I do the same.

"Mom works from home," he says. "She's a writer."

"That's cool. Like books?"

Will nods. "And articles and essays. She teaches writing too, but it's all online. She loves it."

We walk into a kitchen. A woman a little taller than June with a reddish-black bob and bangs stands next to the oven chewing on an eraser and staring at a notebook. She looks up at us and smiles. Her dark eyes and pale nose are the same as Will's, but her face is rounder, her lips fuller. She's wearing an "I Read Banned Books" T-shirt, black yoga pants, and purple fuzzy slippers.

"You must be Luca. I'm Jessica White, Will's mom," she says. Then she wrangles Will into a choke-hold hug with both of her arms. She smashes her lips against his cheek, *mmmmuah*-ing loudly. He scrambles out of her grasp. I hide a laugh.

"Nice to meet you, Mrs. White," I say.

"Oh, Jessica is fine," she says, grimacing at the "Mrs." (Note to self: don't do that again.) Then she says, "Lovely to meet you too. Will's said so many nice things about you."

Will talks about me? To his mom? That makes me linguini noodle in place, but then I'm worried it looks like I've gotta pee, so I stop.

We small talk a little more, and then Jessica sends us off with a plate of freshly baked sugar cookies coated in pink rock sugar. We go to Will's bedroom, where he's got his Nintendo Switch and a small TV. His walls are covered in band posters. Aerosmith. Fall Out Boy. Panic! at the Disco. There's an acoustic guitar on a stand in the corner by his closet.

"I haven't heard of some of these bands," I say, pointing at the wall.

"My uncle Leon gave most of those to me," he says. "He's the one who got me playing guitar. Says I've gotta know the

65

greats if I'm gonna be a real rock star."

His bed isn't made. Pokémon sheets peek out from under the royal-blue comforter. Everything smells a little musty, like old pizza boxes, but it's covered up by cinnamon air freshener.

Will plops onto the edge of his bed, turns on the TV, and tosses me a teal controller from the Switch. "*Super Smash Bros.*?"

"Uh, sure."

I've only played *Super Smash* a couple times with June, but I remember the gist of the game: attack the other person's character until they take enough damage to get knocked out. Will chooses to play as the Pokémon trainer, which doesn't surprise me given his sheets. I stay true to my Italian roots and go with Mario.

It takes me a round to get the hang of it again (Will KO's me within seconds, but when I respawn, I last a lot longer), and then I manage to send him flying in round two. Aside from the occasional "You're going down!" or "Not fair!" we don't really talk as we play. Maybe that's normal for guys? We do break, however, to eat sugar cookies, which are delicious (a little undercooked in the center—perfection). Then Will changes to playing as Lucario. I stick with Mario because I'm finally getting the hang of his best move.

This is so different from hanging out with June. She and I talk constantly when we're together. Like you seriously

66

can't shut us up. So all this not-talking, just-playing with Will means my mind is wandering all over the place. I keep thinking about the face Jessica made when I called her *Mrs. White*. I realize I don't know anything about Will's dad, which might mean he's no longer around. And that makes me think about Ma and Pop. The separation. The D word. Will my mom make faces when someone calls her Mrs. Salvatore in a few months? A year? Soon all I can think about is how we're going to tell Nina and Elio tonight. That I really should be back at the restaurant helping. Doing SOMETHING to keep my family from falling apart. And the more I drift into my head, the more I fall behind in *Super Smash* and end up dead last in our current round.

"Hey," Will says, kicking his socked feet under his thighs. "You okay?"

"What?" I say, embarrassed he could tell I wasn't paying attention. "Yeah, no. I'm fine."

His lips squinch together. "You sure? You got super quiet. If it's annoying that I keep knocking you out, I can play a different character, or we can play a different game if you want. I have a lot—"

"It's not the game," I say before he can go on. I don't want him to think he's the problem. "Really. I just—I have a lot on my mind right now."

"Oh." He sets the red-orange controller on the blanket next to him. "You wanna talk about it?"

My autopilot reaction is "nope, I'm fine," but Will asked the question like he actually wants to hear what I have to say. And for some reason, I want him to know. I can't explain why, but I do. So I say, "Things are weird at home. Last night, my parents—they told me they're separating. My dad's moving into an apartment this weekend. It all just kind of sucks right now."

Will nods like he gets it. "My parents got divorced last year. That's why Mom and I moved back to Chicago. Closer to my uncle Leon and the rest of her family and away from my dad. He's . . . kind of a jerk."

That buoys me a little. Not that his dad's a jerk, but that neither of *my* parents are jerks. They have problems, but they aren't bad people. I feel a little more hopeful, but then I feel bad for feeling hopeful when things clearly didn't work out for Will. "I'm sorry," I say. "Divorce is the worst."

But he shrugs. "It's better this way. Mom's happier. Life is easier without them fighting all the time."

I squeeze the teal controller in my left fist. "But you wish they could've worked it out, right?"

"Not really," he says. "They're, like, *very* different people. I don't think it would have ever worked out."

"Really?" My chest tightens. I don't like this.

"Yeah." He swishes his fingers through his hair. Then he puts his hand on my shoulder. He squeezes gently. Electricity sizzles down my spine. "Your parents will probably be happier too when it's all over. It was ugly for a while, but we're all way better off now."

I shrug his hand away, even though I kinda like the way his touch feels. Warm. But there's no way what he's saying is true. I would never be happier if my parents divorced. NEVER. It would break our family apart. It would ruin everything we have at Mamma Gianna's.

Suddenly, I don't feel like being around Will. In fact, I desperately want to run away from him. I want to be at the pizzeria. I want my parents and my brother and my sister. I need to see them. I need to know they're okay.

I pull out my phone, act like I'm surprised by the time (it's not even five o'clock yet), and say, "Oh, shoot. It's later than I thought. I need to go."

Will drops his controller. "Already? It's only been a couple hours. I was gonna see if you wanted to stay for dinner. Mom can drive you home later. She already said so."

Dinner. Customers. Pizza. All I can think about is what I should be doing right now: helping my family. "Maybe next time," I say, hopping off his bed.

He stands up to follow me out. "Is it something I said?"

"No," I lie, a little too quickly. But I double down. "I just really have to get back to help with the dinner rush."

"If you're sure," Will says slowly. Then he smiles, and I can't stand how cute he looks, even if I am annoyed with what he said. "I'm glad we got to hang out, Friend Luca."

And that does, really, truly, make me smile. For half a heartbeat, I forget I'm anxious about my world falling apart. I've got my first real guy friend. He cares about me. He plays cool video games. And even if he only thinks of me as a friend . . . he still has a very nice face.

Chapter 8

Will and his mom drop me off at Mamma Gianna's at 5:17. There are a couple of cars in the parking lot that I don't recognize. *Customers, I hope.* I thank the Whites for the ride, still feeling guilty and anxious and awkward as heck. Then I bolt to our broken door before I freeze to death.

Right away, Ma comes at me like a bowling ball. "Luca, thank God. I thought you were staying longer, but we need you. Cesar called off sick." She simultaneously shoves me toward the kitchen while stripping me of my winter jacket and talking at me. There's a group of high school boys manging—(that's Italian-ish for "eating")—an extra cheese thin crust and yakking in the dining room. I keep them in the corner of my vision while she shoves me, embarrassed they're seeing me like this. It's not like I know any of them, but still—they're HIGH SCHOOL BOYS. So awkward.

Ma goes on, "Your father's working on the refrigerator, which is on the fritz again. Can you fire up two medium sausage, a gluten-free meat lovers, and a large half–green pepper and onion, half–black olive?"

"Roger that," I say, hurtling past the register and into the kitchen faster than a bullet train. I feel some relief, even in the chaos, being back in my element. Being able to help. Ma turns back to the dining room as I add, "Had a great time at Will's. Thanks for asking."

Her head peeks back around the corner into the kitchen. Her cheeks lift in apology. "How was Will's?"

"Fine," I mumble. I yank on an apron. "Two medium sausage, a gluten-free meat lovers, and a large half–green pepper and onion, half–black olive?"

"You got it," Ma says. "Glad you had fun."

I'm throwing the two medium pizzas into the oven when Pop comes around the corner, hands dinged up and covered in dark gray grease marks. A line of sweat trails down his left temple. He wipes his hands on his paint-stained jeans and nods at me. "What're you doing back? I thought you were at a friend's."

"He had something come up," I lie, readjusting my hairnet. "Besides, you clearly need me here. I'm gone five minutes and look at this place."

Pop chuckles. "Tell me about it." Then he takes a step closer, his voice getting quieter. "How are you today? With the separation?"

My eyes sting. "I'm fine." I focus on rolling out a blob of

gluten-free dough for the next pizza. "Are we still telling Nina and Elio tonight? They're gonna be so upset."

"We are, and I know," he says. "Your mother and I really appreciate you keeping an eye on them. You're such a good big brother. You sure you're okay?"

"I'm—" *Do I tell him the truth? That I almost broke down at Will's just thinking about divorce?* He'd understand more than Ma, but I look at Pop's tired, sagging face. The poofy bags under his eyes. *I can't.* The truth will drain him more. "I'm fine," I say. "Really." I knead out the dough harder. "How's the fridge?"

Pop nods like he believes me. Then he eyes the steel-gray menace. "Fine. But, uh, let us know if Nina and Elio seem off later, okay?"

I want to say: "I'd rather you didn't move out, that you go to therapy and make your marriage work. I'd rather not lie. I'd rather not have to be the 'big brother' right now."

But instead, I say, "Of course."

"You're a champ, kiddo." Pop rubs his hands together like he's trying to warm them up. "Say a prayer for me. This fridge might send me to Saint Peter."

He disappears. Mechanical clanks and scrapes become the soundtrack to my pizza making. Even though I'm doing my thing, worry creeps back in as I envision Elio's and Nina's expressions when they find out Pop's leaving. It makes me want to cry, but I don't because no one ordered an extra-large with tears and a side of snot.

It's around eleven by the time we get home. I'm beat. Gramma Salvatore is already in bed (she sleeps in the guest room when she babysits late), but Nina and Elio are still on the couch watching *SpongeBob SquarePants*. Their eyes are droopy, and Nina's chestnut hair is staticky and sticking up in the back. They sit up and rub the sleepies away when they see us. I can't believe we're going to slam them with the separation *now*. It's so late and they should be in bed. I don't want to hate my parents, but this is making me seriously dislike them.

After we hang up our coats, Ma and Pop start in on the bad news. I barely hear what they say because I'm laser-focused on the twins' reactions. When Pop finally spits out that he's moving into a new apartment this weekend, Nina doesn't flinch. She stares at him dead-eyed, then she stares at Ma, then back at Pop. Elio, though. Oof. He immediately bawls. Instaboogers bubble out of his nose. Chubby tears tremble down his cheeks. But it's a silent sob. He doesn't make any noise other than when he sniffs the gunk back in.

"We love you all very much," Pop says. His hands wring together. "Your mother and I don't want you to think that this changes anything like that."

Elio's little mouth parts. "But—but it changes *everything*."

Ma rubs his back. "I know, baby. That's how it feels. But

74

we promise, you'll think nothing of it soon enough."

I keep watching Nina. She's still weirdly quiet. Elio notices too. "Why aren't you upset?" he asks her.

Unblinking, she turns to our brother. In an even tone, she says, "I'm going to bed."

I've never heard a fourth grader sound more exhausted. It's how I imagine a deflated tire would sound if it could talk. Nina peels off the couch, slips through our tangle of legs and feet, and trudges down the hall toward her bedroom.

"Nin," Pop calls after her. "Stay. Talk to us."

Ironic since Pop's the one leaving us.

"I'm tired," she says without turning around.

"Go after her, Gio," Ma whispers to Pop. She rubs Elio's back in big circles. My poor brother cries harder, burying his face into her shoulder.

Pop heaves himself up and marches down the hall, calling Nina's name.

"I hate this," Elio sniffs. He stares at the empty spot where Nina was. For all they fight about, she's still his other half. "Why isn't she crying?"

Ma looks like she's on the verge of tears herself, but she keeps it together and pulls Elio to her chest. "People show their emotions in different ways. I'm—I'm sure she's upset too."

Instead of arguing with Ma, Elio turns his face into her shoulder and shudders. I hear the feathered gasp of him crying. My heart breaks. He curls his knees into her lap. Her arms cinch around him. A tear escapes Ma's right eye. She catches it with her ring finger before it falls past her nose.

"Want me to do anything?" My voice is hoarse. I clear my throat. I'm overtired, overworked. Not to mention trying to keep my own emotions in check.

"No," Ma says. "Your father and I have got this for tonight. You clean up and get to bed. I'll check on you after I get Elio settled."

I nod. Then I drag myself to the bathroom, brush my teeth, wash my face, and pee. Muffled voices hang in the air as I make my way to my bedroom. I knew this was gonna destroy Nina and Elio. I hate that Ma and Pop are doing this to them. To us.

I close the door behind me and slip into my pajamas. I get into bed, plug my phone into the charger by my nightstand, and I realize I missed texts from Will and June. It's not like it's weird to get texts from either of them, but I have a moment of panic. *What if June found out I was with Will? What if Will doesn't want anything to do with me because I acted like a total loser? What if he's mad I didn't get back to him faster? What if he decided he doesn't want to be friends?*

I take a deep breath and open Will's texts first.

Will: thanks for coming over, friend luca.

Will: maybe next time, ull beat me in super smash

Will: or we can play something else

76

Will: ok c u tomorrow

Okay, so, Will doesn't hate me. PHEW. I don't text him back since it's almost midnight, but I read his texts three more times. *Friend Luca.* My chest warms. Even with me getting all sad and weird and leaving early, he still likes me.

Then I read what June sent, nerves and guilt ramping up again.

June: Just wrapped up auditions and O M G

June: I think I did it. I really think I did it.

June: IT being that I think I'm gonna get Cinderella.
Fingers crossed I get a callback.

June: Um where are you? You okay?

June: Guess I won't hear from you tonight

June: Nope. Not me being worried about you.

June: not worried at all

Her worrying makes me feel even guiltier for ditching her. She's being a good friend. She knows how things get with my family. She's seen it enough. We decided a long time ago that in the BFC silly things like it being midnight on a school night and it being waaaaaaay too late to text someone don't apply to us. I text her back, but I leave out some key details.

Luca: I'm fine. Busy night at the restaurant.

Luca: Ma and Pop told Nina and Elio about the separation.

Luca: But congrats on your audition!!!!!! I'm sure you crushed it.

I'm about to shoot off another text when Ma pokes her head in. "Hey," she says. "No more phone tonight. Get some rest." Then her voice softens. "You hangin' in there?"

I flip my phone upside down on the nightstand, but I don't feel like talking. "I'm fine."

Her mouth slides to the side of her face. "You'd tell me if you weren't, right? We could get someone for you to talk to if—"

"I'm *fine*," I say. The last thing I want is to tell a stranger all my problems. But I turn out my light so she can't see I'm not fine at all.

Ma is illuminated by the hallway light, though. I can see the worry hiding in the shadows on her face. She says, "I love you, Luca. So much. Sweet dreams."

"Good night," I mumble. Then I turn my back to her because if I don't, I'm afraid I'll be messier than Elio.

Chapter 9

My brain won't let me sleep. I'm wide-awake at three in the morning, and since the rules of life no longer seem to apply to my family, I don't feel guilty grabbing my phone despite Ma's orders. I open Instagram, and there's a new post from Travis Parker. *OMG. HOW COULD I FORGET MY ICON WAS MAKING AN ANNOUNCEMENT YESTERDAY?* (Oh, because my family is imploding. WHATEVER.) The text below his video says, "Here it is: what all you pizza heads have been . . . " Instead of clicking the ellipses to read more, I tap the video.

"Travis Parker of *Pizza Perfect* here with another major announcement about the final season of our show." My goateed idol takes a deep breath. "First off, thanks to all the fans who shared their love and sadness that we're wrapping up the series. Y'all rock. We couldn't have gotten this far without you." Travis Parker's lips curl into a smug grin. "But I've got something special to share that'll hopefully sweeten the finale announcement. We've spent six seasons scouting out the best pizza joints in the US of A, but we've missed tons of great za spots. So for this final season, we're looking for pizzerias around the United States to nominate themselves to fill up our eight remaining episodes."

OH.

MY.

GOD.

"Applications open tomorrow, Thursday, January 18"—which I realize is TODAY because this video posted yesterday—"and they're due by February 1. That's two weeks to get your materials submitted. Go to our website for more information. I can't wait to see the amazing restaurants that come through. Thanks for being the best fans ever." Travis Parker ends the video with a wink at the camera.

I swear that wink is FOR ME. Like, Travis Parker is telling me without telling me that this is MY TIME. That I *have* to apply. Grazie to whoever is the patron saint of pizza!

I close Instagram and open the *Pizza Perfect* website. There's a graphic on the homepage calling for applications to be on the final season, but there aren't any links or additional information. I refresh the page. Nothing. I guess it's still *early* on Thursday. I stare back at my ceiling. All those separate yellow lines feel more hopeful now. A light in the dark.

I suddenly sit up. *Omg. This* is the answer to all my problems. All my *family's* problems. Travis Parker and *Pizza Perfect*. If I can get us on the show, not only will my pizza-making dreams come true, but Mamma Gianna's will be FAMOUS. Everyone will want to eat our pies. And if we can impress Travis Parker in the Pizza Perfect Challenge with a single exquisite bite—enough to pay rent and update our appliances and repaint our chipped walls and so much freaking more—Ma and Pop won't fight about the shop, and they'll be able to focus on their marriage and our family and staying together, and then Elio and Nina won't be sad, and Pop will live with us again, and we'll stay together like we're supposed to.

Getting on the show could fix *everything*.

I flatten my pillow under me and fall back. I can't stop smiling. There's hope. Real hope.

I just need to put the best application together that Travis Parker has ever seen. And I will, because I'm Luca Salvatore, and there's never been a bigger pizza fan to ever freaking live.

The application information goes live on the *Pizza Perfect* website while I'm walking to school, and even though it's ten degrees out, I still read through all the info. I've got thumbsicles by the time I walk into Riverfront Junior High, but I don't care.

The application is simple. A bunch of personal info, some short-answer responses, and a five-minute video of footage of the restaurant and me cooking. I've got tons of videos already recorded on my phone, so I can put something together with a few shots of my prepping and cooking. I can do this. I can *totally* do this.

Even at school, the application takes over every part of my brain. I barely register June telling me she made callbacks for *Into the Woods*. I hardly hear Will ask how I'm doing. None of what happened yesterday with either of them matters anywhere near as much as this application. Not if it means saving my family.

While I'm supposed to be taking notes in social studies, I open my red notebook and scratch out and rewrite responses to one of the application questions: "Why is it important for your restaurant to be featured on the final season of *Pizza Perfect*?"

Pizza Perfect has been my favorite show since forever. Seriously. Pizza is my life. Ever since my parents took over Mamma Gianna's, our family restaurant, from my Nonna Zaza, all I've wanted is for us to be on the show. It would be the coolest, most wildly awesome thing to ever happen to me.

I reread it. My eraser tap-tap-taps the paper. It's not special enough. I cross it out and try again.

Pizza is our legacy. Mamma Gianna's has been in our family for generations. My great-grandma started the

business with the little money she had when she came
over from Italy. Everyone used to love our pizza, but
now

I pause. I don't know how honest is too honest. But I
don't think lying to Travis Parker is gonna go over well, so I
keep going.

business isn't going so well. My parents spend every
minute of every day trying to compete with local pizza
chains, but it gets harder every day. We keep losing
money. I'm afraid that if we don't do something quick,
we'll have to shut down. And we can't. It would be like
pureeing my heart in the world's sharpest blender. It
would destroy my family too. You have to understand,
it's my destiny to make pizza. And our pizza isn't just
good—it's the BEST!!! And I swear I'm not making
that up.

You see, Mr. Parker, the reason it's so important
that we get on your show is that it could save my family
from losing everything we love. Everything we've ever
worked for. And not just that—it could save my
parents. They fight all the time. If they didn't have to
worry so much, maybe they'd get along. Maybe they'd
have more time for me and my little brother and sister.

I guess what I'm really saying is, if you don't mind

*me quoting Star Wars, you're our only hope. And that's
the truth.*

Twenty-four hours later, all my written responses for the application are drafted. That just leaves the video. I've got thirteen days before the application is due, but I'm not waiting till the end. I'm gonna be the first to submit. Travis Parker will see how serious I am. That I want this more than anyone else. Since June is queen of performances, I ask her to help me film on Friday night. Ma is at the restaurant and Pop is taking loads of stuff over to his new apartment. June and I are stuck babysitting Nina and Elio, since Gramma Salvatore refused to miss "another night with the gals," which works out because I don't want Ma and Pop to know what I'm up to. *I* know *Pizza Perfect* can save us, but Ma will say it's a distraction and Pop will say it's not worth the risk. WRONG. (*Obviously.*)

My plan if we get accepted: do that whole asking for forgiveness instead of permission thing. Ma and Pop will see that it's a real opportunity. They'll see that I have our family's best interests at heart. They'll have no choice but to say YES, LUCA, YOU'RE THE MOST INCREDIBLE SON EVER, THANK YOU SO MUCH. It'll be PERFECT.

June and I are in the kitchen at my house. I'm wearing a black Mamma Gianna's T-shirt and dark wash jeans. Over that, I've got on my white apron that's splattered in ancient tomato sauce stains that are more yellow-orange than red now. June styled my short, black hair in a sort of messy chic do. She says I look like the poster child for Italian Americans.

"I'm not trying to sound full of myself, but I really think I crushed my callback," she says as she fiddles with my hair. "The cast list gets posted on Monday, and if Anya gets Cinderella, I'm gonna boycott the show. For real."

I flap her fussing hands away. "One: she's not. Two: can tonight please be about me?"

"Yes, chef!" June holds up her phone and points it at me. "Remember to articulate when you speak. Repeat after me: the lips, the teeth, the tip of the tongue. The lips, the teeth, the tip of the tongue. And don't talk too fast."

"Right, right. The lips, the teeth, the tip of the tongue. Got it."

She's been coaching me with her theater skills, and I appreciate it. I have less than negative experience in that area, but I'm gonna have to learn fast if I want to be on TV.

"You look great," she says. "Even Shawn Mendes would be jealous of your hair. Now, here we go. I'll count you down." She holds up three fingers. I shake out my shoulders to get rid of the rest of my nerves. Then she's holding up two fingers. Then one. She points at me to start.

My face pulls wide into a giant smile. "Hello, pizza people! Luca Salvatore here, future master pizza maker and hopeful candidate for the final season of *Pizza Perfect*. The pizza genes have been passed down generation after generation in my family. Ever since my Nonna Zaza let me help her make dough, I've been obsessed with perfecting the pizza.

"While I love the traditional margherita or a deep-dish Italian sausage, I'm excited about adding my spin on the classics. I'm not on our menu yet, but I will be someday. Mark my words. Today, I'm gonna show off a pizza of my own invention: the buffalo chicken pizza."

June is filming me chopping celery when we're interrupted by a shout from the family room.

"ELIOOOOO!!!"

My little sister's shout ruins the take. June groans, tapping the phone screen. "Cut!"

Annoyed, I stomp out of the kitchen into the family room. I already told Elio and Nina to behave so I can finish a VERY IMPORTANT PROJECT, but they keep acting like toddlers. I find them wrestling on the couch, the remote between them like a tug-of-war rope. I use my Older Brother Super-Strength to pry it away.

"That's enough," I shout, dangling the remote above my head. "I've already told you. If you can't act like fourth graders and decide on something to watch *together*, then you can't watch anything. Capisce?"

Elio immediately blubbers. "B-b-but—"

But Nina grips the seat of the couch and shouts back,

"You're not our parent. You can't tell us what to do. Give it back!" She leaps and reaches for the remote. I dance out of her way. Elio whines my name again, but I'm not giving in to either of them.

Elio crosses his arms. "Luca's more our dad than our real one. At least he's here. Not abandoning us like Pop."

I freeze. So does Nina. June gasps softly behind me. (I didn't realize she'd followed me out here.)

"Pop's not abandoning us," I say quickly. I want to sound as confident as I did a minute ago when I was recording, but I stumble over my words. "Ma and Pop are figuring things out. It's temporary. Not forever. He'll—he'll be back."

Nina rolls her eyes. "That's what Olivia P.'s dad said too. Her parents got divorced a month ago. Then her dad moved to Canada."

Elio pales. "That's another *country*."

June steps into the room next to me. "Your dad isn't moving to Canada."

My fingers clench at my side. It's only been a day, and I already hate what the separation is doing to my baby brother and sister. Nina is bitter. Elio is like a sad puppy. Even more reason for me to make sure we get onto *Pizza Perfect*.

"It's gonna be okay," I say, tousling Elio's dark-brown curls.

"Whatever," mumbles Nina.

I sit down next to her and pull Elio to me. "We're going

to be okay," I say. "I promise." But if that's true, I need to get back to filming for the application. "You two fighting isn't gonna help, though. I need you to get along. Just watch a movie. Okay?" I open a streaming app on our TV and shuffle through their favorite movies. *Encanto. Luca. Turning Red.*

Nuzzled in my side, Elio's little chin turns up at me. "How do you know?"

"He doesn't," Nina says, staring at the screen with half-lidded eyes.

"I'm going to make it okay," I say, glancing at June. She's watching me with a sad, side-of-her-mouth smile. "I just—I need you two to get along. Remember: we're in this together. Please be quiet while I work in the kitchen. Can you do that?"

Elio nods.

"Fine," says Nina. "Just put on *Frozen*."

I glance at Elio. He makes a grumpy face, but then he shrugs in surrender. I press play. The opening credits roll. Elio slips away from me and curls at the opposite end of the couch. I drape a blanket over his legs, and then another across Nina. She shoves it away. (*I see why she chose the ice-queen movie. Yikes!*) I don't try again.

Since they're quiet, I leave. June follows. Back in the kitchen, I realize my hands are shaking. That my stomach hurts. I grip the edge of the counter where all my pizza making supplies are spread out. I bend in half, my forehead resting against the cool granite. I close my eyes. Take a deep breath. *I can do this*, I tell myself.

"You okay, Luca?" June asks softly.

I sniff and stand up. "I'm fine. Let's—let's just try filming that again. Before the twins decide their peace treaty is over."

I shake out my limbs. June counts me down. I channel Ma's Dazzlingly Bright smile, just how she's taught me to act in front of customers, no matter how chaotic things get in the kitchen. *Fake it till it's real*, she says. So I do. I pan fry cubes of translucent chicken breast until they're browned and sizzling. I whisk my own buffalo sauce. I blend a bleu cheese sauce. I keep smiling for the camera even though my insides are breaking. I can't get Elio's and Nina's faces out of my mind. But I'm doing this for them. This video will keep our family together. Just keep smiling.

I'm about to put the dressed buffalo chicken pizza in the oven when another shout comes from the family room. June groans. But now I'm not annoyed. I'm angry. I tell her to wait in the kitchen while I give the twins a piece of my mind.

"What's your problem?" I shout when I get into the family room. Nina is pressed against the right armrest of the couch, the blanket up to her chin. Elio is sprawled out. Tiny hills of his blanketed feet are just shy of grazing Nina.

"His feet are touching me," she snaps. "I told him to back off, but he won't listen."

I sigh. "Elio, can you please scooch over?"

He balks. "What? I'm not even touching her!"

"I don't care," I say. "Just do it. I told you I'm doing something important, but you two keep getting in the way. Don't make me call Ma or Pop."

Nina glares at our brother. Elio reluctantly drags himself toward the far end of the couch. "Fiiine. You guys suck."

Nina sticks out her tongue at him. I shoot her a "none of that" look, and she turns her head back to the TV, fidgeting with the remote. They're quiet again. I march back to the kitchen and smile for the camera as I slide the pizza into the oven.

June films me angry-washing dishes. It feels good to get my aggression out on the pans and mixing bowls. We watch through the glass oven door as the pizza cooks. We pull it out twenty minutes later, and I'm just cutting into the pie for the camera when Nina and Elio start shouting. I drag my hands down my face. I'm so freaking tired of this.

"Should we go in there?" June asks. Nina shouts something about feet and toe cheese.

"No. Keep filming." I nibble on a pizza crust, grinning and *mmm*-ing like a cartoon. "Now this is pizza perf—"

FWUMP! In the other room, it sounds like a pillow being thrown. Elio shouts at Nina to stop acting like a jerk.

"Maybe we should go check on them," June says, glancing at the kitchen doorway.

I shake my head. "They're fine. I just need to get this last—"

Nina screams, cutting me off, "STOP TOUCHING ME WITH YOUR FEET!" Then—*CRACK!* It's a nauseating whacking sound. Two hard objects colliding.

My stomach roller-coaster drops.

"AAAAUGHHHH!"

The scream is high-pitched. It's pained, not angry. My blood chills. June and I bolt from the kitchen. In the family room, Nina is standing next to the couch. She's whiter than fresh burrata, staring open-mouthed at Elio, who's on the floor clutching his face. Streams of red strain through his fingers.

Blood. *Oh no, no, no. Luca, you idiot! You could have stopped this!*

He screams louder. Dark spots spatter the wood floor. I rush to him, knocking aside the remote at his knees. "What happened?"

Through his sobs, he sputters, "Sh-sh-she threw the remote at me!"

My head whips at Nina. Her head shakes, as if she can't believe what she's seeing. "I didn't mean it."

This is too big for just me. I point at my phone in June's hand. "Call my parents."

She tucks her blond hair behind her ear. "On it."

I turn back to Elio. My joints feel achy, the way I get when I have a fever. But I can't be weak. Not now. "Let me see." I pull Elio's hand away. An inch-wide gash cuts above his right eyebrow. I've nicked myself dozens of times in the kitchen, so I've seen blood plenty, but this is different. It won't stop gushing.

I grab the blanket closest to me and press it against Elio's head. "Hold it tight against your forehead," I tell him. "We need to stop the bleeding."

He sobs. "Am I gonna die?"

"What? No," I say, but now all I can think of is Elio dying and it being all my fault. I hold my baby brother in my arms. "You're gonna be okay."

I steal a look at June. She's pale too. "Can't get ahold of your mom," she says. Her fingers flit across the screen, then she presses the phone to her ear. "Trying your dad now."

"Thanks." My teeth grind together. *Please pick up. Please pick up.*

Nina tiptoes closer, her hand covering her mouth. "That's a lot of blood." She looks me in the eye. "He needs a doctor."

Elio cries louder.

"I know, I know," I say, rocking him like an infant. "As soon as Ma or Pop gets here, we can get you to the hospital."

"Luca," June says, her voice feather soft. "Your dad's not picking up either. We need to do something." She points to my little brother, the blanket pressed to his head. "It's coming through."

Sure enough, sticky crimson is seeping through the fabric onto my fingers. It's warm and smells like old pennies. My insides squirm. Of course we can't get ahold of my parents. And Gramma Salvatore already told us she's not around. All the adults are always gone when we need them. My stomach squeezes. I can't believe the next words out of my mouth.

"Call 9-1-1," I say. "Hurry."

Chapter 10

I ride in the ambulance with Elio. I sit next to him on a too-small seat smashed between medical supplies and beeping machines. Andi, the Latina paramedic checking Elio's vitals, wears a mask, but her hazel eyes are kind. Her muffled voice keeps telling me it'll be okay.

It'll be okay.

Headlights bob in the windows of the double doors of the emergency vehicle. A minivan drives behind us. It's June's mom, June, and Nina. We got ahold of Mrs. Mason right after we dialed 9-1-1. Of course, Mrs. Mason answered right away. She always does. She's a good mom.

The ambulance races through the dark streets, siren wailing. It's a clear night, but there's slush in the streets. We stutter to a stop as we pull into the emergency entrance of the hospital. Elio moans, his chubby bottom lip trembling. Andi applies more pressure to his forehead.

It'll be okay.

Elio's gurney is lifted out of the ambulance. He's wheeled into the hospital, where two people in scrubs ask questions about his vitals and his bleeding and allergies to medications and other things I don't understand or have the answers to. They take Elio down a busy yellow-and-gray hallway. I follow like a duck paddling after a speedboat, trying to keep up.

A nurse named Chuck sits with me in a small waiting area while Elio is taken to a room. He'll need stitches, Chuck says. Mrs. Mason got ahold of our parents, he says. Here's some water and a package of crackers. I don't eat the crackers, but I sip the water. Chuck tries to ask me about what happened. I answer him, I think, but it's like someone is puppeting my tongue, my lips, my lungs. He writes down what I say. He tells me it'll be okay.

It'll be okay.

Ma and Pop arrive together, almost fifteen minutes after we get to the hospital. Pop's eyes are glassy. He bear paws the top of my head in greeting. He calls me champ and tells me I did good. He smells musty and a little like stale bread, like he hasn't showered, like he's been somewhere I don't recognize. Drinking a beer in a new apartment that isn't *our* home.

Ma wraps me in a hug. She asks me questions, more questions than Chuck did. But she doesn't write anything down, and her questions come faster than I can give her answers. *What happened? How long was Elio bleeding? Did you see it happen? Why didn't you try calling Gramma Salvatore? What were you doing that you didn't see Nina throw the remote? Do you know how expensive ambulances are? Why was Nina so upset? Did you lock the door when you left? Was the oven off?*

I keep my cool until Elio gets wheeled into the room. He's stunod—loopy, out of it—from whatever meds the doctor gave him. He looks so small in the giant hospital bed, wearing that mint-green gown and covered in the coarse white hospital blanket. There's an angry red line above his right eye. Five stretches of thread, like stitching on a baseball, seal the gap that wept blood minutes ago. The injury is swollen and shiny from whatever ointment they slathered on it. It's not until I see my baby brother that I finally break. I sob into my hands in the hard-backed chair next to his bed.

"Oh, baby," Ma says, cradling me in her arm. "He's all patched up. See?"

I feel stupid that she's comforting *me* when I'm not the one who looks like a rag doll. She should be fussing over Elio. I shove her off. Tell her I'm fine. She tries to say something else, but the doctor comes in. She's short, maybe South Asian. Her skin is warm golden brown. I swipe the tears from my cheeks while she tells Ma and Pop that Elio will be fine. The cut was clean, not too deep. His stitches will need to be taken out in five to seven days. That he should

96

rest this weekend. That he'll be good as new. Shouldn't be much of a scar either.

When the doctor leaves, Ma and Pop stand over Elio's bed, looking at him like he's a work of art. Pop gently sweeps the curls off his forehead. Elio yawns. Then something happens that I don't expect. Ma wraps her arms around Pop's waist. Pop wraps his arm around her shoulder. He kisses the top of her head. Wires and gears spark in my brain. *System malfunction!* My *separated* parents are acting like they love each other. *What is happening?*

They hold each other like that for a full minute. Like it's natural. I am so confused.

I watch them talking with Elio, standing together like a married couple should, and I wonder if Elio's injury, us ending up in this chaos, isn't a total disaster. If, maybe, it's the best thing that could have happened. I mean, of course I don't want Elio to be hurt, but . . . maybe all Ma and Pop needed is seeing what's most important: their kids. Their family. Maybe they needed a reminder about why we're a family. To see what happens if we don't stick together.

But then Pop lets go of Ma, and Ma lets go of Pop. They separate. Ma says she'll stay here with Elio, but that Pop should take me and Nina home.

"I don't want to go," I say. It feels wrong, leaving Elio here, when I was responsible for him. When this is my fault. I should stay until we can all go home.

"It's been a long night, kiddo," Pop says. "You and Nina need to sleep."

"I'm here," says Ma. "You did good getting Elio to the hospital. Leave the rest to us."

I stare at the floor. "But it's my fault he's here. I should have—"

Pop walks over and tips my chin up so that I'm forced to look at his eyes. "It was an accident. It's nobody's fault."

"But—"

"No buts," he says. "Now, come on. Let's get you and your sister home."

Out in the waiting area, Pop thanks Mrs. Mason for all her help. I hug June and thank her for everything. She whispers in my ear, "That's what the BFC is for. Best friends take care of best friends."

Pop is near the automatic exit doors, holding Nina's hand. "Luca, time to go."

"Us too," Mrs. Mason says to June. "Let's go."

We say one more round of goodbyes in the parking lot, and then Pop, Nina, and I pile into his red sedan.

When we get home, it's almost eleven thirty. Pop tucks Nina into bed. While he does, I clean up the mess in the kitchen. June and I left our pizza-making stuff everywhere. I load the dishwasher with as many of the measuring cups and bowls as I can. I put the flour back in the pantry. I wrap up the buffalo chicken pizza and stash it in the fridge. When I finish, I find Pop in the family room, scrubbing Elio's blood off the floor. I'm surprised to see the stack of pillows and blankets he's been sleeping with stacked at the end of the couch. After the way he and Ma hugged in the hospital, I thought maybe—*maybe*—something had changed.

"You're sleeping out here again?" I ask.

He looks at me funny. "Of course."

"But I thought—you and Ma hugged at the hospital," I say. "You kissed her."

Pop folds the wet rag in his hand. He sighs. "That, uh, well. You see, Luca, your mother and I, we still love each other. And we've known each other so long that we know how to comfort each other when life gets rough. But that doesn't change anything. We're still separating. I'll sleep on the couch just like I have been for a while now."

A while. It hits me just how much I've missed. I knew it had been a few days of Pop on the couch, but not *a while. How long is that? Weeks? Months?* My head feels like a hot-air balloon. My knees shake. I'm so tired and overwhelmed and disappointed and confused that I almost cry again, but I rub my eyes to stop myself and play it off like I'm tired. "So you're still moving out this weekend?"

"I am." Pop pats the couch cushion next to him. "You wanna talk about it?"

I consider telling him how I really feel, but I don't think I could get through what I want to say without crying. I'm too tired to control my emotions. And I don't want to add more stress to Pop's day than I already did by being the worst babysitter/big brother ever.

"No, that's all right." Then I head to my bedroom.

At the hospital, for a fleeting moment, I thought maybe we didn't need *Pizza Perfect* to save us, that getting on the show could just be for me. For *my dreams*. But now it's clearer than ever: operation *Pizza Perfect* is a must. Pop just said he and Ma still love each other. If that's true, then there's still a chance they can fix their marriage. If Elio's accident could bring them together, even a little bit, just imagine what being on TV would do!

I plug my phone into the charger next to my bed. When I open the lock screen, I notice the green text message icon with the number two in a red circle. It's Will. Warmth flutters in my chest.

Will: Hey! Wanna hang again this weekend?

Will: We can play a different game if you want.

In this hurricane of an awful night, his messages are a lighthouse. Everyone else's problems swirl around me, and I can't fix them, but there's this boy. This friend. This friend who is a boy with a face that I like. He makes me feel like I matter. And what's even better is that I don't have to share him with anyone else. Like a secret. I want to hold on to that and never let go.

I text back without a second thought.

Me: I do.

Chapter 11

The next day, despite our massive Salvatore dumpster fire of a Friday night, Pop STILL loads up his buddy Tony's truck with clothes, the old kitchen table, the futon from our basement, and boxes of other random things that belong here, in *this* house. It's like, I *knew* the move was going to happen because Pop said so, but I can't *believe* it's happening. Like, it doesn't make any freaking sense.

Elio sleeps most of the day, which means he misses the last few hours of Pop living with us. When he wakes up, he's got dark circles under his eyes and his forehead is bulging like a milk carton full of sour milk. Ma directs him to the couch, where she feeds him painkillers and pancakes along with a dose of as much *SpongeBob SquarePants* as he wants. Honestly, aside from wincing when he tries to raise his eyebrows, Elio acts like this is the best day of his life.

Nina, however, won't leave her bedroom. At almost three in the afternoon, she's still in her pajamas. Ma sends me in to try and talk to her, but she won't look up from the graphic novel she's reading—*Twins* by Varian Johnson, which she's read a million times already. I get her not wanting to talk. I'm sure she feels bad about hurting Elio. Probably as bad, if not worse, than I feel about letting it happen.

Gramma Salvatore comes over to help, so Ma can run the restaurant. I go to Will's that afternoon because I need a freaking break. He tries to talk to me, ask me how I am, but I don't want to talk. I just want video games and time with him. That's all. But he keeps asking me questions because I guess I'm acting like more of a weirdo than usual. So I end up spilling about what happened with Elio and Nina. I even tell him about my *Pizza Perfect* application. I show him some of the videos I recorded, and we end up spending most of our time together editing down the videos into something five minutes long. It's not quite done by the time I leave, but I notice how much lighter I feel when I walk out of his apartment. Being there was like a vacation.

I'm surprised that I tell him so much. But he makes me feel safe. Seen. And weirdest of all—listened to. Like, he *really* hears me when I talk, which June only does when I'm about to break down, and my parents . . . well, they almost always miss that mark. The fact that he *wants* to know more about me, the good and the bad, makes me warm and tingly. Turns out Will's not just cute and funny.

He's kind. Like, really, truly kind.

Gramma Salvatore ends up staying the night so Ma can head to Mamma Gianna's in the morning and Pop doesn't have to come back. He's busy settling into his new apartment, but I hear Gramma Salvatore on the phone with him after she sends all of us to bed. She's not good at whispering. "Gio," she blares, "I can't lend you more than I already have. I got you out of this house, but I can't keep funding your life. You need to find a way to pay for the hospital bills on your own. Sell the restaurant. I don't care what you do!"

I can barely sleep after I hear that. I feel betrayed. Gramma Salvatore never liked the restaurant, but now I feel like she's helping break my family apart. She *wants* us to get rid of the restaurant. She *wants* Pop out of our house. I want to break into the guest room and tell her off, but I don't. Instead, I rewatch the video Will and I put together. I'll show her what the Salvatores are made of when we land one of the final episodes of *Pizza Perfect*. We'll get rich and famous, and Pop'll never have to ask her for money ever again. That'll show her.

On Sunday, Gramma Salvatore leaves nice and early (good riddance) and Pop comes over to have breakfast with us. He says this is what it'll be like. Sometimes we'll be with him at his apartment, and sometimes he'll come over to have meals and hang at our house. He calls it "your house," like it's no longer his. Like he's no longer a part of *us*. That makes me angry. Sad.

Maybe Nina was right. Maybe he is abandoning us. Maybe he *will* move to Canada like Olivia P.'s dad. To stop myself from obsessing about Ma and Pop's marriage, I tweak the application video. Thinking about us getting onto *Pizza Perfect* makes me feel better. I stay up late editing the video until it sings. I attach it to an email along with my written responses, shoot a quick prayer to whoever is the saint of applications, and hit send.

I eventually drift off thinking about what it would be like to shake Travis Parker's hand. To show him around the restaurant. To have one of those signature heart-to-hearts with him. To watch his face melt into that goofy grin when he eats one of my pizzas. How he'll make my family whole again.

When Monday morning rears its ugly head, I want to smack it in the face. I don't feel rested at all. Staying awake for seven classes is going to be a C-H-A-L-L-E-N-G-E. Although she usually says it'll stunt my growth, Ma lets me take a thermos of coffee with cream and sugar on my walk to school. I don't even like coffee. But June will have to piggyback me to class if I don't take drastic measures.

She and I have advisory together first thing. I'm a little worried about seeing her. We texted some over the weekend, but she still doesn't know I've been hanging out with Will, and I don't know *when* to tell her because, at some point, she's gonna find out. And even though Will asked me

104

to hang out and she didn't, I feel like I picked him over her. She was there for me with Elio at the hospital, and now I'm keeping this secret from her that keeps getting bigger.

She's waiting for me outside Mr. Maylar's classroom. Her hair is a little greasy and pulled into a low ponytail. She's wearing an oversized green hoodie. When she throws her arms around me it feels like a warm blanket. I hug her back. She smells like strawberries and vanilla.

"How are you?" she asks, her voice still a little froggy. "How's Elio?"

"I'm fine. Tired. But fine. I think." I lead the way into Mr. Maylar's room. We take our seats near the back. "Elio's okay too. He tried to stay home from school, but Ma couldn't find anyone to babysit. His forehead looks a lot better than it did Friday night."

"I'd hope so," says June. Then she breaks into a giant grin. "I've got news."

I lean closer. "What?"

"Cast lists are posted . . . and I got Cinderella!" She strikes a pose, hands framing her face. I envision a glittering Instagram filter making her cheeks sparkle.

I raise my hand for a high five. "Dude! That's awesome. I knew you would get it. Congratulations!"

She high-fives me. "I mean, I *hoped* I would, and I felt really good about my callback, but Anya was great too. Better than I let on last Friday, I just—I'm so happy. This is my first lead role. I even have my own song."

"Just the beginning of the rest of your big famous life."

She laughs. "That's a little dramatic."

"Well, it *is* thee thee-ah-ter, dahling."

She giggles. Mr. Maylar gives us "quiet down" eyes. We chat in hushed voices about the rest of the casting choices for *Into the Woods* until the bell rings and the morning announcements start. There's the standard safety reminders and hallway expectations, along with the Pledge of Allegiance, but there are also two new announcements.

"We're still months away from the seventh and eighth grade spring dance," the secretary says over the PA, "but student council is seeking volunteers to help plan the event and raise funds. If you're interested in joining student council to make this the best dance ever, stop by Ms. Tyler's room at three thirty on Tuesday."

June whispers in my ear, "Our first ever dance! Think you'll go?"

I shrug. "Will *you* go?"

"Maybe," she says. Her cheeks redden. "If someone asks me."

My nose wrinkles. "Getting asked isn't a requirement to attend, you know."

"I *know*, but—"

Mr. Maylar waves his hand at us to be quiet. We hush but giggle because he literally has a grumpy-cat face in the morning. It's hilarious. Mr. Maylar wags his head at his computer, totally clueless about why we're laughing.

The last announcement for the day is about another spring event: "Riverfront Junior High, are you ready to rock? This year's Battle of the Bands will be here before you know it. Students are encouraged to sign up to compete before the end of March. If you have questions, talk to our band director, Mr. Lewis. Students of all skill levels are encouraged to participate."

Rock bands make me think of Will. Will reminds me that I've been a bad friend to June. When the announcements end, I lean closer to her ear so Mr. Maylar can't hear me. "I know you're going to be busy with the musical, but wanna hang out soon?"

She flips through her planner, keeping one eye on Maylar. "Rehearsals are every day now." Then she winks at me. "But I'll see if I can pencil you in."

I roll my eyes. "Such a diva."

At lunch, we're allowed to use our phones. While I'm waiting for June and Will to get their hot lunch, I refresh my inbox. Zilch. *I mean, c'mon, Luca. Your* days *ahead of the application due date. It's not like Travis Parker is sitting around twiddling his thumbs, waiting for* your *submission.*

Will makes it to the table first, and I stow my phone. He's wearing a camo Green Day T-shirt and a gray zip-up hoodie. His hair, of course, is shiny and perfect as ever. "Guess what," he says, chomping on a carrot.

"What?" I ask.

June plops between Will and I as he answers, "I talked to Mr. Lewis about signing up for the Battle of the Bands. Since I don't have a band yet, he told me he'll keep an ear out for other kids interested in starting something. He might even have a drummer already!"

"That's so cool," I say. I'm happy for him, but a little voice in a dark corner of my mind tells me he's going to find new friends. Cooler guys he can hang out and play video games with.

"You know, I could talk to the musical cast," says June. "There're a lot of band kids in the show. Since we don't have a real pit orchestra, everyone's a vocalist. And I know a lot wish they had a chance to perform with their instruments instead."

Will brightens. "That would be great!"

She grins, all satisfied with herself. I wish I'd thought of that. Then I'd have something special to do for Will. The last thing I need is for him to realize that June is much cooler than me.

Then Will asks June, "Would you want to hang out with us sometime? Me and Luca?"

Her face lights up, and I can feel my special guy-guy friendship evaporating. She doesn't even look at me to see if that's okay. All of a sudden, I imagine Will and June hanging out without *me*, and I lose my appetite.

"Definitely, but I'm going to be pretty busy with the musical," June says. "But I mean, Luca and I hang out all the time. We've been best friends since forever. Right, Luca?"

I fidget with my foil Doritos bag. "That's right. Till death do us part!" I joke, so Will doesn't think it's like a *thing* he's excluded from. But then June and Will both make weird faces, and I realize I made a MARRIAGE joke, which is the OPPOSITE of what I want either of them to think about me and June. I quickly add, "As friends. Like, best friends. But forever."

"Yeah, I got it," Will laughs. He stares at me an extra second, though, and I feel like he's trying to say something without saying something. I just can't tell what. Then he says to June, "But maybe you'd consider letting a new friend into your exclusive club?"

June chomps a potato chip. "For you, I think we can make an exception."

Will and June keep talking, and I already feel like they're making something new between the two of them. Something I'm not part of. And I do not like that. He was supposed to be mine. Someone just for me. And now, I feel like I've lost that too.

Chapter 12

Pop's new apartment smells like cabbage. It might even be made of cabbage. The walls in the kitchen are peeling and a gross pea-green color. Flecks of paint cluster near the dusty white floorboards.

It's Friday, one week since the remote fiasco, and the first night Nina, Elio, and I are seeing where Pop lives. It's a tiny, one-bedroom apartment, so he says we can't sleep over. Not unless we all want to cram on the futon, which we don't. Elio snores and Nina is a kicker. We settle for dinner. Pop hovers over the stove, stirring a pot of red sauce. Spaghetti boils in another pot. Garlic bread toasts in the oven. The familiar smells of home only somewhat mask the odor of this weird, grimy place.

The twins and I crowd around the small kitchen table that used to be in our basement. Pop's *humming*. Nina gives me a "what the what" look. I shrug. Pop is *not* a hummer.

He stops and spins around like he can hear us not

talking about him. "So, what's the latest?" he asks. "I miss you guys."

Elio perks up. "I get my stitches out tomorrow."

Nina winces at the mention of stitches. She hasn't been her normal bossy self all week. I watch her scrutinizing the reddish line above our brother's eye. It looks better than it did a couple days ago. The skin isn't so raw or angry, and the swelling has gone way down.

"That's right. Your mother's taking you while I man the restaurant," Pop says. He blows on a spoonful of sauce, tipping it into his mouth. His lips smack together, satisfied. "You're gonna look like a real tough guy with that scar."

Elio grins. "Will you call me Scar Face?"

Pop chuckles. "Maybe we can come up with a less . . . murderous nickname."

"You really think it'll leave a permanent mark?" Nina asks. That perks up my ears. It's like the only thing she's said since we got here.

Pop doesn't seem to pick up on her gloomy mood because he says, "Oh, sure. It'll look wicked awesome. Check out mine." He bends close, showing off a jagged mark of discolored skin near his hairline. "Hockey puck. Six years old. Man, that hurt. But don't I look badass?"

Elio snickers. "Totally."

There's a beat of silence. Nina's eyebrows squeeze together. She looks like she's about to say something but then decides against it. Without another word, she leaves the kitchen.

Pop finally seems to be aware of his surroundings. He gives me a chin nod to go check on her. I wish *he* would, since he's the one who brought up the whole permanent scar thing. But I'm the big brother, and I sort of feel like I need to redeem myself after I royally screwed up babysitting last week. I follow her.

Nina is tucked in the crease of the futon, her knees pulled under her chin. She picks at the chipped lavender nail polish on her big toe. I sink into the worn, fluffy mattress, a few inches from her. A poof of dust motes cloud in the air.

"You okay?" I ask.

She tilts her chin on her knee so that her face is out of view. "I'm fine."

I know that line all too well. It's one of my favorites. "Fine" doesn't mean she's anywhere close to it. But getting past "fine" to her true feelings requires some excavation. Time for a different tactic.

"Elio's so clumsy." I laugh, scooting closer and prodding her knees gently with mine. "I'm surprised it took him this long to get a scar."

"He didn't *get* a scar," Nina mumbles. A triangle of lavender lifts off her toenail. She rolls it between her fingers. "I gave him one."

"It was an accident. You didn't mean to hurt him," I say.

Nina buries her face in her thighs. Her muffled voice says, "Maybe I did." Her hair falls around her shoulders. Her back shakes. A sniffle emerges from behind the veil of hair.

I chew my lip. That can't be true. Nina gets angry, but she's not EVIL. Sheesh. I get out my pick and brush and dig a little deeper.

"What do you mean?" I ask, rubbing her back the way Ma used to for me when I was upset. "You *meant* to cut Elio's head open?"

"Okay, I mean, no." She shakes her head vigorously, but she still won't look at me. She cries harder into her knees.

I glance at the doorway to the kitchen, wishing I had reinforcements. That Pop would come in and help me make her feel better. But he doesn't. This is one of those times when I can't tell the difference between what it means to be Nina's brother and Nina's father. All I want is to be her big bro, and even that I've sucked at lately.

So I admit the truth that's been eating at me. "Nina, maybe you were frustrated and overreacted, but what happened isn't your fault," I say. "If anything, I'm to blame. *I* was supposed to be watching you and Elio."

She peeks an eye out from behind the shroud of chestnut hair. "You didn't throw the remote."

"No, but I should have been there to stop you before it got that far."

Then she says something that really surprises me. "It's not your job. Ma should have been there. Or Pop. It's—it's *their* fault I was so angry anyway."

"Oh." I need to recalculate. I switch the position of my legs under me. "So you weren't mad at Elio?"

She sits up, showing her face. Tearstains track down her cheeks. Her eyes dart to the kitchen entrance. She whispers, "I mean, I *was*, but that wasn't all I was upset about. I couldn't stop thinking about Pop moving out." She looks around the sparse room. "Everything's changing. I hate it." She sucks in the clear snot invading her upper lip. Her voice gets harsher. "He seems happier, doesn't he? It's like he *wants* to be away from us."

My stomach twists. I can't argue with that. Pop does seem different. Lighter. But I can't let my baby sister think her family is falling apart. "But *we're* here. You, me, and Elio. *That's* why Pop is happy."

She shrugs, then goes back to picking her toes. "If we made him happy, he'd never have moved out."

"He moved out because he and Ma are having problems. Not because of us."

"We should have been enough for him to stay."

"He's not gone forever. It's a *temporary* separation."

Her eyes slide to me. "For now."

Well, *this* isn't working. If I didn't think I was losing my touch before, it's clear I am now. We could talk in circles about why Pop moved out into infinity. I grab hold of Nina's legs and spin her so we're face-to-face. My voice is stern. "Remember what Ma and Pop said. This isn't about *us*. It's about them. They're gonna figure this out and then Pop'll move back in."

Nina sniffs. "You really think so?"

"I'm gonna make sure of it," I say, not adding anything about how I'm hoping *Pizza Perfect* will save the day. But my phone suddenly feels heavy in my pocket. This would be the perfect moment for a notification to buzz with an email, but it doesn't.

"But how?" she asks. "You can't make people fall in love. That's, like, a *rule*. Haven't you seen *Aladdin*?"

I laugh. "You're right. You can't. But I'll tell you a secret." Her face brightens. I lean toward her ear. "Ma and Pop still love each other. Pop told me so. So there's hope. I have a plan to make sure they know how important it is that they stay in love. For the restaurant. For the family. For us."

Now she seems genuinely interested. "What's the plan? I wanna help."

"I can't tell you yet," I say, "but as soon as I can, I will. I'll need your help to pull it off."

"Really?" she asks, eyes wide.

"Really." I nod to the kitchen. "But if we're gonna save our family, we need to put on happy faces for Ma and Pop. If we're sad or angry, it makes their lives harder. So, what do you say? Can we head back into the kitchen for dinner?"

Nina chews her lower lip. "You promise to tell me the plan later?"

"Pinkie promise." I stick out my little finger. She wraps hers around mine. We shake. Then I stand up and offer her my hand. "Care to join the banquet, m'lady?"

She tips her fingers into my hand with a giggling eye roll. "Fiiine."

I take her arm in my elbow and lead her back to the kitchen. She sits in the chair next to Elio this time, saying, "I decided you'll look cool with a scar. You're welcome."

Elio laughs. "Next time you want to make me look cool, maybe give me a heads-up?"

Nina shrugs. "We'll see."

When Pop scoops dinner onto our plates, he gives me a wink and mouths "thank you." He means for talking to Nina. My chest warms. I sit up taller in my chair. I'm glad he can see what I'm trying to do. How I can help. He trusts me to put us back together. I hope that means he'll have my back if—*when* we get the email from the *Pizza Perfect* people. If either of my parents is gonna need some convincing, it's Ma. I'll take all the backup I can get.

Now, if I could just hear back from *Pizza Perfect*, I could get to fixing everything.

Chapter 13

I'm a lot of things: a master pizza maker, a big brother, an oldest son, a decent-to-average student. (Okay, fine. Just average. But a guy can't be everything!)

One thing I'm definitely *not*? Patient.

No matter how much I resist refreshing my email hoping a *Pizza Perfect* subject line will come through, I end up doing it every two minutes. Seriously. By Thursday, February 1, the application deadline, I'm dragging my thumb down my screen without even thinking about it. But it's always more of the same: a whole lot of nothing. Each time I don't see something come through, I'm more and more convinced I'm not going to hear back.

I mean, I'm just a *kid*. They probably won't even take me seriously. Maybe it was a bad idea to keep the application from Ma and Pop. I mean, it wouldn't be the first time I've been written off because I'm a kid. When I was nine, Nonna Zaza took me to help at a soup kitchen over winter break. We filled ready-to-go meals for the unhoused of Chicago. I oversaw opening cans of corn and filling little containers. One of the adult volunteers (Marge) kept trying to move me to a simpler task (putting the packed Styrofoam containers in plastic bags). She thought opening cans was too much for a nine-year-old, obviously missing that I grew up in a kitchen. I mean, I could've baked her a whole corn casserole all by myself! Nonna Zaza stepped in twice to tell Marge to back off. It drives me bonkers when adults don't think kids can do stuff, but it happens all the time. What if that's what's happening now? If Ma, Pop, and I had worked on the application together, maybe the *Pizza Perfect* people would have emailed us back already.

Fortunately, on Deadline Day, I get a welcome distraction from thinking I bungled the whole thing. Will invites me over again. I don't even have to worry about asking June if she wants to join us because she's at *Into the Woods* rehearsals every day now. She'll just never know. And Will still gets to be *my* friend.

My I-wish-he-was-more-than-a-friend friend.

Hanging out with Will is changing. It's getting easier. I'm not so in my head about what I say or do. Today, instead of playing video games, we microwave movie theater butter popcorn and take turns showing each other our favorite funny videos. Most of mine are cooking blunders and kitchen mishaps. Most of Will's are about kittens, which surprises me. I didn't take him for a cat video kind of kid. Mamma mia, was I wrong!

The three hours he and I are together are the longest stretch I go without looking at my email. Partly because my phone is in full-on funny-video mode, but mostly because Will keeps scooting closer to me and our elbows are touching, and I can smell his coconut shampoo. I legit can't focus on anything else. *What is happening to me? Why is he doing this?* Like, is he trying to get closer to *me*, or is he just getting a better view of the screen?

I. DON'T. KNOW.

In either case, my parents, Nina and Elio, the restaurant, even *Pizza Perfect*—it all fades away when I'm with him. My brain takes a break. I relax. I don't have to *try* to be anything other than me. And he doesn't judge me for being weird or liking pizza so much, which even June does sometimes.

I used to think I just didn't get along with guys. I mean, there're plenty I'd never have anything to say to, but now that I think about it, the same goes for lots of girls too. And Marin in my social studies class is nonbinary, and we have lots in common even though we don't hang out. So maybe it's not about gender. Maybe it's Will. Maybe it's me. Maybe we have something special. Not a best-friends thing like me and June but something different. Something good. I'm just not sure what it is yet, but whatever it is makes me feel safe. *He* makes me feel safe. Like I can tell him anything.

So before I lose my nerve, I ask, "Have you ever, uh, *liked* someone?"

He looks at me. His perfect hair sloshes a half second late in the same direction. "I dunno. Maybe?" He smirks. "Have *you*?"

I didn't expect him to turn the question back on me so fast. "Oh, uh. Maybe?"

He laughs but not in a mean way. "You don't sound so sure."

"Well, how do you *know* if you like someone?"

He flips his phone around. "I don't know. For me, it's— it's a *more* thing. Like that person makes you want more. To *be* more. And they make you feel like you can do anything. *Be* anything. At least, that's what it's like for me. Does that make any sense?"

"Yeah, actually."

"*Actually*?" He shoves me, laughing. "Don't sound so surprised."

"I'm not—I just . . . I've never talked to a guy about this kind of stuff." *Oh my God.* I can feel the words bubbling up. "Because, you know, I think they'd get weird. With me liking boys."

Again, me being gay isn't a secret, but you don't exactly announce the gender you wanna date when you meet someone. I'm not sure if Will knows or not, so this is me kinda coming out to him. I hold my breath. I have no idea how he's gonna respond. I stare at my hands. I wait for him to get awkward. To tell me he doesn't want to hang out anymore.

An extra-long pause hangs between us, but he doesn't scoot away. Then he says, "I don't think it's weird."

I look up. He's smiling. "Really?" I say.

"Really."

"Cool."

"Cool," he says. Then he grabs his phone. "Have you seen the video with the cat in the bathtub? It's *classic*."

I can't decide if it's weird that he changed the subject or not, but I'm kind of glad he does. I'm not sure I want to talk about crushes anymore either, but I'm glad that, at the very least, he knows the truth about me now. And that he still wants to be my friend. I just wish I knew if he likes boys too. But since he didn't just come out with it, I'm guessing not? I don't know. UGH. Why is everything else with him so easy, but this is so hard?

But now I know one thing for certain: Will White makes me feel *more*.

Thinking about him takes up a lot of brain space after Thursday. I'm still thinking about him on Saturday at Mamma Gianna's. It's a quiet night. Mostly delivery, on account of the nasty sleet coming down sideways, which means Pop has been on the go since late this afternoon. Ma and I have been playing hot potato answering the phone, sorting online orders, and firing pizzas with Cesar. Nina and Elio are sitting in separate booths reading Dog Man books. We've only got one dine-in table, so it's no biggie for the twins to take up so much space.

Our only diners are two high schoolers, and they're clearly on a first date. The girls are dressed *way* too fancy for our joint, and they keep giggling at everything the other says. One girl is tall and super-skinny with amber-brown skin and platinum-blond hair. The other girl is rounder with glittery, glossy lips and dark brown skin. Their feet touch under the table like overlapping slices of pepperoni.

Whenever I steal a glance at them, Will pops into my mind. Despite my best efforts not to think about him this way, I picture the two of us in that booth. We're older, in high school. We're taller. More muscly but not *too* muscly (I don't do sports; Will doesn't either). I imagine us wearing high-top Converse like the two girls. His are black with pen doodles on the white edges. Mine are tomato-right-off-the-vine red. When the girls' feet touch, our feet touch. An oven ignites in my chest.

My phone buzzes in my pocket. I snap out of my daydream. My first thought is Will. Like he could sense me thinking about him. If he's got superpowers, he's gonna be in major trouble for not dishing sooner! My fingers slip into my pocket and pull out my phone. When I see the notification, I nearly drop it on the register. I shiver all the way down to my toes.

It's not Will.

It's an email with the subject: Greetings from the Pizza Perfect Crew!

Ohmygodohmygodohmygodohmygodohmygod.

I swipe up, unlocking my phone. My hands shake so bad I've gotta tap the email app twice because I miss it the first time. And there it is, sitting at the top of my inbox. THE EMAIL. My tongue goes bread-crumb dry. My thumb hovers over the small rectangle showing the start of the message. I debate waiting to get home to open it, but I can't wait. Not patient, remember? Like taking the Polar Plunge into Lake Michigan, my index finger dives at the screen.

Dear Luca and Mamma Gianna's,

You're receiving this email because you applied to be featured on the final season of the hit food series *Pizza Perfect* hosted by award-winning celebrity chef and restaurateur Travis Parker. Our committee is committed to thoroughly reviewing all applications and determining which restaurants will be the best fit for our program.

Our team loved reading your responses, especially from such a young pizza enthusiast. Luca, when we watched your video, we knew we had to meet the personality we met on camera in person. Your energy and passion for pizza is infectious. So, without further ado, we are thrilled to share that Mamma Gianna's has made it to the second round of candidates to be featured on *Pizza Perfect* season seven. Congratulations!

There's more in the email about next steps and keeping all this super-confidential and blah blah blah, but I stop there and reread that second paragraph over and over. It takes everything in me not to leap onto one of our tables, scream, and do a victory dance. I can't believe it. Everything I've been hoping for, all I've done to save my family, our restaurant, it's within grasp. I think I'm gonna cry.

The front door opens in the middle of my fourth reread. Pop busts in, an empty pizza carrier under his left arm. He's dripping half-frozen wet all over the floor. He takes off his hood and nods at me. "Are we closed yet?"

"Not even close," I say. But this is perfect timing. I need to tell Ma and Pop about the email, and I've got them in one place, which doesn't happen all that often these days. (I'm one step closer to fixing that!) I zoom around the counter and take his hand before he's got a chance to load up with another round of deliveries. I lead him into the kitchen. "I need to tell you and Ma something. Something BIG."

Pop ditches the pizza carrier on the counter as we pass the register. "Uh, okay."

Ma's pulling an extra-large black olive and mushroom out of the oven. She looks at us strangely, like she can sense something's up. "What's wrong now?" she asks.

Pop shrugs. "Luca needs to tell us something."

She dusts her hands on her apron. "Did something happen at school?"

"Nothing like that. Nothing bad," I say. I take a deep breath, toes tingling, and come out with it. "So, you know how I told you *Pizza Perfect* is ending after this next season? Well, they asked restaurants to nominate themselves to be on the show . . . so I filled out an application and recorded videos and sent them in. And I just heard back." I pause for dramatic emphasis. Ma looks alarmed, like she isn't breathing. Pop's mouth is hanging open. "They, like, *loved* what I sent in, and they're sending out a scout in three weeks to talk to us and see the restaurant in person before they make the final decision. You guys! We might *actually* be on TV!"

Ma is the first to recover. "Luca, I— Is this for real? Can I see the email?"

"Of course it is." I hand over my phone.

Her eyes rapidly scan the screen. "Looks legitimate," she says. "I just— I'm in shock. *Us?* We're not that— I mean, now isn't exactly the best time. I don't think we can—"

Pop claps me on the shoulder, cutting off her buffet of incomplete thoughts. "This is incredible, Luca." I think he could see my face falling. Pop gives Ma a look. Then he says,

"I'm blown away you did this for us, kiddo."

But Ma doesn't appreciate Pop's almost-glare. She grinds her heel into the tile and pretzels her arms. "Gio, how can we possibly do this? You and me? With . . . *everything*. We can't. We can barely keep our heads above water as it is." Then she looks at me. "Luca, it's sweet you applied, and I'm sure you did an amazing job, but we—*I* don't have the capacity for anything else right now."

No, no, NO! This is exactly what I was afraid of!

Pop squeezes my shoulder, but he looks at Ma when he says, "Maybe we can discuss this later, Christine?"

I breathe a little easier. If at least one of them is on my side, we might have a chance. Clearly Ma isn't thinking this through. "Getting on the show could save the restaurant," I say. "Think of the exposure! People all over the country would know about us. They'd travel to Chicago just to eat *our* pizza."

Ma looks at me like I'm a sad puppy. "Baby, that's not how it works. Even if we get on the show, no one's coming to Chicago to get *our* pizza when they could get it in their hometown, let alone one of the big-name pizzerias down the street."

"That's not true," I say. "I read about it online. Restaurants featured on the show get famous. People *do* travel to them, even if they're in hard-to-get-to places."

Pop tilts his head at Ma, a smug grin on his face. "Think

back, Chris. When we were first married, didn't we love to check out local dives? Whenever we traveled, we always hunted down the best of the best. That one Memorial Day trip we took to Minneapolis? We spent the whole weekend hunting down Michelin stars and local faves."

Ma rolls her eyes. "But that's *us*. We're Italian. We're foodies. That's what we do."

"You *really* think we're the only two like us on the planet?" Pop says dryly.

Ma's jaw opens, but words don't come out. She's cracking. Time to go in for the kill.

"And that's not all, Ma," I say. "If we get on the show, if we impress Travis Parker in the Pizza Perfect Challenge, he'll gift something to Mamma Gianna's. That's part of the show. Not everyone gets cash—but a new oven, a new fridge? And there could be real money, Ma. We could give the place a facelift. Maybe even hire someone else to help."

Ma fidgets with the gold pendant around her neck. She stares at me, then looks to Pop, then back to me. Finally, she says, "There's no denying we could use the financial help." She hands back my phone. "We'll—I'll *think* about it. Your father and I will discuss this later."

Turn up the gas and let's get cooking! This. Is. HAPPEN-ING. I bear-hug Ma. "Thank you, thank you, thank you!"

"I didn't say yes yet!" she gasp-laughs, patting the top of my head.

"Well, you'll have to decide kinda quick," I say. "We've only got until Monday to respond. There's a couple of forms we need to fill out too, and—"

Pop says, "Forward us the email. We promise to get back to them before the deadline."

"You swear?" I say, already pulling up the email so I can forward it.

"You have our word," says Pop.

Ma nods in agreement. "Now get your little behind out there and man the register like I asked."

I salute her. "Yes, ma'am!"

I'm flying high, but I falter when I see one of the teen girls standing at the register looking lost, her wallet in hand. Oops. I apologize for not helping her sooner. She's whatever about it. I ring her up, give her a box for the leftovers, and then I watch her and the other girl walk out hand in hand.

I smile. For the first time in a while, I feel good. Hopeful.

My plan is working.

Chapter 14

Pop comes over on Sunday afternoon. Things feel normal with him in the kitchen, talking business with Ma. They tell me I've gotta stay in my room while they discuss the *Pizza Perfect* sitch, but this isn't my first rodeo. I keep my door cracked and eavesdrop best I can. This is the biggest thing to ever happen in my life! They're kidding themselves if they think I'm missing out on important details. But they know my tricks—all I make out are garbled words. When Pop leaves for his apartment that evening, neither of them let on about how it went. Needless to say, I don't sleep that night.

Then they drag it out allll day, and freaking finally, on Monday afternoon, they share their decision with me.

"Look, Luca," Ma says, "this really couldn't have come at a worse time for us. Your father and I— You understand things in our marriage aren't good. We talked through a lot yesterday, and we've come to a decision."

Pop clears his throat. "What goes on with our family is our business, and we know these reality-type shows sometimes dig into people's lives too much. Personal information gets out for the whole world to see. We don't want that. Not about our marriage."

My hands wring together. I don't like where this is going. I can feel my chance to save my family (and meet Travis Parker) sifting through my fingers like flour.

"*But*," Ma says, eyes darting at Pop, "your father and I agree that, while this opportunity has come at the worst possible *personal* time for us, it couldn't have come at a better time for Mamma Gianna's." She takes a deep breath. I hold mine. *Omgomgomg.* "We'll meet with the scout so long as we can all agree that they won't film or discuss our personal lives."

"Well, our marriage primarily," adds Pop.

"Yes! Fine! Whatever!" I jump around, shouting. "I can't believe this is happening!"

They full-tooth smile. Ma gives me a side hug. "We're happy you're happy."

Pop says, "That's what's most important to us."

I send off the confirmation email in a flash, copying Ma and Pop on it this time. I'm still grinning like a clown when I get to school on Tuesday. I'm supposed to keep everything about *Pizza Perfect* SUPER SECRET, but I can't not tell June and Will. SOMEONE else has to know. Soon as we're in Culinary Arts, I spill.

June goes starry-eyed. "OMG. You're going to be famous! And before *me*! Can I be your publicist when you're fancy?"

"I wanna help too," Will says, holding up a pinkie. "I'll be your taste tester. I've got a very refined palate."

I raise my hands. "Guys, cool it. Shh." I glance around at the other kids, but none of them are listening. "Nothing's official yet. First, we need to impress this scout person. If she doesn't give us the thumbs-up, we don't get on. We've got three weeks to clean up the restaurant and prepare something extra special for her."

Will slumps in his chair. "Guess that means we won't be hanging out much. Who am I gonna play video games with?"

I freeze. *OH. NO.*

He did not just say that. Not in front of June.

She still doesn't know about my out-of-school friendship with Will. I almost clap my hand over his mouth, but it's too late. June absorbs the news in slo-mo. Her smile wobbles, and then she just looks confused. "You two have been hanging out?"

Will side-eyes me. "I mean, yeah. A bunch of times. Luca's like my best friend here."

Best friend. C'mon, Will. You had to use BEST?

"Oh, um." June hesitates, glancing at me. "I didn't realize you guys were getting so . . . close."

Damage control, Luca! SAY SOMETHING. I shift in my

chair. "I mean, you've been busy with the musical. I just didn't have time to mention it."

Now *Will* looks at me like I said the absolute wrong thing. Which I realize I did. Like I was only hanging out with Will because June wasn't around. *Luca, you're making a mess!*

"You have a phone," June says. "And the musical isn't *all* the time. But maybe you don't need to text me if you have a new best friend."

The bell rings. I feel so uncomfortable, trapped between Will and June. I want to say more, but Mrs. Ochoa greets us in her Riverfront fleece and dinosaur apron. She tells us we're making a tres leches cake, a traditional Mexican dessert that uses three different kinds of milk: sweetened condensed milk, evaporated milk, and regular old whole milk. The cake is soaked in milk and topped with a creamy frosting. It's served chilled. I've had tres leches before, and I just about died it was so good. Our assignment is to make the cake today and prepare the whipped topping. Tomorrow, we'll soak it and top it. Wednesday, we mange!

As soon as Mrs. Ochoa sends us off to work, I can tell we're gonna have a problem. To get the cake baked today, we need to have our batter in the oven within the first ten minutes of class. Unfortunately, the tension between me, Will, and June is thicker than a flourless chocolate cake but nowhere near as delicious. June starts bossing Will around, nudging him out of the way when he reaches for an ingredient or a measuring cup.

"I can read a recipe, June," Will says. "The difference between a quarter of a cup and two-thirds is pretty obvious."

"But you were measuring the flour wrong." June demonstrates with her hands. "Pack it in like this so you get an accurate measurement. This is how Luca—my *best* friend—showed me."

My eyes slide to the left, but I stay on task, separating egg yolks from the whites for the batter. We need to whip the whites into stiff peaks before adding them to the rest of the ingredients. It'll give the cake a light, spongy texture. Keeping my tone bright, I say, "I mean, it's okay if it's not—"

"I bake cookies with my mom all the time," Will interjects as he digs his measuring cup into the bag of flour. "I can measure just fine."

But June reaches over his shoulder and grabs the full measuring cup before he tips it into the mixing bowl. "That's too much!"

"Guys, stop. Mrs. O—"

"Let go!" Will yanks back, attempting to dump the flour into the bowl. Instead, it flies into the air. A white arc snows to the floor.

"You guys!" I come between them, dusted in flour. "We don't have time for this!"

Will ignores me and barks at June. "Look what you made me do!"

"*You* were gonna ruin our cake!" June says haughtily, not giving an inch. "I saved it."

Mrs. Ochoa appears in front of our workstation. "Ah-*hem*." We freeze. I'm mortified. Mrs. Ochoa *never* has to talk to our group. I mean, *I'm* the best chef in class! I bite my bottom lip as she surveys the disaster like a helicopter filming a highway accident. "What happened here?"

Will and June point literal fingers at each other.

"I was trying to stop him from messing up."

"She doesn't trust me!"

Mrs. Ochoa says, "Tres leches is about finding harmony in three similar yet distinctly different ingredients. While you're tasked with baking a cake, the real test is if you can work with others to meet your goal." Her finger drags across our flour-dusted table. "If you can't work together, you won't have cake. Teamwork means respectfully communicating what you need and humbly listening to your partners." She glances at the clock. "If you don't get this batter in the oven in the next seven minutes, it won't bake in time. What's your plan?"

"We'll fix it," I say quickly. "Sorry, Mrs. O."

She nods, already on the move to check another group. "Better work fast."

When she's gone, I look both my friends in the eyes.

"I don't know what's going on, but if we're gonna make it, I need to be in charge. June, you clean up the mess. Will, you measure the dry ingredients while I finish whipping up these egg whites."

June pouts. "Why do I have to clea—"

I turn on the hand mixer, beating the frothy mixture. I talk over the *whiiiir*. "No time to argue. Just do it."

I don't mean to be rude, but that's how it goes in a kitchen sometimes. There isn't time for hurt feelings. For drama. Not when food is on the line. And June, of all people, knows how seriously I take my food. With an eye roll that could get her cast in a horror film, June gives in and wipes up the flour storm. Will silently remeasures the flour and adds it to our mixing bowl.

I finish folding in the white waves of egg into the beige batter just in time and slide the pan into the oven. None of us talk as we clean up our station. I'm frustrated with both of them, but I also know I'm to blame. I never should have lied to June, but she is way overreacting. I'm allowed to have other friends, just like her. It's not *that* big a deal. And she has tons of friends. She doesn't get to act jealous. I'm not jealous of *them*.

Our cake is the last to come out of the oven, right as the bell rings. When we test it to see if it's cooked all the way through, I'm relieved that the knife comes out clean.

I usually take pride in fixing other peoples' problems,

but today I'm angry. Will and June *shouldn't* be a problem. At home, I'm used to it, but school isn't home. I've never had to manage two friends not getting along. (Mostly because it's always been just me and June, but STILL.) Part of me thinks it would be easier to tell Will we can't be friends anymore, but that's not fair. I want to be *more*. I like that he makes me feel like I matter.

June is going to have to be okay with that.

That means they've gotta get along. And one way or another, I'll make sure that happens.

Chapter 15

When school gets out, I grab Will and drag him to talk with me and June before she starts rehearsal. We find her just outside the cafetorium. I clutch my red notebook, which I've been using to brainstorm recipe ideas and write notes to myself about how we can impress the scout from *Pizza Perfect*.

"Look, June," I say, "I'm sorry I didn't tell you Will and I were hanging out, but what happened in Culinary Arts today—that can't happen again. I need you. *Both* of you. If there's any chance of me and my family getting on Travis Parker's show, I need your help. But if you're acting like babies, that's not helpful. Can I trust you to be my friends or not?"

June hugs her script binder to her chest. Her eyes lift to look at Will. He glances at her, runs his fingers through his hair, and shrugs.

"I—I don't know, Luca," June says reluctantly, swaying

on her toes. Her eyes flit to Will, then back at me. "You really hurt my feelings."

I don't have time for this. "I already said I was sorry. Can't we just move on?"

She glances over her shoulder. "I need to go. Rehearsal is starting."

"But—"

She walks off. Doesn't even say goodbye. She abandons me. Just like Pop. I'm a simmering teapot.

"Well, *okay* then," says Will, cringing. "Do you still, uh, wanna hang today?"

Now I want to stick it to June. "Yes. Yes, I do."

We head over to the elementary school to pick up Nina and Elio before we make our way to Mamma Gianna's. When we get to the restaurant, I'm surprised to see Mr. Cheeks, our landlord, sitting in a booth with Ma. There's a binder and papers laid out between them. Ma is fidgeting with her necklace. She gives me a quick wave, but Mr. Cheeks doesn't even glance in my direction. He goes right on talking, his loud, nasally voice spewing something about "margins" and "action." I wanted to introduce Will to Ma, but now is clearly not a good time.

Nina and Elio hole up in their usual booth, and I take Will into the kitchen. I've decided that the only way I can hang out with him is if he's willing to help me clean and prep the restaurant for the scout. He doesn't seem put off by the idea, which makes me feel buttery warm. We start with a deep clean of our finicky refrigerator.

"Who was that out there?" Will asks while he washes his hands.

"The woman is my mom," I say, "and that guy is our landlord, Mr. Cheeks. I've only seen him a couple times. He's never around. Not unless something's wrong."

Will turns off the water, drying his hands on a paper towel. "*Is* something wrong?"

I sigh. "The list of wrong things is too long to get into right now. Best thing we can do? Get cleaning so we can impress that scout."

For the next hour, we pull out all the items from the fridge, temporarily stashing them in the walk-in freezer. We scrub every tray and rung. While we work, Will tells me about his plans for the Battle of the Bands competition. Mr. Lewis found him a drummer, an eighth grader named Allison Gufferson, so now he just needs a bass player and a vocalist. He says they need to start practicing soon if they're going to be ready for the spring. "But I'll still make time to hang," he promises, his shoulder sliding against mine.

Hello, butterflies. "Good," I say, nudging him back.

As we're refilling the clean(er) fridge, Ma appears, looking sad as dried-out mashed potatoes. I want to ask her what happened with Mr. Cheeks, but she wouldn't like talking business around someone she doesn't know. But her face lights up when she sees us.

"You must be Will," she says in her Dazzlingly Bright voice, which weirds me out. I don't want him to meet Mamma Gianna's front-of-house personality; I want him to meet my mom. She holds out a hand. "I'm Christine, Luca's mom. So nice to meet you. He talks about you all the time."

Aaaaand presto! I'm a cherry tomato. "Ma! Not *all* the time."

But Will laughs, shaking her hand. "Nice to meet you too. I really like your restaurant."

There's nothing Ma likes more than a compliment about her family's legacy. Pride fills my chest, not only because of Mamma Gianna's but because of Will. She grins. "Thank you very much. Should I put a pizza in for you two? Or maybe some cheesy garlic bread?"

Will looks at me. "Oh. I don't have any money."

Ma tosses her hair. "Hon, your money isn't good here. You're in my kitchen. You're as good as family now. What do you say?"

For as much as Ma drives me bananas, she can also be the most welcoming, loving person on the planet. She means it too, even if she's using her fake-happy voice and smile.

"Then I say yes, please." Will grins.

Ma walks off, shouting over her shoulder. "One order of cheesy garlic bread it is. Thanks for cleaning out the fridge!"

Will leans on my shoulder. My stomach flutters at the

140

weight of him. I'm still having a really hard time thinking of him as just a friend. The butterflies flap faster when he whispers in my ear, "No wonder June is your best friend. Unlimited free food all the time? DUDE."

I laugh, shoving him off. "It's not just the free food. She loves the hard labor and occasional fridge scrubbing."

We both laugh but talking about June—it makes me more sad than mad now. I mean, I'm still frustrated and annoyed that she reacted that way, but I *did* lie to her. And she is my best friend. We've shared so much together. But I also don't think I should feel bad about Will.

The rest of the week, Will and I tackle different parts of the kitchen and dining room. Elio and Nina, to my surprise, help with things I normally do—folding pizza boxes, wiping counters and tables. That way, Will and I can do some of the more demanding work. We wash booth seats and chairs. We polish woodwork and reorganize the bulletin board, tearing down fliers from a decade ago. We get on our hands and knees and scrub the floors while we listen to Will's play-list of essential rock music that his uncle Leon made. We're sweaty and gross by the end of each day, but I'm having the time of my life. Hanging out with Will only gets better, and he doesn't seem to mind cleaning to spend time with me. Not even June is willing to do the un-fun stuff.

She and I still aren't good. She's been awkward and even started sitting with the musical kids at lunch. Now it's just me and Will. I get that she's upset, but I said sorry, and I don't have more energy to convince her otherwise. I've got bigger pies to bake.

I spend the entire weekend trying out new pizza recipes. I'd ask Will to come over, but he's with his dad for the weekend. I text June to hang, but she leaves me unread. WHATEVER. Her freaking loss because on Saturday I cook up a deep-dish that's my take on a seven-layer taco dip. Nina and Elio give it three and half out of five stars even though they devour three slices each. ("It's just too . . . goopy.") On Sunday, I make a thin crust trio inspired by Thanksgiving dinner. Pizza one: a white pizza with cranberry drizzle and brie. Pizza two: a smear of mashed potatoes, a garlic butter sauce, and sausage. Pizza three: turkey, stuffing, and a drizzle of brown gravy. Gramma Salvatore comes over to eat with us while Ma and Pop work (ever since the remote injury, Ma and Pop have limited my babysitting opportunities . . . I'm mostly okay with that). She says I've just reinvented how we'll be doing the holiday from now on. Honestly, coming from the grandma who hates that we own a pizzeria, that's high praise. I add her comment to my red notebook.

We still have two weeks before the scout from *Pizza Perfect* arrives. With all the work we still have to do, it'll be just enough time to get the restaurant into camera-ready shape. Even Ma and Pop have kicked their effort into overdrive. Pop has been around the restaurant more, and he and Ma seem to be getting along better than they have in weeks. My plan is working. If they can see what's worth fighting for—us kids, this restaurant—they'll quit this stupid separation and get back together. By Thursday night, they haven't fought for a whole forty-eight hours, which is a small miracle. At this rate, Pop'll move back in after the scout gives us the green light.

We're all at the restaurant on Friday afternoon, one week before the scout is supposed to arrive, when I get an email. When I read the notification, I feel like I just stepped into our walk-in freezer.

Subject: Urgent Pizza Perfect Update
Dear Luca and Mamma Gianna's,

We apologize for the inconvenience, but due to a scheduling error, our show associate, Candace Goodwater, needs to conduct her visit to Mamma Gianna's earlier than expected. Please prepare for Candace to arrive no later than 3:00 p.m. tomorrow (Saturday). She is looking forward to her visit.

Again, our sincerest apologies. Please let us know if you have any questions or concerns.

All our best,

The PP Team

"Mamma mia! No, no, no, no, no!" I shout at my phone. This can't be happening. We're not ready. *I'm* not ready.

Pop appears in front of me. "What's wrong?"

I show him my phone. "The scout from *Pizza Perfect* is coming TOMORROW. What're we gonna do?"

My gaze travels around the pizzeria while Pop reads. There's still so much to do. We haven't filled in or painted the chipped walls. Two of the tables are still wobbly. The bulbs in the illuminated sign out front need to be replaced. And our door's bell is *still* broken. We're gonna look like total rookies!

Pop hands my phone back. Then he cracks his knuckles. "It's time to call in the reinforcements."

While I call Will and Gramma Salvatore to see if they can help us, Pop calls in his pal Tony, our handyman, and then he catches Ma up to speed. I overhear them arguing about whether we should close for the night to make our final preparations. Pop thinks we should ("This could change the game, Chris. We can't mess this up."). Ma thinks we shouldn't ("Are you out of your mind? We literally can't afford to close our doors for even a minute. I'd add a day to the week just to keep our doors open longer if I could!"). I can't believe they're wasting time arguing when they should be working. I barrel between my parents and pull out a card I rarely use: their first names.

"Christine! Giovanni!" I shout. Their traps shut and their eyes go wide. Before they can stop me, I go on. "You don't get to fight and ruin this. I've worked too hard. Much

144

as I think we should close early, we won't have to with the extra help. I'll tell everyone what to do. You focus on running orders. Capisce?"

Ma's jaw tightens. Pop's knuckles whiten. They look like fussy children. Silent. Stewing. The silence boils me. Now I'm really angry. I raise my hands in a double *ciao*. (Serious business.) My voice rises. "I said, *capisce*?"

"Eh," Pop relents. "Capisce."

Ma nods. "Fine."

I double knot my apron around me. "Good. Now let's get to work."

Chapter 16

I realize there's one more person I want helping us: June. We've been on shaky ground for weeks now, but our friendship is stronger than Will coming between us. So that she knows I mean it when I say I need her, I do something drastic—I call her. (GASP.)

June picks up on the second ring. "Hello? Luca? Are you okay?"

"Yes and no," I say, relieved she answered. More so than I expected to feel. Maybe I've missed having her around more than I realized. "Look, I—I know things have been weird between us. I was a bad friend, and I haven't been the best lately. I'm sorry."

It's quiet on the other end. I hear her breathing. Then, "I'm sorry too. I just—I was afraid I'd messed up. That I was losing you because I'm doing the musical."

"You aren't losing me," I say. "And Will isn't replacing you. He's just . . . more."

I legit hear her eyebrow arching. "More? Luca, is there something you haven't been telling me about you and Will?"

I almost drop the phone. "What? No! I—"

"If there was, you could tell me."

"We're, uh, I—" *Should I tell her I have a major crush on Will? But, I mean, what's the point? I don't even think Will likes me like that. He made it clear we're friends, and I feel like he would have said something by now . . . right?* I clear my throat. "We're just friends. Really." Then I rush into the meat of my call, hoping to avoid any more prying questions. I tell her about the scout and us busting it to be ready.

Before I can ask her to help, she says, "I'll ask my mom to drop me off. See you soon."

It's like a massive sack of flour has been taken out of my arms hearing her say that. It's not just that she's helping— it's that we're okay. That we'll *be* okay.

June and Will are a little awkward around each other, but I put them in different parts of the restaurant, so they don't have to see each other as much. They both leave a little before eleven o'clock, and Gramma Salvatore takes Nina and Elio home just before midnight. But Ma, Pop, Tony, and I rearrange and scrub and prep until three in the morning. I've had so many second winds that by the time we get home, I'm too wired to sleep. I lie on my back, staring at the ceiling and all those parallel lines of light until four. At least, that's the last time I remember looking at my clock.

I wake up to Ma gently rubbing my shoulder. "What time is it?" I squint against the brightness invading my bedroom. My heart jump-starts—*it's tomorrow*! "Did I miss Candace Goodwater?"

Ma steadies me as I bolt up. "It's all good. It's only ten," she says. "You worked your butt off last night. You deserved to sleep in."

I rub my eyes. "But Candace will be here in"—I count on my fingers—"in five hours. There's still so much—"

"Hon, we have five whole hours to make it happen," she says. "Besides, your father and I have been up for a while already working on little details. He polished up the chef statue near the bathrooms, and I gave all the cutlery a look over and pulled out the dingy ones."

I lean back against my headboard. I'm impressed. I didn't think either of them was really, truly on board with this whole show thing, but maybe I was wrong. Maybe they want this as much as I do. Which means, deep down, maybe they also want their marriage to work.

I roll out of bed ten minutes later. Ma makes me a cup of coffee which is fifty percent hazelnut creamer. Delicious. That little bit of caffeine kicks me into high gear. By noon we're at the restaurant. I'm wearing my favorite Mamma Gianna's T-shirt: it's heather red with our full-color logo across the chest. I roll the sleeves twice so they're higher up on my arms. I'm wearing my favorite dark wash jeans, and my good sneakers. My black apron is ready to go, freshly washed in a midnight load of last-minute laundry.

Everything in the restaurant looks and smells fresh. I've never seen it like this before. I don't think Ma or Pop have either. We never have time to give the floors and walls the love they deserve. Don't get me wrong, it's still the same old Mamma Gianna's but it's a version I'm proud to show off.

Around one o'clock, the minutes start to take extra long to pass by. We're all feeling the anxiety. Nina and Elio get cranky and kick each other in one of the booths. It starts out like a game, the two of them laughing. But sure enough, two minutes later, Elio is crying because Nina kicked too hard and that's not fair and now his day is ruined.

Then Ma and Pop get into it because Ma thought Pop was paying attention to the twins, and Pop thinks Ma is overreacting. I'm all nerves and can't deal with any of them today, so I go to my sanctuary within my sanctuary: the kitchen. I need to focus.

My hands gravitate to the fridge, the pantry, pulling ingredients. I get a pan heating on the stove. I cut open an eggplant, brush it in olive oil, and shove it in the oven. I grab a chicken breast and pulverize it with another frying pan until it's flat as a pancake. Then I lightly bread it and get it frying with lemon and garlic. The oil spits and bites at my exposed skin. I don't mind. I'm in the zone. While I cook, I imagine what it'll be like when Candace gets here. I imagine her being one of those sharp, bossy exec types in the lawyer shows. A blond updo, a pressed blazer, a leather portfolio. Glasses on the tip of her nose. I imagine her scouring our restaurant, slowly cracking, warming up to us. Then, when she tastes our pizza, completely melting and saying, "Luca Salvatore, this is the most delicious pizza I've ever eaten! You did it! We must have you on *Pizza Perfect*."

I'm putting my original pizza concoction in the oven, not even realizing what time it is, when I hear the front door open. My whole heart is an artichoke lodged in my throat. I swallow the prickly leaves and step out of the kitchen.

Ma and Pop are shaking hands with a short Black woman with dark brown skin and cropped, blond hair. She has an earbud in her left ear and small silver triangle studs in each lobe. Her septum is pierced, a thin silver ring dangling above her top lip. Her striking hazel eyes are hidden behind thick, black-rimmed glasses. She's in a purple "Protect Trans Lives" shirt and black pants. A silver belt bag is strapped across her chest.

Dang. She is *way* cooler than who I imagined. But also, way more intimidating. She's unsmiling, nodding at Ma, who's going on and on about how grateful she is Mamma Gianna's is being considered for *Pizza Perfect*. (*Oh* is *she now?*) Candace's face lights up when she sees me, though.

She extends a hand in my direction. "Candace Goodwater, she/they. You must be Luca Salvatore, child of the hour.

I recognize you from your fabulous video."

She/they. I make a mental note to switch up my pronouns when I'm talking about Candace. My entire body tingles with pride. "Thank you" is the only thing I can think to say.

They glance at their watch. "I apologize in advance for needing to keep this brief. I'm doing a whirlwind tour of Midwest pizzerias. I've only got an hour before I've gotta jet."

Ma displays the dining area with an open palm. "Shall we conduct the tour, then?"

I grimace. Why does Ma sound like a medieval lady in waiting?

But Candace nods. "Lead the way."

I follow behind Ma and Pop as they tell Candace about the history of the restaurant and how we took it over a few years back. Candace nods along, snapping pictures and taking notes with her phone. I watch her face. She smiles at the right times, but she keeps flipping her wrist up to look at her watch. It doesn't seem like she's really invested in being here. I keep waiting for her to be wowed by something, but the more Ma and Pop go on, the less interested she seems. Every now and then, her eyes tilt to me, as if she's expecting me to step in. But every time I try, Ma or Pop cuts me off.

When we walk into the kitchen, that's the first time I see Candace's face light up. They comment on the savory scent, and I know they smell the za I've got in the oven.

They ask about where we get our ingredients. If they're locally sourced. If they're organic. What we do with leftover food at the end of the night or week. They take more notes, a silver glimmer in their eye.

Half an hour into our time with Candace, we bring her samples of our three most popular pizzas: the traditional Chicago deep-dish with our homemade sauce and extra mozzarella, our barbeque chicken thin crust with Canadian bacon, and our signature pizza inspired by great-grandma's thick, almost focaccia-style pizza with light sauce, lots of herbs, and a sprinkling of cheese. She seems most impressed by the last pizza, making an audible "mmmmm." But overall, I can't tell what she's thinking. This isn't going at all how I expected. She should be falling head over heels with us. With our food.

"Did you make these?" they ask me.

I point to myself. "Me?"

She laughs. "Yes, you. You called yourself a master pizza maker. I want to make sure I'm sampling your expertise."

I shift on my feet. "Well, I mean, I made the dough for those pizzas, but I didn't finish them."

"*I* baked those," Ma adds. "We had a long night preparing for your visit. Luca is an excellent chef, but his creations aren't on our menu."

Candace's smile falters, but her eyes stay trained on me. "That's too bad. I'd hoped to see you in action. Travis was quite taken with your enthusiasm."

Excuse me? I can't have heard that right. "Travis . . . Parker?"

They laugh, tinkling and light. "You got it, hon. He insisted we meet you."

"Whoa." My legs are shaking.

Candace dusts her hands on her pants. "I think I've seen and tasted all I need, but is there anything else you think I should know before I report back to the crew?"

That makes me nervous. She hasn't even been here the full hour. Maybe she's not impressed. Ma and Pop look at each other and shrug. Neither of them can think of anything else, and frankly, they look relieved that Candace is wrapping up. But how can they not see that this isn't a surefire win for us? If Candace *really* wanted us on the show, she'd say it. She'd gush about our restaurant, our pizza. This is all wrong.

I raise my hand. The three of them look at me. Candace smiles like a question mark. "You don't have to raise your hand. This isn't school, baby."

I blush. "Right." My hand falls to my side. "I, uh, well, I just want you to know how important this is, to all of us. Being on *Pizza Perfect* has been my dream forever."

Candace leans forward. "Say more. Tell me what this would mean to *you*."

To me. Her request feels weighty. Like the next words

153

out of my mouth matter more than anything Ma and Pop have said. I clear my throat. "This restaurant has been in our family forever. It's our legacy. Getting to share that with the world would honor my great-grandma's memory, and my Nonna Zaza, who we took it over from. It would mean we get to keep sharing our family recipes with people. My family—"

Candace holds up a hand. "I'm going to stop you there." Their lips purse. They travel my face with hazel eyes like they're searching for a constellation at dusk. "Don't get me wrong, Luca. All of that is lovely, but it's not what I asked. I want to hear about *you*. Just you. What would this mean to Luca Salvatore, boy pizza master?"

For a second, I'm confused. My forehead creases, but then I realize what she's saying. All I did was talk about my family. What it means to *us*. Nothing about me. I didn't even realize I'd done that. I fidget with the string on my apron. "Can I think for a second?"

They nod. "Take your time."

I look around the restaurant. At the murals of Italy on the walls. The broken bell above the front door. The black-and-white photo of Great-Grandma Gianna on the wall on opening day of the restaurant. I think about the feeling of dough in my hands. The smell of cheese melting in the oven. The way crust crackles between my teeth. Sparkling warmth flickers up from my toes.

I hold on to that feeling as I answer Candace a second time. I can't bring myself to look her in the eye; I stare at the table as I speak. "Being on the show would mean that I matter. My whole life is pizza. I learned to make pizza from my family because I was born a Salvatore, but I make pizza because I love it. When I'm rolling out dough or preparing toppings, I'm free. I'm the most me I've ever felt." I laugh and look up at Candace. "That sounds stupid, doesn't it?"

Their chin rests in their palm. For the first time since they arrived, I can see all their bright-white teeth. They're really smiling. Their voice comes out soft as summer wind. "It doesn't sound stupid at all." They sit up tall against the chair. "Baby, look, I smell something else going on in that kitchen. You sure you don't have something of *yours* I can taste?"

I glance at Ma and Pop. They both shrug. They don't know what I was making, and I've never made this particular pizza before. But this feels like my last chance to wow Candace.

"I'll be right back," I say.

I come back out with my pizza in hand. I place the creation in front of her. Her eyes twinkle. "What do we have here?" she asks.

"Just something I whipped up," I say. "It's my take on a chicken piccata pizza with roasted eggplant and a garlic butter sauce. It's topped with a blend of asiago, Parmesan, and mozzarella. Oh, and some fresh arugula."

"But to be clear," Ma interrupts, "that's not on our menu. Luca is very creative, but—"

Candace stops her. "I'd love a piece."

Considering the fact that *I* have never tasted this creation, I'm a squirming mess of nerves as I serve them a steaming slice. I hold my breath as they lift the whole plate to their nose. They inhale deeply. Their eyelids flutter. "Oh my," they mutter. "Oh *my*." They set the plate back on the table, raise the slice to their lips, and take a generous bite. The reaction is instant: a blissful moan of joy. I exhale. *Ohmygod. They like it.*

She doesn't even finish chewing before she says, "Luca, this is exceptional. Damn!" Then she giggles, holding a hand over her lips. "Apologies for talking with my mouth full of food, but—oh, hot *damn*, this is good."

For some reason, the cussing makes me believe them. They really mean it. I—Luca Salvatore—have impressed the *Pizza Perfect* scout who has no doubt eaten one billion different pizzas. "Thank you," I say.

"What inspired this?" She takes another bite. "What recipe did you use?"

"Oh, I was just playing around in the kitchen," I say. "No recipe."

Their left eye twitches. "And how old are you?"

"Twelve."

"And you make other pizzas? Like this?" She shoves the

half-eaten slice an inch away from her as if it's too tempting.

"Well, yeah. It's like my favorite thing to do." I feel myself relaxing into this moment of someone really seeing me. What I can do.

Candace suddenly scoots the chair out from the table. "Excuse me," she says. "I need to make a quick call. Do you mind if I step away somewhere private?"

Ma directs her to the kitchen. "Of course. Please. Do whatever you've got to do."

Candace flashes Ma a smile. "Thank you."

While Candace is out of the dining room, we huddle in a booth, me next to Ma and Pop across from us. In hushed tones, we debate what the phone call is about. We eat a slice of my pizza while we do. Ma and Pop both give me a "what the what" look and tell me how outrageously good my food is. I gotta admit, it is delicious. *Now that Ma's actually tasted one of my creations, maybe she'll consider letting me have* something *on the menu. . . .*

Twenty minutes later, putting them well past the hour they were supposed to spend with us, Candace emerges from the kitchen, cell phone pressed between their palms. "Well," they say. "Thank you for your patience, and all your time today. I've thoroughly enjoyed myself."

"We really appreciate you coming in," Pop says.

Ma adds, "It's meant the world to us to be considered, especially to Luca."

"I can tell." Candace beams at me. "And it's because of

Luca, and that particular bite"—she points at the half-eaten chicken piccata pizza—"that I'm thrilled to share that, after confirming with the showrunners and Travis Parker himself, Mamma Gianna's will join the lineup of restaurants featured in the final season of *Pizza Perfect*."

Ohmygod.

OH MY GOD.

I just about pee my pants. "Are you serious?"

"Very," Candace says. They look at their watch. "I'll send you more details on Monday with next steps, but I've gotta leave now to make it to my next stop. Again, congratulations."

"Thank you," I say. "Thank you so much." I can't help myself. I leap up and wrap them in a big hug. They laugh and give me a squeeze.

On their way out the door, they turn back and look at Ma and Pop. "You got one hell of a kid there."

Ma grins. "We know."

Their eyes slide back to my pizza one last time. "And I might not be a restaurateur, but I think you should reconsider adding Luca's creations to your menu, starting with that *inspired* concoction of flavors. Ciao."

Soon as the door closes, Ma and Pop wrap me up in a giant hug. "Travis FREAKING Parker is coming to Mamma Gianna's," I shout. We whoop and scream and dance in a circle. I'm sandwiched between them, and I don't budge from the near-suffocating embrace.

I'm beyond excited about getting on the show, but I'm also highly aware that my parents aren't just hugging me. They're hugging each other. They haven't done that in weeks. And here we all are, joined together because of me.

I can just tell: this is when our lives change for the better.

Chapter 17

On Monday, just like Candace said, we get an email with more details and forms to sign. It also includes a tentative filming schedule. Travis Parker will be filming with us for a full WEEK at the end of April, which is only like two months away. AHHHHHH!!!

I want to start prepping immediately, but Ma and Pop tell me to slow down. Celebrate the win. Recover before the main event. I argue there's no time to rest, but if I'm being honest, after everything we did to impress Candace, I'm more tired than a cliché. Not to mention behind on homework. But now that Travis Parker is officially coming, preparing for him feels like the only assignment that matters.

I'm still flying high a week after Candace Goodwater told us we are going to be on *Pizza Perfect*. But a trio of events clip my wings and send me hurtling back to earth.

One.

On Saturday, a week after Candace's early visit, June, Will, and I hang out for the first time. It's June's idea. Ever since we all came together *Avengers Assemble*–style to get the restaurant shining for Candace, she and Will haven't had another fight, but there's still something awkward between them. ("I really do want *all* of us to be friends," June reassures me.)

So we go to June's house to play board games. Mrs. Mason is a part-time journalist for the local paper, and Mr. Mason is a fancy-pants lawyer. June is a mini-replica of her mom, all the way down to how she talks, fast and a little out the right side of her mouth, like she's always grinning. Mrs. Mason hugs me as soon as I walk in the door. "Luca, it's been too long!"

"Good to see you too, Mrs. Mason," I say. Then she gives Will the same treatment even though they're meeting for the first time. That's just the kind of person June's mom is.

June pokes her head out from the kitchen. "I've got everything ready in here!"

A pyramid of board games stands on the wooden kitchen table. I see some of my and June's favorites: Exploding Kittens, Monopoly, Settlers of Catan, Munchkin, Clue. For all the video games Will plays, he's never heard of most of the board games. We ease him in with a round of Munchkin.

Things are fine until we're a little over halfway through the game. Will's a natural, quickly picking up strategy and keeping pace with us. He stops June in her tracks every time she thinks she's got a winning card. I can tell she's getting frustrated by her huffing and how, instead of sitting in the kitchen chair, she perches on her knees, leaning over the table.

Will seems to pick up on June's attitude because all of a sudden, June wins the game. She's overly braggy about it too. Which is weird. *Has she always been this competitive?* Then I think about the musical. *I'll boycott the show if I don't get Cinderella. There's no way Anya's getting it over me.* Maybe I've just ignored this side of her because she's my best friend.

We play Exploding Kittens next, and again Will starts off strong. June gets huffy, but now I can tell Will is getting annoyed with her moaning and groaning. He keeps biting his nails and shooting me looks. I shrug, trying to play Switzerland. This time, though, Will wins the game. June immediately insists we play another round. She claims she got a bad hand of cards to start. So we do, and she loses again.

"I don't feel like playing anymore," she declares, gathering the cards before Will or I get to have an opinion.

"Do you want to play something else?" Will asks.

"Not really," says June.

And she doesn't say anything else, so now I'm totally confused. She invites us over to play games, claiming that she wants all three of us to be friends, and then she decides she doesn't want to play games? WHAT THE WHAT?

"You wanna do something else instead?" I ask.

She looks around her kitchen. She leans back in her chair and holds her stomach. "Actually, I'm not feeling that well. I think I might be done for today."

Will and I look at each other. "Oh," I say. "We can go if you want."

"Well, I just—" Then she looks at Will. "Are you sure you've never played Exploding Kittens before?"

He laughs awkwardly. "I'm very sure. My mom and I aren't game people."

"You swear?" she says.

Now Will looks uncomfortable. "I'm not lying."

I try to catch her eye. Why is she pushing this? I don't understand why the three of us can't just get along. I make a face and say, "That would be a weird thing to lie about. He's telling the truth, June."

She doesn't let go of it. "But you won both games, and I'm pretty sure you let me win Munchkin."

A sharp edge creeps into Will's tone. "I didn't. I *was* winning, and then you won. Fair and square."

I lean across the table to June. "Why are you acting weird? Aren't we all supposed to be *getting along?*"

"I'm not acting weird," she scoffs.

Am I hallucinating? "Um, yeah. You are."

Her eyes clamp shut. Her cheeks pink. "I need to lie down. You guys should go." Then she stands up, walks into the living room, and curls up on the couch.

Will gives me a questioning look, but I just shrug. "I'll call my dad to come get us."

I text June later that night to see if she's okay, but she doesn't respond. I don't get it. It was *her* idea for us to get together. I don't know what's getting in her way. Why can't she see that Will is important to me? That it doesn't mean she *isn't* important to me? And if I can't be friends with her *and* Will, does that mean I have to let him go? I mean, she's my best friend. We're like family. I can't lose her. I won't.

Two.

On Tuesday, I'm at Mamma Gianna's with Ma. Pop has the twins for the night.

I'm in the kitchen when I hear Ma laughing at the register. Not just a giggle or polite customer laugh. A full-on belly laugh. I haven't heard her do that in a long time. Curious, I leave my batch of dough and poke my head around the corner of the kitchen doorway.

Leaning against the counter by the register is a man. He's tall, white with creamy skin and golden blond hair that falls in fluffy waves. He's old but even still I'd say he's handsome. Like, *really* handsome. And Ma is acting like I've never seen her before. She's like a teenager, covering her smile with a curl of her fingers. She sways a little from side to side, eyes locked on this man I don't recognize.

A stone plunges deep into my stomach. Is Ma *flirting?*

Guard dog instincts kick in, and to end their conversation I almost bark that I need Ma, but something in me shatters and instead, I back into the kitchen. My chest rises and falls faster and faster. I hold my hand to my heart. Weird pressure builds up. Sharp pain crackles against my rib cage.

If Ma is flirting, that means she *like*-likes something about that man. That man who looks *nothing* like Pop. Who *isn't* Pop. And my parents might be separated, but they aren't divorced. They're still *married.* Do separated people get to flirt? Is that a thing?

Or does this count as *cheating?*

Then I get angry. I go back to my dough, and I punch all my feelings into the golden mound. Who does she think she is? Does our family mean nothing to her? Is she not gonna fight to keep the Salvatores together?

When the laughing ends and I hear the door open and close, I muster up the courage to go back out there. To look my mother in the face.

I find her shuffling a stack of receipts. Her expression is serious again, like a spell has been broken. Relief washes over me. Maybe that's all it was. A temporary enchantment.

But I can't help myself. "Who was that?"

She looks up at me, blank-faced. "Who?"

I nod at the door. "That guy. You were laughing. Do you know him?"

"Oh, no. Just some customer," she says, going back through the receipts. She doesn't actually look at me.

Because I'm me and I've gotta know what she's really thinking, I say, "He was cute. Like a movie star."

Now she rolls her eyes at me. "A little old for you, kiddo." But then she glances at the smudged door. "But I guess he was, wasn't he?" In the same breath, she catches herself and turns to me. "Dough coming along all right?"

I try to keep my face emotionless. "It's fine."

"Good." She goes back to her receipts.

I slip back into the kitchen and knead the dough until my knuckles are sore.

Three.

On Thursday, Pop and I are at the restaurant when Mr. Cheeks barrels through the doorway. His gray beard is thicker than it was before. He's wearing a red baseball hat and suspenders over a plaid button-down. "Salvatore, we need to talk."

No hello, no how are you. Straight to business. *Madone, I can't stand this guy.*

Pop keeps his tone even. "Mr. Cheeks, how can I help you?"

"You can start by paying me the three months' rent you owe me."

I stop sweeping the floor. *Three months' rent?* That's not possible. We're tight on cash, especially now that we have all those hospital bills for Elio's ambulance ride and stitches, but there's no way Ma would lapse on rent. At least, not by *three* months! If we don't pay for our building, we don't have a business.

Pop seems just as surprised as me. His lips twitch. "What are you talking about? We fell behind at the holidays, but Christine's been paying you, hasn't she? She got caught up, right?"

Mr. Cheeks looks disgusted. "Is that what your wife's been telling you? Gio, I haven't seen a check from your business in months. I approved an extension for Christine on good faith that she'd have the money, but I still don't have anything."

"Mr. Cheeks, I had no idea," Pop says. "I'm sorry. I'll get to the bottom of this. I promise. You'll have your money today."

Chapped lips make the ugliest frown I've ever seen on Mr. Cheeks's face. "Heard that before. I'll believe it when I see it." He glances around at the empty booths. "And if I don't, I'll have to evict you from the premises. From the looks of it, no one's gonna miss the joint."

I drop the broom. "That's not—"

"Luca." Pop's voice lowers an octave. That never happens, but when it does, I know I need to shut my trap. Pop exhales. He white knuckles the counter. "You'll have your money. Today. I'll find a way."

Mr. Cheeks sniffs. "Good. Drop the check off to my house by five o'clock. Otherwise, I'm taking legal action. Understood?"

I want to punch Mr. Cheeks in the face. Pop keeps his expression steely. "Yes."

Then Mr. Cheeks waddles out the door. Pop taps the counter. "Luca, watch the register. I'm calling your mother."

He disappears into the kitchen. I pick up the broom and stand it in the corner behind the counter. I'm nauseous. Everything I love feels like it's crumbling, and just when I thought I'd fixed everything by getting onto my favorite TV show. Now my best friend is super awkward with me, my parents clearly don't love each other, and we might lose our family business.

And if there's no business, there's no *Pizza Perfect* featuring Mamma Gianna's.

Just like that—one, two, three—every good thing I felt while Candace was here evaporates into nothing.

Chapter 18

"How is it already time for dress rehearsals next week?" June says as we walk to Culinary Arts at the end of the first full week of March. "Terrance, who's playing the Baker, still doesn't have his lines memorized. And our choreography for the opening number is sloppy. We'll never be ready in time for opening night!"

"Your first performance isn't until next Thursday, right?" I say, gently nudging her shoulder with mine. "That's plenty of time. Three whole days next week to get all that right."

June holds her armful of binders tighter to her chest. "Is that how you'd feel if Travis Parker were coming in three days and you had a giant mess to clean up?"

I start at the mention of my icon's name. "Not so loud," I whisper-shout. "That's supposed to be a secret."

June flaps her hand at me. "No one's listening," she says. "My point is that I'm worried it won't come together, and I want it to be perfect."

I nod. "Yeah, I get it."

Ever since Pop and I found out we were massively behind on rent, my parents have reached a new boiling point. Pop asked Gramma Salvatore for emergency funds to cover us, but she refused. ("I'm not adding another sliver of duct tape to that sinking ship, Gio! I already covered your move out of that house, *and* I fronted for Elio's hospital bills. I'm. Tapped. *Out*. It's time to bail.") Obviously, I wasn't supposed to hear that, but what can I say? Gramma Salvatore is on my poop list.

So Ma and Pop had to sell some furniture and take out another loan to pay off what we owed Mr. Cheeks plus some for March, but now we literally have negative money. And Mr. Cheeks is being a total jerk. He says if we're late again, he's kicking us out. As in NO MORE MAMMA GIANNA'S. Every time I walk through our front door, I picture a "Permanently Closed" sign taped to the glass. The thought of losing Mamma Gianna's after all we've been through straight up makes me want to vomit. The only good news is that we won't be kicked out before Travis Parker arrives to film. We need him and *Pizza Perfect* more now than ever. And not just the show—we need to crush the Pizza Perfect Challenge. Winning is the difference between us staying open and closing for good.

Ma and Pop got into a huge fight last night over me. I keep trying to convince Ma that one of my pizza creations could tip the scales for us, especially after what happened with Candace. But Ma keeps saying, "We show off what we know best. Our traditional pizzas, the ones Great-Grandma Gianna made that first put us on the map. Anything else, it's just not worth the risk." But Pop disagrees. BIG-TIME. He exploded on Ma last night. ("Chris, you're missing the magic. *Luca* got us this far. He'll get us the rest of the way.") They sent me, Elio, and Nina to our rooms when I tried to intervene, but angry Italian voices are just fleshy megaphones. I heard a lot. How much Pop believes in me. How much Ma doesn't.

"Hey," June says. "You okay?"

Madone. I got totally lost in my thoughts. I pretend like I'm shaking cobwebs from my brain as we walk into Mrs. Ochoa's classroom. "Yeah, no. I'm good."

She looks hurt. Offended. She knows I'm lying. "You sure? I feel like, I don't know, like—like you don't talk to me the way you used to."

She's right, but I don't say that. Ever since our failed game day with Will, I don't feel like I can trust her to be on my side. Plus, Will's been around. He's a better listener than June, but I don't want her to feel bad that I'm going to him instead of her. I flash a Dazzlingly Bright smile. "Girl, I'm *totally* fine."

She fidgets with her pencil. "You sure? I just—"

"You guys!" Will bounds into the classroom. His backpack crashes onto our workstation. A mile-wide smile makes his whole face sparkle. "I did it! I got my whole band together. We officially have a drummer, bass, me on guitar, and Melissa Berg on vocals. I'm so excited. We're gonna crush this."

June's face scrunches. "Melissa *Berg* can sing?"

"Totally," he says, dropping into the seat on my left. "Her voice is cool, raspy. She sounds way older. It's awesome."

"I wonder why she's not in choir," June says. "She should have tried out for the musical."

Will fiddles with a cowlick near his left ear. His hair's grown longer, almost to his neck, but it looks better than ever. (I catch myself staring.) "I think she's like a real singer," he says. "You know? Like *real* music. Not show tunes."

Oh. Snap. I can feel June turning to ice next to me.

"Show tunes *are* real music," she says, each word covered in frost.

Will shifts in his chair awkwardly. "I mean, yeah, its music, but not like on the radio. It's not like people listen to show tunes all the time."

"*I* listen to show tunes. All. The. Time. Lots of people do," she says. "And who even listens to the radio anymore? Were you born in like 1989 or something?"

Now Will's eyes scrunch. "You don't even know what you're talking about."

"Neither do you."

"You guys," I say, finally finding a gap to wedge myself between them. "You can like different things."

The bell rings. Mrs. Ochoa pulls the classroom door closed.

"Yeah, but he's wrong," June spits. "And rude."

"I'm not being rude," says Will. "She doesn't even know what she's talking about."

"You're an idiot."

"You are!"

Mrs. Ochoa suddenly looms over us. "Ahem." Her eyes hop from Will to June to me. "Is there a problem over here?"

June doesn't miss a beat. "There is. I need to work with a different group."

My jaw drops. "What? June! No."

She ignores me, her glare glued to our teacher.

"Did something happen?" Mrs. Ochoa asks, more serious than before.

The other kids in class are watching us. I'm so embarrassed. I can't believe I let June and Will get to this point. They're fighting because of *me*. It's not about the music.

"Will's annoying and rude," says June. "I just—Can I work with Jill and Danny instead?"

Will spurts, "I wasn't being rude! I was stating my opinion. Sheesh!"

Mrs. Ochoa's forehead creases. "Take a breath, please. You've been doing so well this semester. I'm not changing groups because of a disagreement. Work this out. If you can't, we'll reconsider groups on Monday. Understood?"

June huffs. "Whatever."

Silently, we make monkey bread, a sweet, cinnamon-sugary dessert. I stand between June and Will like a seawall keeping the waves from crashing against the land. Everything at home is a mess. I need my friends—both of them—even if things are weird with me and June right now.

"I need to tell you guys something." I stir the dough that we'll eventually coat in cinnamon sugar, too many emotions and thoughts tossing inside me.

"What?" asks June. Will leans in a little closer to me too.

"Mamma Gianna's is in trouble. Like, *way* worse than I thought." I tell them about being behind on rent, the loan we had to take. How we don't get another chance to fall behind. How next month—April—is going to make or break everything for us. June covers her mouth, repeating "I'm so sorry" and "oh no." Will is quiet, but his eyes track me with hawklike intensity. He surprises me, taking hold of my hand. He squeezes it. I squeeze back, grateful to hold on to someone. "It's, like, *really* bad," I say.

"Dude," Will says. He gives me a side hug. "That majorly sucks."

"I'm so sorry," says June. "I can't believe I didn't know. How can I help?"

You would know if you weren't always so focused on your-self. I snort-laugh. "You can't. Not unless you can come up with a way to drum up more business."

She deflates, and I feel guilty. It's not like I gave her a chance to know what was going on. Even still, there's nothing she could have done.

"Maybe my mom can write a book about you," Will says, half joking.

"Well, *my* mom's a journalist," June snipes, not joking at all. "If anyone's mom is writing anything, it's mine. I was Luca's friend first."

That sets them off yapping like territorial dogs. I drag my hand down my face. *So not what I need from them right now.*

As we get our monkey bread in the oven, June says, "Well, if *I* can do anything to help you, Luca, let me know. I've got your back."

"Me too," says Will.

As we're leaving class, June stops at Mrs. Ochoa's desk. "About changing groups," she says. "I'd still like to work with Danny and Jill."

"Are you sure?" our teacher says.

I can't believe she's being such a diva! "June, don't—"

"I'm sure."

Then she walks out the door, not even glancing back to see if I'm behind her.

Chapter 19

I'm in the kitchen at home on Sunday trying out a new pizza recipe when Ma busts in and thrusts her phone in my face. "Did you see this?"

I take the phone from her. "What is it?"

"Just read." Her foot taps anxiously against the wood floor.

Her screen displays a local news website. At the top is the headline: Local Pizzeria Poised for *Pizza Perfect* Stardom. I read it twice to make sure I'm not hallucinating. *Oh. No.* My armpits start to sweat. I scroll through the article. *Why is our CONFIDENTIAL stardom on a website for EVERYONE to see?* I mean, the post is short, just a couple paragraphs, but the damage is done. *Madonna mia, this can't be happening.* It says Travis Parker is featuring Mamma Gianna's on the final season of *Pizza Perfect*. That was supposed to be SECRET. Like, we signed *legal* documents saying we wouldn't spill!

"How did this happen?" I ask.

Ma wags her finger at me. "Scroll to the top, and you tell me."

"What are you—" My eyes bulge when I see who wrote the article: Sally Mason. As in *Mrs. Mason*. "June's *mom* wrote this?"

"That's what it says. She needs to take it down. Immediately. There's already a dozen comments. People are reading it. Word is getting out, and I don't want to screw up this opportunity now that we have it. I didn't want to admit it before, but we really need it."

Ma doesn't get beaten down. She's a fiery Siciliana, but ever since it came out that she was lying about paying the rent on Mamma Gianna's, she's seemed smaller. She says she was too embarrassed to tell us how deep in the hole we were. That she'd convinced herself she could make it work. That she couldn't stand the idea of letting down Nonna Zaza or facing anymore ridicule from Gramma Salvatore. But all her lies led to exactly that. Today, she's barely a smolder. A bonfire on its last log. And I'm not a fan. Even if I'm mad that she doesn't get how great I am with pizza, I'd still like my inferno back please.

"I'll call June." I give Ma her phone and pull mine from my pocket. June answers right away. "You told your mom about us being on *Pizza Perfect*? What were you thinking?"

June stutters. "Hi, uh, I— Are you mad? I thought—I

177

thought it would help. You said you needed more money for rent, so I thought if people knew, they'd get excited and buy—"

"JUNE." I cut her off. My heart is a time bomb in my chest. "The article needs to be deleted now. RIGHT. NOW. We signed papers saying we'd keep the filming secret." I cover the phone with my other hand. "I wasn't supposed to tell you or Will. I mean, no one should know we're on it until the episode airs. If the *Pizza Perfect* people find out we—*I*—blabbed, they won't film us at all!"

June gasps. "Oh crap. Oh crapcrapCRAP! I'm so sorry. I was trying to help. After what you said last week, I—"

"Stop! Help me now and get it off the internet!"

Her voice cracks. "I will. I'm sorry, Luca. I'm so, so sorry." It sounds like she's crying, but I don't care. I'm mad at her. I'm mad at myself. I'll explode if she ruined my chance of getting on *Pizza Perfect*. Our one final shot at rescuing Mamma Gianna's. My fingers squeeze my phone case tighter.

"Just tell me when it's done." Then I hang up.

The article comes down fifteen minutes later, but I'm still seething. Mrs. Mason calls Ma to apologize for posting the article without confirming with us. Ma accepts the apology, but I'm still a rage monster when June calls an hour later. I don't answer. Ma says I shouldn't be so mad. "Mrs. Mason said June was trying to help," she says. "She just went about it the wrong way."

But what I'm most mad about isn't June. It's me. I shouldn't trust people so much. Not June with secrets. Not my parents with our family or the restaurant. Maybe not even Will. I'm the only one I can count on, and I let myself down. I'm such an idiot.

Ma and Pop decide it's best to be up front with Candace Goodwater and the *Pizza Perfect* crew about what happened instead of them finding out on their own. I help them write the email. I'm mortified admitting that I blabbed to my best friend. I'm terrified Candace will write back and tell us it's over. That we broke contract. That Travis Parker isn't coming.

Once again, I'm obsessively refreshing my email but not in the fun way. There's no immediate response. Instead of giving in to the endless spaghetti tangle of worry knotted in my brain, I go with Ma to the restaurant. I need to be where I feel safe. On our drive over, June calls again, but I still don't pick up.

Despite the article coming down quickly, word travels fast, which is a blessing and a curse. The blessing: Mamma Gianna's is busier than it's been in months. The curse: people are calling in, asking if it's true we're gonna be on TV. Ma plays it cool, neither confirming nor denying what's going on. Then, slick as a freshly mopped floor, she asks everyone if they want to place an order. Soon we're firing pizzas left and right. I get lost in the rhythm of the work, and I almost forget about the whole mess until June walks through the door.

She's paler than usual, and her hair isn't combed. She slinks to the counter, hands in her pockets. "Can we talk? Please?"

I focus on refilling our red pepper flake shakers. "I'm really busy right now."

"Luca," June pleads. "Just a minute?"

Ma appears next to me, phone pressed to her chest like she's on the line with someone. "Luca, talk to June. I've got this."

"But—"

"Shoo!"

Reluctantly, I leave my red pepper flakes and pull June to an open booth. "What is it?"

She tucks blond wisps behind her right ear. "Luca, you gotta know, I'm so, so sorry."

"Sorry isn't gonna convince Travis Parker to come here."

June turns the color of snow. "Did you lose the show?"

I stare in silence, letting her sweat before I say, "Not yet, but I don't know what's gonna happen." I lean on my elbows. "How could you do this? I trusted you."

"I really was trying to help."

"You could've helped in other ways! I need a friend, not a publicist."

Now she looks frustrated. "I've been trying, but you haven't made it easy. Everything is about Will all the time now! You barely talk to me anymore."

"Well, you abandoned me for the musical. What else was I supposed to do?"

"I can do other things. The world doesn't revolve around *you*, Luca."

I snort. "That's rich coming from you. It's always the June Mason show. I finally get something for me—*my* turn to be in the lead role—and all you can do is focus on you. Best friends should be happy for each other. I needed you."

"I was trying to fix that! I—I wanted to do something big, something only *I* could do as your best friend. Luca, I care about you. I know I haven't been around much. I'm sorry. And I *tried* to make up for it, but obviously I crashed and burned." She swats a tear away, but another chases after it. "Ugh. I hate crying. So stupid."

My shoulders slump. *Ugh.* This whole situation really *is* my fault. I shouldn't have shut June out. This is why I shouldn't put myself first. I just end up hurting people I care about. "You're not stupid."

"I am if I ruined everything for you." She sniffs.

"We don't know that yet." I shove the napkin dispenser to her. She grabs one and dabs her nostrils. "I—I'm sorry I didn't tell you what was really going on. That I made you feel like you weren't important."

"I'm sorry too. I know I can be selfish. Can you forgive me?"

"Of course. And Ma and Pop think it'll be okay, with the show and everything," I say. "What's more important—*yes*, even more important than Travis Parker—is you and me. You're my best friend, and I want to be yours."

Her lips squinch to the side of her face. "You sure? You've been spending a lot of time with Will."

I squirm in the vinyl booth. She says it almost like she knows I have a crush on him. I already made a mess not telling her the truth about Mamma Gianna's and my family problems, but look at what she did trying to help. She made an even worse mess. If I tell her I like Will, will she blab to other people? To Will? What if she tries to "help" again and then Will wants nothing to do with me? I want to trust her, but I can't. Not right now. So I say, "He's a friend. A good friend. But not my best friend."

"But you talk about him all the time!" She leans across the table, napkin clenched in her fist. "You hang out with him whenever you get the chance!"

I blush, but I say, "You gotta trust me on this. No one beats out June Mason for best friend status." I hold out my pinkie. "I swear."

She glares at my inchworm finger like it's a trap. I shove it closer, and she gives in, wrapping hers around mine. "I'm really sorry, Luca. I've just been overwhelmed with the musical and thinking about you. It's been a lot. I know you've got more going on than me, so I feel ridiculous. UGH. Do you forgive me?"

I'm still frustrated and upset about what she did, but I mean it when I say, "I forgive you. Just swear you'll keep things quiet from now on. And do you think you, me, and Will can try to be actual friends?"

"I swear." She pulls her hand back and drags her finger under her nose. "We can try to be friends. But he's gotta change his tune about show tunes first."

On Monday morning we get an email from Candace Goodwater and the *Pizza Perfect* crew. She thanks us for being forthright about what happened. Since Mrs. Mason doesn't work for a national media outlet and the article was removed within an hour of posting, their team agrees that Mamma Gianna's can still be featured on *Pizza Perfect*. Candace ends the email sternly stating that if something like this happens again before Travis Parker arrives, they'll be forced to find an alternative restaurant. My heart hiccups when I read that line.

I let June know right away that we're safe and that she hasn't done any permanent damage. She gets all soppy and apologetic again, and now that I know Travis Parker is still coming, I give her a more enthusiastic reassurance that our friendship is okay. But I still need to figure out how to make things right between Will and June. I want all of us to be friends. So I text Will and make a bold move.

Me: Hey I was wondering if you want to see opening
night of Into the Woods tomorrow.

Will: With you?

Me: No. By yourself.

Me: OF COURSE WITH ME

Me: LOL

Will: I'm not that into musicals

Me: I promise it'll be good.

Will: Don't make promises you can't keep. Lol.

Me: I always keep my promises.

Will: But isn't June in it?

Will: I don't think she likes me that much.

Me: She is.

Me: But I want you two to get along. Showing we
support her will help.

Me: Do it for me?

It took him an extra minute to respond, but then:

Will: FINE

Will: Let me ask my mom

While I wait for his next text, warm bubbles percolate in my stomach. Will and I have hung out plenty of times now, but something about this feels . . . different. My ears heat up. I close my eyes and picture us sitting in the Riverfront Junior High cafetorium watching the musical. I imagine our knees close together. Our hands touching.

My eyes snap open. *OMG LUCA*. It's not a date. This is NOT a date. Even if you *want* it to be a date, he's your friend. *Just* your friend. He might be cute, and it might seem like he's flirty sometimes, but he's not into you like that. You would *know*.

I would *know*. Right?

My phone buzzes.

Will: I can go!

Stomach bubbles float between my lungs. I sit up.

Will: I hope I don't regret this

Me: lol you won't.

And I hope that's true.

We have front row seats, and the house is packed. The plastic folding chairs are super uncomfortable, and they don't allow for the knee touching I'd daydreamed about. But when the curtain opens and the music starts, I forget all about it.

The *Into the Woods* cast is really good. They belt out the opening song over the prerecorded pit orchestra. June comes out in her raggedy costume as pre-ball Cinderella. She looks terrible, like she's supposed to. I can pick her voice out of all the actors singing together. In a good way. She stands out because she's more mature, surer of herself. Her vibrato warbles like an adult's.

I keep Will in my periphery throughout the musical. He slowly leans forward, more and more, a big dopey grin expanding between his cheeks. He's way more into it than I expected. By the time June gets to her big solo, "On the Steps of the Palace," he's beaming at the stage, reflecting all the energy she's pouring into the audience. I grin. My plan is working. I think he's legitimately enjoying himself and maybe finding some newfound respect for June too.

When the show's over, he and I are the first to leap up and applaud. The cast bows, and June smiles right at me and Will. This is the happiest I've ever seen her.

"She was, like, *so* good," Will whispers when the curtain closes. His breath is hot on my ear, and I try not to shiver. "Better than I realized."

I elbow him. "Told you so."

And I have this weird urge to hug him. To wrap my arms around him.

To hold his hand.

But I don't. Because we're friends. FRIENDS.

On our way to congratulate June, Will drags me over to a table where parent volunteers are selling silk roses to give to cast members. To my surprise, Will stops and pays for one. I guess he *really* liked June's performance. And he is one of the kindest people I know.

We find June in her gold costume dress talking to her parents. When she sees me, Mrs. Mason apologizes again for what happened with the article. I tell her it's okay, but I'm mostly distracted by the way Will is levitating around June. I've never seen him like this.

He hands her the rose. "You were amazing. Seriously. I had, like, no idea."

"Thank you." She blushes, taking the fake flower from him. "I'm surprised you came."

Will tilts his head at me. "Luca twisted my arm," he says. "But I'm glad he did. You're super talented."

Their eye contact makes me squirmy. *Are they* . . . *flirting?* THAT'S NOT THE PLAN.

I cut between them. "Yeah, you were outstanding." I lean forward and put a hand in front of my lips like I don't want others to hear. "Like *way* better than everyone else."

June sways in her dress, all smiles. Her eyes, though, are still on Will. I'm so confused. I thought she was mad at him? Now she's acting like he's Prince Charming! "Take back what you said about musicals not being real music?" she says.

Will nods vigorously. "A million percent. You completely convinced me."

"Well, good."

They hold eye contact for another second too long. My feet itch. Even if Will never would or could like *me*, the worst thing he could do is like my best friend. "Well, we'll let you talk to your other adoring fans," I say. "See you tomorrow." I drag Will away by the arm.

"Thanks for coming," June shouts after us. "And for the rose, Will!" She shoves her nose in it like it will smell like something other than fabric and plastic.

Will waves at her. "You're welcome!"

While we wait outside for his mom to pick us up, Will goes on and on about how incredible June was and how he's gonna listen to the soundtrack and maybe she'll have to sing with him sometime when he plays guitar and blah blah BLAH. Listening to him go on and on makes me feel like I'm being filleted alive. Like, I'm glad they finally found some common ground, but now I'm worried they found too much of it.

Chapter 20

The thing about owning a restaurant is that you don't really get to take vacations, and it can get lonely. Spring break is the last week of March, about a month from when we film. June and her parents fly to Cancun for an all-inclusive week of food and sunshine. Will gets shipped off to Cincinnati to spend a week with his dad. He loathes every second of it, texting June and I the play-by-play of his misery.

Yeah, so, June and Will are good. Like, better than ever. But I'm not as much of a fan of their friendship as I thought I'd be. While I essentially become a full-time employee at Mamma Gianna's for a week, once again trying to convince Ma to let me put one of my pizzas on the menu, the two of them keep blowing up my phone with selfies and random photos of palm trees and Will's dad's collection of fishing lures. I chime in when I can, but I'm not like them. There's never a break for the Salvatores, especially not when Travis Parker is on the line.

Between gathering paperwork for tax season and celebrating Easter, the days go quickly, and soon we're two weeks away from Travis Parker and his film crew arriving. We're in all-out prep mode. On a sunny April Sunday, Ma, Pop, and I debate rearranging the restaurant to maximize our vibes.

Pop points at the chef statue near the front door. "Should Mr. Chef relocate to the register? He's sorta in the way when people walk in, you know?" He mimes someone walking through the entrance and nearly colliding with the three-foot statue.

Ma cocks her head at the door. "I'm more concerned about fixing that bell. Probably shouldn't have Travis Parker here with such an obvious thing in disrepair."

"Yeah, yeah, you're right," says Pop. "I'll take it apart today."

Ma and I give him an eyebrow. Then she says to me, "How many times have we heard that one before?"

I count on my fingers. "Eh, I don't know. 'Bout two, three, seven hundred times?"

"Hey," says Pop, inching away from the door. "What's all this ganging up? Thought we were in this together." But he doesn't sound like he's actually offended. He weaves behind the counter. "I'll grab the ladder and check it out. For real."

Ma waves her hand at him. "I'll believe it when I see it."

I press the corner of the last wobbly table. I've been

carefully checking each one, adjusting the circular screws under each of the legs to make sure they're flat on the floor. Well, as flat as they can be on this ancient, warped tile. The table doesn't budge. *Phew.*

"Tables are good to go," I say, wiping my grimy hands on my jeans.

"Thanks, Luca," says Ma. The phone rings. She hands me an orange bottle of Goof Off and a rag. "How about you spend some quality time with the gunk on the front windows. There's gobs of ancient tape and sticky goo left from fliers. I want all that gone so we can give the windows a real wash before filming starts." Without taking a breath, she answers the phone. "Thank you for calling Mamma Gianna's. This is Christine speaking. How can I help you?"

While she takes an order for two medium deep-dish, I hike up my sleeves, spritz some orange cleaner on the rag, and press it against a dust-filled patch of tape residue. The glass is cool, but the sun is shining. It's a perfect spring afternoon. The birds are back. A robin made its nest in our sign. The babies' chirps make me feel hopeful.

While I'm scrubbing, I miss who walks up to our front door. I don't register who it is at first, but after a double take, I recognize him. It's that blond dude Ma was flirting with a few weeks ago.

I'm kind of stunned, and a little confused, seeing him again. This time, since I'm not stealing a look, I give him a full once-over. He's tall—taller than Pop by a good three inches. His shoulders are broader, and his chest extends farther than his gut. He's wearing a navy puff vest over a gray long-sleeve thermal tucked into tight jeans. A matte-gold buckle sits on his waist. He's wearing brown boots, and the cuffs of his jeans are rolled up to show off his boring brown socks. He's not model attractive, but he's objectively good-looking in a dad sort of way.

When he approaches the counter, Ma seems genuinely surprised to see him too. At first, I think she's wearing her Dazzlingly Bright smile, but when I look closer, I realize it's her real smile. I don't like that.

"Uh, hi," the man says to Ma. "How's it going?"

"Good for a slow Saturday," Ma says. "Tidying up before the dinner rush."

The man's square jaw nods. "Right. Right."

Ma slides a paper menu to him. "Can I get you something, uh . . . ?"

"Chris," says the man. "My name's Chris."

Ma laughs. She holds out her hand. "Well, I'm Christine. Ha ha. Chris. Christine. That's funny." She blushes. *Ew. What is happening?* Then Ma rubs her hands down her shirt like she's trying to collect herself. Like she's embarrassed. "I, uh, own the place."

Chris laughs. "Oh, I remember."

Sticky window cleaning comes to a halt. I'm completely

distracted by this train wreck of flirtation happening in front of me. Does this Chris guy seriously have no idea that he's flirting with my MOM? And right in front of me? I want to scream, "She's a MARRIED woman!"

"Well, Mr. Chris," Ma says. "What can I get for you? Deep-dish? Thin crust?"

"Actually," he laughs. "Just a pen."

Ma's lips squinch. "A pen?"

"A pen," he repeats.

She slowly pulls a ballpoint from under the register and hands it to him. He takes it, leans over the counter, and writes something on the takeout menu. Given Ma's shocked expression, I think she and I are both feeling surprised and weird about what's going on here.

"I never do this," says Chris, "but, uh . . ."

He slides the menu back to Ma. At this point, I have completely given up on the window gunk that now smells like artificial citrus. Ma's eyes flutter as she reads whatever he wrote. Her hand slowly lifts to cover her face, which has turned a dark shade of crimson.

Ma's about to say something when Pop barges in from the kitchen with our metal, paint-stained ladder. "We gotta reorganize that supply closet. Nearly killed myself trying to get to this—Oh, sorry, didn't know we had a customer."

Pop nods to Chris, who nods back like it's no big thing. Ma quickly folds up the menu in her hand, covering up whatever is written there. Meanwhile, I'm sweating. Sweating and confused. Sweating and angry. Sweating and sad.

"It's all good, man," says Chris. "I was just leaving." Then he looks at Ma. "But, uh, if you want to, uh—well, you know how to reach me."

He gives me a closed-mouth smile and a wink as he walks out the door. He moseys down the sidewalk like the Cubs just won the World freaking Series.

Pop's brow furrows. He looks at Ma as he opens the ladder. "Did I miss something? Who was that guy?"

Ma stuffs the menu in her back pocket. "Some guy. Chris. He, uh, ordered from us before." Then she looks at me like I didn't just witness the whole dang thing and says, "Go on, Luca. Keep scrubbing. Clock's ticking."

I must be dreaming. Ma's pretending like that guy didn't just hit on her. Like she isn't hiding whatever he wrote on that menu in her back pocket. My shock ferments into frustration and anger. "What did he write on that menu?"

I move out of the way so Pop can open the ladder under the broken bell. Ma clicks her nails against the counter. "Nothing. Just scrub, Luca."

I can't believe it. "You're lying," I say.

Finally, Pop catches on that something majorly not cool just happened. That Ma is keeping *another* secret. "Christine, what's he talking about? Do you know that guy?"

"No! I swear," she says. "He's only been in here once

before. A few weeks ago. I don't know." Her hands are flying all over the place in that famous flustered-Italian style.

Pop's voice drops. "But he didn't order anything." It's not a question.

"No."

Pop struts forward, thumbs holstered in his pocket. "Then what was he doing here?"

Ma pales. She looks from Pop to me and back to Pop. She fiddles with her necklace, eyes darting around like she's looking for a way out. When neither Pop nor I give up our staring, she breaks. "He gave me his number! Okay? But it's no big deal. It's not like I'm gonna call him!"

Pop laughs, disgusted. "Un-freaking-believable. Wow, Christine. Just . . . wow." He waves his hand at the ladder and the broken bell. "You fix the bell."

"Gio. *Gio!*" Ma shouts as Pop walks out the front door. "Oh, very mature! That's right. Leave, just like you always do. Lot of good counseling has done us!" Pop flashes a rude gesture from outside, something I've never seen him do. Then he disappears out of sight. Ma slams her hand on the counter. I jump.

"Luca." Ma's voice is brittle. "Watch the register." She doesn't wait for me to answer before vanishing into the kitchen.

I'm shaking. My eyes sting. My insides are at a full boil. There's a tightness in my chest, in my throat. Teeth gouge into my tongue as I try to keep myself from breaking down. *Don't you dare cry, Luca. Don't you dare.*

But I do.

It's not a sob. It's like leaking. A soft, defeated cry that I wipe away as I fold up the ladder and stash it in the corner. I stand alone at the front door, hoping Pop will come back. That Ma will come out with her cell phone pressed to her ear, trying to explain what happened.

But they don't. Instead, the phone rings by the register and, once again, it's on me to run the show. I suck up the snot dripping from my nose and clear my throat.

"Thank you for calling Mamma Gianna's. This is Luca speaking. How can I help you?"

Chapter 21

The phone number fiasco with Chris haunts me the rest of the weekend. He doesn't show up again at the restaurant, but his presence lingers like three-bean-chili farts.

Now Ma and Pop are worse than they've ever been. They say they need even more space. They can't even be at Mamma Gianna's at the same time. That means I'm doing double the work with each of them to run the business and get ready for Travis Parker.

I feel like a total failure. Everything I've done to keep them together hasn't changed one thing. They're still fighting. They can't agree on anything. Pop's not moving back in.

But I'm not giving up yet. I know in my gut that when Travis Parker gets here, that'll be my last shot at helping Ma and Pop see the truth.

By Monday morning I feel like the mashed potatoes we fold into our pizza dough. June and Will ask if I'm sick, but I tell them I'm fine. Just tired. (I wish I were sick. The stomach flu would feel better than my heart weighing like an anchor in my chest.)

I'm stunod all day, even in Culinary Arts, where we're tasked with baking a three-cheese ziti. You'd think I could do this recipe with my eyes closed and my hands tied behind my back, but I can't channel Houdini to save my life. Flashes of Chris leaning over the counter, writing his phone number on that menu, slipping it to Ma—they drain all my magic. She says she won't call, but what if she does? Or what if it's not Chris, but some other guy Ma falls for? If it's not just my parents falling out of love—if it's them falling for someone else, how do I fix that?

Will and June, to my surprise, take charge. It's strange being told what to do. *I'm* always the leader. The head chef with my trusty sous-chefs. But I'm so foggy that I don't argue. I can't.

It does weird me out, though, that my friends are getting along *so* well. Ever since the musical, it's like a switch flipped. June rejoined our cooking group. Now she laughs at Will's terrible jokes, and Will listens to June talk about her dream roles on Broadway like he cares. Don't get me wrong—I'm glad they're not fighting, but I also feel like something I had with Will, something special, slipped away. A stick of butter that melted through my fingers.

At lunch, Will plops his tray next to me with a grunt.

"What's wrong?" June asks, snapping a chip between her teeth.

Will curls a bang of black hair around his index finger. "You know how Melissa Berg was doing vocals for my band?"

"Yeah." June drags out the word like taffy.

"Did something happen?" I pick the crust off my salami and mozzarella sandwich, but I don't eat it. I'm not all that hungry.

Will grumbles, "She quit. I guess her grades suck, so her parents told her she can't do anything extra until she's got As and Bs. But the Battle of the Bands is like a month away!" He cradles his face in his hands. "We spent so much time practicing, and now it's all for nothing. We can't perform without a singer!"

"I'm sorry," says June.

"I mean, *could* you perform without a singer?" I ask.

Will gives me an "are you bananas?" look. "Not if we want to win."

June pops another chip into her mouth. She chews slowly. "A month is still a lot of time. We blocked and choreographed an entire musical in a little more than four weeks." She swallows. "What if you found another vocalist?"

"It took me weeks to find Melissa," Will says. "Where do you think I'm going to find someone who can—"

He stops because we can both read the expression on June's face. Her lips are pursed in an almost-smile, eyes shifting side to side as if to say, "Um, *hello*." All I can do is watch as the trains collide in front of me.

"Wait—*you* want to sing in my band?" The pitch of Will's voice goes up.

June laughs, smoothing her hair behind her ear. "I mean, yeah, I guess that would be cool. If you want me to. I've got time now that the show's over."

"But you don't know any *band* songs," I blurt. I mean, it's true. June's playlists are all musical theater, but I can't decide if I said that to sabotage their plan or just state facts.

"I can learn," June counters. "Look how fast I memorized my lines and all that choreography. A few rock songs? *Psh*. Easy peasy."

Will beams. "We only get to perform three songs. You can learn those in three weeks, right?"

"Sure!"

What have I done? Will and June will be hanging out together. Without me. Alone. I can't stomach it. "But what about helping me with things at Mamma Gianna's? How will you have time to learn music *and* make sure we're ready for"—I lower my voice—"Travis Parker?"

"We can do both," says June. When I give her a look, she adds, "Really! I'm good at multitasking. I'll make sure Will is too."

"Totally." Will leaps up. "June, this is seriously amazing. Thank you so much. I'm gonna tell the rest of the guys right now."

He dashes to Allison Gufferson and Brendon Alvarez. I watch him telling them the "good" news over my shoulder, absently picking at my sandwich but not eating any of it.

"Luca," June says. I turn to look at her. "You're acting weird."

I smoosh a piece of bread between my finger and thumb. I roll it into a tiny brown ball. "No, I'm not."

"You totally are." She wags a chip at me. "I know your tells. I'm your best friend, remember?"

I roll my eyes. "I'm fine."

She whispers, "I thought you *wanted* me to be friends with Will."

I hate that she's right. "I do." I sigh.

"Then why are you acting like you don't want me to join Will's band?"

I'm being stupid. I do want them to get along, but I can't tell her that I'm jealous. That I'm sad she'll get to spend time with Will without me. That I'm worried they'll end up becoming closer and I won't be a part of their friendship. That maybe they'll ditch me, and the band will become their everything. That they won't need me. That she and Will will end up *like*-liking each other. My toes curl in my shoes. Will probably *does* have a crush on June. She's amazing. And talented. And pretty.

And a girl.

I've gotta stop being selfish. June's right. I did what I set out to do: I brought Will and June together. I exhale. "Sorry.

I just have a lot going on right now. I totally want you to be in the band if that's what you want."

She smiles. "It's weird, but I kinda really do." She offers me a chip from her bag. I don't take it. "I'm sorry things are tough for you right now. But just think—in less than two weeks, you're gonna be hanging out with a famous person."

A butterfly escapes the swirling storm in my stomach. It flutters across my rib cage. Knowing Travis Parker will be here does make me feel a little better. I grin. "It doesn't feel real. Like, I know it's gonna happen, but still—does that make any sense?"

"That's how I felt before opening night," she says. "Like this couldn't possibly be my life. People buying tickets to watch *me* sing and act. It was like a dream. And then it wasn't, and it was the best feeling in the world." She eats another chip. "I guess that's why I'm so excited about the band. I love performing."

Will hops back into his seat and tells us the band is excited about June joining. The rest of lunch, Will and June talk about practice schedules and he shares a playlist of their songs. He tells her how Melissa sang them, the riffs she added, how Brendon can get a little behind sometimes, so she really needs to know her counts. It's complicated, listening to them. I'm happy they're getting along. I just never imagined I'd be on the outside of what brought them together.

But I *did* bring them together. I made sure they got to know each other and that Will went to see June perform. And if I can get these two to get along, then maybe I haven't lost my touch. Maybe there's still a chance for Ma and Pop, even if wrenches like Call Me Chris keep getting thrown at me.

That just means I've gotta go bigger and bolder as I draft the ultimate recipe to save my parents' marriage.

Chapter 22

When every part of your life is a dumpster fire, it's hard to know which flame to put out first. Do I focus on keeping my parents together? What about Mamma Gianna's staying open? What do I do about Will and June getting flirty? I need advice, but I can't go to my parents. Not when *they* are part of the problem. And Gramma Salvatore is team Pop *and* anti-Mamma Gianna's. Plus, she tells "the gals" EVERYTHING. I've learned to only tell her things I want going out in the neighborhood newsletter. Which leaves me with only one other adult.

Nonna Zaza used to be my go-to. I could tell her *anything*. But ever since she moved to Florida, she started this whole new life without us. She lives in a retirement community, spending most of her day by the pool, and she's getting . . . *old*. Like, she doesn't-remember-things old. Even the way she talks is different. So sometimes, I feel like I can't or *shouldn't* go to her. But we're two weeks out from Travis Parker–palooza, and I need her.

"Luca, bambino!" Nonna Zaza shrieks into the phone. "How's my number one?"

Number one. The firstborn. I'm always reminded that, as the oldest grandchild, I have the most responsibility. "Good, Nonna, I'm good," I say, doing my best not to stare at her up-close nose. "How're you?"

"Oh, fabulous, fabulous. What's there to complain about with all this sunshine?"

I try not to cringe on camera. Leave it to me to be the rain cloud in her life. "Right, right. Uh, actually, I, uh, wanted to talk to you about something."

"What's on your mind?"

What isn't *on my mind?* I don't want to worry Nonna, so I choose my words carefully. I'm not sure what Ma has been telling her. "Things at the restaurant are going okay, but they could be better. You know how I make my own pizza recipes, using *your* dough of course. Well, I've been trying to convince Ma to let me add one of my creations to the menu, because I think it could be good for business, but she won't—"

Nonna holds up a finger. "Luca, love, I'm gonna stop you right there. Mamma Gianna's is your mother's now. She's the donna of the establishment. What she says goes."

I swallow. "But—"

"You're so sweet," she interrupts me. "Always thinking about how you can help. But I'm done with that life. I earned my time. Why don't you tell me about something else? How's school? Your friends?"

I tell her a little about June and Will. A little about Culinary Arts. But I end the conversation short because I feel betrayed. Nonna's in Florida, loving her life, and we're drowning. She can't even bother to listen to me. Her *number one*? So much for that.

So, like always, I'm on my own. When Ma and I are at the restaurant a couple days later, I say, "I've been thinking about what Candace Goodwater said about that pizza I made."

Ma stares at the spreadsheet on her laptop. "Oh yeah? What about it?"

All she does is work, which I get, but she's been as much a mom as Nonna Zaza has been a grandma lately. And Ma LIVES IN THIS STATE. I mean, Pop isn't much better, but every now and then he tries. With the two of them scrambling to figure out their own lives and Mamma Gianna's, it's like Elio, Nina, and I only get the leftovers of our parents.

"She said we should get my pizza on the menu." I toss the rag I used to wipe down the counter over my shoulder. "I think we should. We could promote it as a Luca-the-Kid-Chef special. Weekly, specially crafted pizzas that switch up to showcase our master chef kid."

Ma lowers her screen but doesn't close her laptop. "Luca, we've talked about this a million times. We can't go changing things right now. Not with—"

"But Candace knows what she's talking about. We could just try—"

206

"Luca!" She massages her forehead. "I said no. I can barely balance our budget as it is, let alone think about how we'd afford a new pizza on the menu. Please. Keep doing what you're doing. *That's* helping."

"But—"

"ENOUGH." She straightens her laptop screen and turns away, ending the conversation. I struck out two for two, and I'm feeling like a stinky, broken garbage disposal. This angry, anxious woman isn't my mom, and I don't know how to get her back.

When we get home that night, I can't stop thinking about how I felt at the restaurant. I get missing Pop since he's away in his apartment, but it's weird missing a person you live with. Even if you're angry with them for making stupid decisions. My parents feel so far apart—and so far away from me—that it feels like now or never to get Ma and Pop back together. I'm not just rescuing their marriage now; I'm rescuing *them*.

I'm a master planner, but I'm overwhelmed. I need help, and my grownups have abandoned me, so I resort to two people I've never thought I'd ever go to for help. Ignoring that it's lights-out, I sneak into Elio and Nina's bedroom. I whisper, "Hey. You two awake?"

There's a beat, and then from the darkness, I hear, "We are *now*."

"Good." I close the door behind me and flip on the

switch. Amber light from the lamp on the nightstand between their twin beds fills the room. Nina squints, holding the back of her hand over her eyes, but Elio is alert and wide-eyed as an owl. I sit on Nina's bed. "I know it's late, but . . . I need your help."

Elio flops back on his pillow. "If this is about chores, I'm going back to sleep." He fake snores into his pillow.

"It's not," I say. "It's about Ma and Pop."

Elio cuts his act and sits up. Nina crosses her arms, but she watches me expectantly. I go on, "I'm sick of Pop living in that stupid apartment and the two of them fighting all the time. They love each other deep down, I just know it. But *they* need to remember how much they love each other. *Why* they love each other. And we can help them remember; I just don't know how to do that exactly. Not yet. Which is why I'm here."

Nina and Elio glance at each other, doing that twin thing where they have a whole conversation without speaking. Then Nina says, "You want *our* help? You never want our help."

"Yeah," says Elio. "You just want us to do stuff."

"This is different," I say. "The three of us know our parents better than anyone else. If there's anyone who can come up with a plan to keep them together, it's us."

Nina sits up and pulls her knees to her chest. "What if you're wrong? What if they don't want to be together?"

I scoot closer and put a hand on her knee. "They might think that now, but they need to remember all the good times. They need to remember us. *We* are why it's so important to stay together. Family is the most important thing, right?"

Nina nods.

"We could write them letters," says Elio. "Or put a movie together of old videos and us saying nice things. Ma always loves watching our baby videos."

"Maybe," I say. "But I think it needs to be bigger than that."

"Like send them on a vacation?" says Elio. He scratches above his scar. "What's that thing called that people who just got married go on?"

"A honeymoon?" I say. "That's bigger, but it's a little too big. We can barely afford to keep Mamma Gianna's running. I don't think we can manage a cruise along the Amalfi coast. But their anniversary *is* coming up in May. Maybe we could do something special for that?"

Nina *hmms*, then says, "Maybe we can't send them away, but what about a date?"

"A date." I chew on it. "Not a bad idea. But it would have to be one heck of a date. Not just dinner and a movie, you know?" Then something sparks and I have the most brilliant idea. My heart pounds. "Wait. Nina, that's it!"

She beams. "What? Really?"

I drag Elio onto Nina's bed. Then I whisper my idea. They both light up. We spend the next hour brainstorming how we're going to pull it off.

I interrupt June and Will's band talk on Wednesday, a week and a half before Travis Parker is set to arrive, to tell them my Salvatore marriage mission and ask them to be a part of it. We won't be able to pull it off without their skills. They're hesitant at first, but they eventually agree when I bribe them with a month of free pizza.

"You're sure it's a good idea?" June asks. "Seems kinda risky."

"Definitely." I've played out the plan Elio, Nina, and I cooked up a dozen times. Each time, I can see my parents falling back in love. Hugging me and Nina and Elio. Being a normal family that lives under one roof, grinning and running Mamma Gianna's until it's famous and thriving so that someday me and the twins can run it with our kids.

"I'm in," Will says. "I'll take any opportunity to play music." He glances at June. "We'll have to find extra time to rehearse outside of band practice, though. Can you stay a little longer this afternoon? My mom can drive you home when we're done."

"Oh yeah," she says. "I don't mind. I've been having a lot of fun."

Will smiles. "Me too."

They haven't fought at all since June joined the band, and it's been as awful as I thought it would be, knowing they're hanging out without me. Their overly friendly, almost-flirting makes it even worse. It's gotta be cosmic payback for me lying to June about hanging out with Will. I deserve this.

June turns to me. "That *person* is gonna be here in just a few days, right? Are you ready?" She's decided it's safest to always talk in code about *Pizza Perfect* and Travis Parker. She's still embarrassed about her mom's article.

Queasy slugs squirm in my gut. "Yeah. No? I don't know. I'm excited, but super nervous. He'll be here a week from Sunday, and there's still so much to do."

Will squeezes my shoulder. A tingle shoots through me. "Dude, you've got this. No one knows more about pizza than you. Plus, you're the coolest guy I know. That *person* is gonna love you."

I'm the coolest guy he knows.

"Yeah?" I grin. Heat creeps up the back of my neck. No matter how I try, I can't shake how much of a crush I've got on him. How much I miss spending time alone with the one person who really listens to me.

"For sure," he says. "It's gonna be the best week of your life."

Later that night, I'm daydreaming about what my week with Travis Parker will be like, when I get a text from June.

June: I need to tell you something.

June: I think I have a crush

June: on Will

June: 🙈😳😍

My eyes sting. The floor falls out from under me. *I should've known*. I mean, I *did* know. When Will started at Riverside in January, she totally thought he was cute. But then it was just me and Will for those first few weeks, and I thought maybe . . . maybe he could like *me*. And then June was mad at me for hanging out with him, which meant she was angry at Will, so no crush. But now we've made up and they're friends. Will is undeniably adorable, and June is just magnetic. This was inevitable. I just didn't want it to be.

This is just my luck. OF COURSE my best friend in the whole world has a crush on the same person as me. And the worst thing is I'm pretty sure Will feels the same way about June. He's been gaga over her ever since the musical.

There's no use fighting this. My fingers tremble as I type.

Me: He is pretty cute.

June: I KNOW RIGHT

June: Do you think he'll ask me to the spring dance?

The spring dance. With everything else going on, I totally forgot that was a thing! It takes everything in me not to type: No. He never will. He's definitely into boys and I'm really hoping he asks me even though he's been spending all this time with you and I don't care if that hurts your

212

feelings because it's the truth and there are lots of other boys you can ask to the dance but please don't ask this one because he's the one, THE ONLY ONE, I want to go to the dance with.

But I don't. Because that wouldn't be nice. June deserves to be happy too.

Me: Maybe he will.

June: I HOPE SO.

I can't text her back after that. It hurts too much.

Chapter 23

Friday, two days before Travis Parker and the *Pizza Perfect* crew are set to arrive, a massive storm rolls over the Midwest. Every spring, we get nasty weather, but this is the most epic rain-thunder-tornado-ish mess I've seen. We watch funnel clouds forming in nearby towns on the news. Around dinnertime, golf-ball-size hail and sideways rain pelt us. Tornado sirens go off a little after midnight. The sky is ghostly green, and our house shakes. We hunker in the basement. Elio cries, worried about Pop being alone in his apartment. Ma holds my little brother while we Face-Time our dad. Pop's knees to chest in his bathtub, saying it'll be okay. I'm pretty freaked out too, but I try to stay calm. Without Pop here, I'm the man of the house. I need to keep it together. For Ma and the twins.

Between the noisy light show and worrying about Travis Parker showing up on Sunday, I barely get any sleep. We head back to our beds around two. When dawn breaks through my blinds, my blanket is on the floor and my sheet is tangled in my legs. A sour taste coats my tongue when I push myself off my mattress, yawning at the gray morning light. I peek out the window. Branches and garbage litter our yard. Our neighbor's lawn furniture is upended.

With all this damage, my gut says to head right to Mamma Gianna's. I'm worried about what we'll find. I imagine windows smashed in, kitchen flooded, roof gone. But Ma tells me to slow down. That our alarm system would have gone off if something happened. She forces me to eat breakfast, but I'm so nervous about Travis Parker and all we still have to do, that I can barely gulp down my eggs and toast.

It's Pop's turn to open the shop. He picks me up around ten, while Ma is in the shower. Rain pelts the windshield as we drive.

"You doing okay?" he asks. He's in his weekend comfies—ratty jeans and a faded Cubs sweatshirt. "Those circles under your eyes are darker than mine, kiddo."

I fidget with the seat belt strapped across my chest. "Just nervous about Travis Parker. I want everything to be perfect when he gets here. I want to make him the best pizza he's ever tasted. Show him what I'm made of."

Pop flicks the turn signal as we round the corner, two blocks away from Mamma Gianna's. "Kid, you've got nothing to be nervous about. The restaurant's never looked better, and you've still got a full day to play around with whatever recipes are filling that little brain of yours. It's gonna be good."

I draw a smiley face in the fog on my window. "If you say so."

A car cuts in front of us, and Pop hits the breaks a little too fast. My body juts forward. The seat belt cuts into me, followed by Pop's clothesline arm.

"Sorry 'bout that, kiddo," he says. "People forget how to drive when it storms. Sheesh." He tilts his head closer to the glass, looking out at the sky. "Hope it clears up soon."

"Me too." I always feel gloomy when it rains. Maybe that's why I feel off.

When we walk into Mamma Gianna's, I relax. The roof is still on. The windows aren't broken. The floor isn't flooded. But then I realize how weirdly quiet it is. Too quiet. And too cold, even for late April.

"Does something seem strange to you?" I ask.

Pop flips the light switch. The lights don't come on. He toggles it again, and still nothing. He frowns. "Crap."

"What's wrong?" I ask.

"Power must be out." He reaches into his pocket and pulls out his phone. "Frickin' storm. I'll give Tony a call. You call your mom—tell her to bring coolers and ice packs. Quick."

It hits a half second later why he says that, and my insides melt. Without power, our fridge and freezer won't be running, which means all our ingredients haven't been cooled in who knows how long. All our ovens run on electricity too, which means we can't bake anything until the power comes back. I can't mix. I can't blend. I can't do *anything*. My chest tightens. Travis Parker will be here in twenty-four hours, and nothing'll be ready!

I sprint to the kitchen, using my cell phone flashlight to guide my way. I whisper a silent prayer to whoever is the saint of power outages. *Please let the food be okay. Please let the food be okay.* Holding on to the frayed threads of my optimism, I check the finicky refrigerator. Usually, it hums and clanks like a tractor, but it's silent. *Not good. Not good. Not good.* Holding my breath, I inch the metal door open. Not even a whisper of cool air seeps out. Our meats, our veggies, our cheeses, our milk—all warm. *No, no, no.* The door handle slips from my fingers.

The freezer, thank God, is still cold—not Arctic cold, but cold enough—but it won't be for long if we don't get the power back on.

I call Ma. She curses when I tell her what happened. She hollers that she'll be over in a few minutes. That I shouldn't go into the freezer again. That we need to conserve as much cool air as possible. That if the fridge has been out for over four hours, we've gotta junk everything in there. It'll be unsafe to serve.

That's hundreds of dollars of food going to waste. That means more money spent to replace product we can't even sell. Which won't even matter if we can't get the power back on to make pizzas.

Tony shows up half an hour later. He's tall and Black, with dark brown skin and a full salt-and-pepper beard. I can tell by the way he whistles when he walks in that things aren't good. Ma arrives a few minutes after him, wheeling two giant coolers. While she and I salvage what we can from the fridge and freezer, which isn't much, Tony tells Pop to call the utility company.

"Nothing much I can do," he says, scratching his elbow. "Not sure why your backup generator didn't kick on either. That could have saved the fridge at least."

"Talk to Christine," Pop says loudly. "We were supposed to replace ours a year ago."

Ma's face turns sharp as jagged glass. She drops a bag of shredded mozzarella into a trash bin and shouts, "We didn't have the money, Gio. What did you expect me to do? Sell a kidney? And it worked the last time I kicked it on. How was I supposed to know?"

Pop shouts back, "Well, now we're both gonna have to sell kidneys to get us out of this mess."

Ma stomps out of the kitchen, hands flying in the air. "*You* could have done more, Gio. Gotten another job. I already put in double hours and sell makeup—"

"Oh not this crap again," Pop snorts. "Are you forgetting

how much my mother has given us? How much we still owe *her* on top of all the loans we've taken?"

Their voices become the fizz and crackle of a broken TV. Just noise. That's all it ever is. They aren't trying to make anything better. All they know how to do is make things worse.

But I can't let them ruin the best thing that's ever happened to me. That's ever happened to *us*. Not when we're so close to a real opportunity to change our lives. I storm out of the kitchen, shove myself between them, and shout at the top of my lungs. "THAT'S ENOUGH!"

Ma and Pop freeze. Tony shudders.

I keep going before they can start up again. "Fighting isn't going to fix this. Travis Parker will be here tomorrow, and we don't know when the power will come back on. We need a backup generator right now. Pop, you call the utility company. Ma, you and I can go to the hardware store to buy one. Then we're getting this restaurant up and running. Capisce?"

Ma cringes. "It's not that simple, Luca. Do you know how much a generator costs? Enough to power a place like this?"

"I don't care," I say. "You have credit cards, don't you?"

"Yeah, but—"

"If we can show Travis Parker what we can do, it won't matter. He'll give us money that'll cover the generator and all the ingredients we lost and make up for the months of rent *you* lied about paying." Ma recoils like I smacked her, but I don't care. I'm tired and angry and so close to seeing my celebrity icon. To fixing the mess *she and Pop* made. I take a deep breath. "Being on his show is the answer to all our problems, but we're not gonna be on the show if we don't have a restaurant."

Pop scratches the top of his head. "Kid's got a point, Christine."

"But we're already drowning in debt," says Ma. She laughs but not in a funny way. "Not even. We've drowned. There's nothing left."

"I know, I know," Pop says. He chews on his thumb. "I can try taking out another loan. I mean, I guess I could go back to my mom, but—"

Ma snorts. "She'd never. Your mother hates me."

Pop's eyes roll. "You *did* kick me out of my own house."

"Don't you dare," Ma says, finger jabbing the air. "But maybe I *should* have. No, *I* should have left your sorry—"

"STOP," I shout. My eyeballs sting. Fingernails dig into my palms. "Just stop!"

There's a sudden flicker. The lights stutter and go on. Power hums. From the kitchen, waking machines beep and clink. *Grazie to all the freaking saints!* I could cry I'm so relieved, but in the fluorescents, I can see the damage is done. Ma and Pop glare at each other like they're ready to commit murder.

"Welp," says Tony sheepishly. "Looks like you got lucky.

I'll, uh, be on my way." He nods at Pop and slinks out the door.

I check my phone. It's almost two o'clock, just a couple hours before we open. "We still have time," I say. "We just need some fresh ingredients, and we can run service tonight."

"Right." Ma checks her watch. "You're right. Gio, can you run to the store?"

But Pop shakes his head with a disgusted laugh. "You're kidding, right?"

"What?" Ma asks.

"You think you're better off without me," says Pop. "You think you can do this on your own? Fine." He smashes his palm against the glass front door. It flies open, rain pouring in. And he walks out.

Ma runs to the door, shouting after him. She apologizes, but she doesn't chase him. She says she was angry, frustrated. That she didn't mean it. But Pop doesn't come back.

Ma sinks into a booth, her head in her hands. "I can't do this anymore. I just can't do this."

I slide into the seat across from her. I hate seeing her like this, but I can't understand how they fight this way. Not when they're supposed to love each other. Not when they're *family*. Why can't they listen to each other? Work together? They're freaking *adults*. They're supposed to be better than this.

"Ma," I say quietly, knowing if I say the wrong thing,

she'll snap at me too. "We can't give up. Travis Parker will be here tomorrow morning. Please. Go to the store. Get what we need. I'll start a fresh batch of dough. We *can* do this. You and me. And Pop . . . He'll come back. He always does."

She stares at me, eyes shiny as peeled onions, her hand covering her mouth. I can't tell what her lips are doing.

"*Please*," I say again.

She sighs. "Okay." She inhales slowly. "Okay. You're right. We can't give up." Her dark eyes rove the empty restaurant. "You sure you're all right getting set up without me?"

I nod. "I could run this place blindfolded."

She almost laughs. "I know you could, baby. I know."

Five minutes later, she leaves, reassuring me that she'll be as quick as possible. She says she'll call Cesar and see if he can come in early to help me out. I tell her I'll be fine.

But when she leaves and I lock the door behind her, it's just me, alone in our sinking ship that I love with my whole freaking heart. And I'm out of duct tape. We're supposed to be the Salvatores. A complete recipe. But right now, we're separate ingredients, and I don't know how much longer I can keep fighting all by myself to be something we're so clearly not.

Chapter 24

The patron saint of dysfunctional families and Midwestern storms must be looking out for us because we only open Mamma Gianna's half an hour late. While Ma was out, I flailed like an octopus, getting as much ready as I could. She, Cesar, and I keep firing orders until close.

Pop never comes back Saturday night. He ignores the first three texts I send him and even when I resort to an actual phone call he doesn't pick up. That stings. I mean, I'm his *kid*. I'm not Ma. *I'm* not the problem here. And I need my dad. Ma, Nonna Zaza, Gramma Salvatore, and now Pop—everyone is letting me down.

With Travis Parker hours away from landing at O'Hare airport, I collapse into my bed when Ma and I get home that night. My brain tells me I should be making the pizza recipe I've been dreaming up all day, a brand-new one that sounds life-changingly good, but my muscles are jelly. My bones are breadsticks ready to snap. I just can't do anymore.

Before I pass out from exhaustion, I text June and Will about everything that happened at the restaurant. Neither of them responds, which makes sense since it's almost midnight, but part of my brain tries to convince me they're together, becoming best friends—or worse, *flirting*. Which is stupid. Of course they're not together. And June is still my best friend. And Will, well, I'm not sure how I feel about him. He's my friend, and I still have FEELINGS, but how can I have feelings when June is crushing on him. (And what if he likes her back?) GAH! I smash my face into my pillow and scream.

Then, before I know it, I'm waking up to my alarm. Sunday morning. Travis Freaking Parker Day is HERE. I catapult out of bed.

Candace Goodwater notified us that Travis Parker will arrive at the restaurant between one and three o'clock this afternoon. That we should be ready and waiting so the film crew can arrive ahead of him to record our initial meeting in all its authentic glory. *That* means we should be at Mamma Gianna's by eleven a.m. at the very latest. But Ma tells me to slow down. That we've got a long week coming on the heels of a difficult Saturday. That we gotta rest in the final hours before we're on our toes twenty-four seven.

But I can't rest. Not NOW. Instead of catching Sunday morning cartoons with Nina and Elio, I mess around in our kitchen with my recipe idea. It would be PERFECT for the

Pizza Perfect Challenge, if only Ma will let me use it.

"I want to celebrate our history," she says. "Besides, that's too much pressure on you. If the challenge goes sideways with one of your pizzas, I don't want you beating yourself up. You've got enough going on as it is, you know?"

I don't know what hurts more: that she doesn't think I'm made of tougher stuff or that she doesn't believe in me and my pizzas to bring home the big bucks for us.

June and Will text me as Ma, Nina, Elio, and I are walking out the door at noon.

> **June:** Oof. What a mess. Sorry last night was so awful, Luca.
>
> **June:** BUT OMGOMGOMGOMG TRAVIS PARKER AHHHHHH!!!!
>
> **Will:** Dude. It's HAPPENING. Good luck today! Tell us everything.
>
> **Will:** I want to know what it's like to meet a famous person

I tell them I'll keep them in the loop, and that, if they're lucky, they'll get to meet Travis Parker too. That gets me a whole bunch of excited emojis.

After the power outage yesterday, I half expect Mamma Gianna's to be on fire when we get there because the universe seems to have a vendetta against us, but it's not. Every machine is whirring and clinking and humming. *Phew.*

But I still haven't heard from Pop. It'll be weird if he's

not here when Travis Parker arrives. They're expecting a *family*-run business. I send him another text, but still nothing.

With everything in order by ten to one, the twins, Ma, and I pile into a booth. Ma's wearing a red blouse and black slacks. Her makeup is extra on point. Nina, Elio, and I are in black Mamma Gianna's T-shirts and clean jeans. Elio and I have product in our hair, which we only do for fancy occasions. Nina's hair is pulled into a tidy ponytail that Ma wrapped in a hot iron so it dangles in a single curl.

"Look," Ma says, "whatever happens this week, no matter what money or gift we get—*if* we get anything at all—I hope you just have fun. We need some fun, don't we?"

Nina's face contorts in mock confusion. "What's fun? I don't know what that is."

"Maybe Travis Parker will give me a hermit crab!" Elio grins. "That would be fun *and* the best prize. Then I could use the money I've been saving for a HUGE habitat!"

I lace my fingers and set my hands on the table. "You all can have fun, but not *too* much. This is serious business for me."

Ma wraps her hand around mine. "I know. But we don't know how it's gonna go. I don't want you getting your hopes up. No matter how much we want something, life doesn't always work out the way we want."

I pull my hands back. "It will. It *has* to."

At 2:26, Candace Goodwater appears at the front door with two men and a woman. Candace's hair is electric purple now. She greets Ma and I with a hug and then introduces the cameraman, Doug; the sound woman, Esther; and the makeup guy, Billy. Butterfly wings bat against my chest. This is real. This is happening.

While Doug and Esther set up equipment, Candace runs down what we'll shoot today, and Billy blots my nose with something he says'll keep me from getting too shiny on camera.

"It'll mostly be introductions, some banter, and then a tour of the restaurant," Candace says, eyeing the tablet in her palm. "Mostly the foundational 'Dough' part of the episode, which we'll add to tomorrow. We'll aim to be done by five today." Candace's eyes flit around the room. "Is your husband coming? I'd love to get a shot of the whole family when TP arrives."

I shift on my feet. Ma fidgets with the gold pendant around her neck, and says, "He got held up with something. I'm not sure he'll make it."

Ma's too good at avoiding the truth. I don't think I realized how good she is at it until now. But she's determined to keep our personal business out of the show. I shouldn't be surprised.

"That's too bad," Candace says. "Well, we can circle back, introduce him, and get a family shot later. No sweat."

Maybe *they're* not sweating, but I'm all sweat. I'm practically dripping when the front door opens at 3:07, a choir of angels sings, and Travis Parker glides through the door followed by another cameraman and a guy holding a fuzzy microphone on a long stick.

MADONNA MIA. THIS IS IT!!!

Fireworks fizzle and unfurl in my bones. My nerves are rockets and firecrackers. He's here. My inspiration. My icon. The man I've watched for years. He's in *my family's* restaurant. I can't take my eyes off him. *Madonna mia, is this my real life?* He's taller than I expected. The tips of his hair are inches from the top of the doorway. He's wearing a purple-striped button-down, dark wash jeans, and brown leather sneakers. Classic Travis Parker.

He beams from the doorway—at *me*. His voice, coming not from a speaker but from his actual MOUTH, says, "Buon giorno, Mamma Gianna's! How's it hanging?"

"Mr. Parker, it is such an honor," says Ma, waltzing across the tile. "I'm Christine Salvatore, and these are my children, Elio, Nina, and Luca."

"*The* Luca? The one my team has been chittering about for weeks?" He winks at me. "How's it going, man?"

I float to him. My hand is suddenly shaking his. I'm TOUCHING Travis FREAKING Parker. "I—I'm amazing," I say, breathless. *You sound like you just ran the mile. Get it together, Luca!*

His skin is softer than I expected, but his grip is strong. Clearly someone who's opened a million jars and chopped thousands of veggies and pulled and stretched and rolled countless discs of dough. He laughs, "I hear you run the joint. The youngest master pizza maker in the country. Isn't that right?"

I swallow back phlegm. I grin. "That's right."

I can't believe he *knows* about me. He hasn't even tasted my pizza yet, and he *knows* who I am. I could die right now and that would be okay.

Okay. Not true. He's at least gotta try my pizza first.

The next half hour, we walk Travis Parker around the restaurant. We start in the dining room and talk about how Great-Grandma Gianna opened the shop over fifty years ago. Ma tells him how she came over from Sicily with a few hundred dollars, a little hope, and a killer pizza recipe. We talk about how her friend, Angelina Bruzzo, painted the murals of Italian landscapes on the walls from her memory and the photographs they brought from Italy. Travis Parker laughs at the chef statue we have by the bathroom. "You know it's an authentic pizza joint when you've got one of those hanging around."

We take him around to the kitchen and show him our setup. The ancient fridge and oven, the same plastic bins we've been using for a decade to store ingredients and ferment dough, the sink we've scrubbed with steel wool and still can't get some stains out of. The camera crew maneuvers around us, one pair ahead while the other hangs behind.

I keep waiting for Travis Parker to get bored—I mean, the guy's seen a bajillion kitchens. Ours can't be *that* special. But he doesn't lose interest. In fact, he's like *actually* fascinated by everything we say. This is better than I ever could have imagined. He asks a lot of questions: What kind of prep do we do each night? How many employees do we have? What's our most popular menu item? What's our favorite pizza?

Ma tackles most of the questions, but every now and then, she'll toss one to me, saying something like, "Luca knows better than I do."

Each time that happens, a pilot light reignites behind my ribs. I always talk like I run the restaurant, when it's really Ma and Pop who do the heavy lifting, but her acknowledging that I know things—that I *really* help—makes me feel ten feet tall.

It's almost five o'clock and everything is going great. Then Pop walks in the back door. He's wearing a gray T-shirt with pit stains and a hole near his belly button and jeans with a tear in the knee. And, even in the tomatoey-garlicy aroma of our kitchen, I can smell him. My nose wrinkles. He smells yeasty, like beer. His eyes are glossy. A little red.

"Hey! Look at that. The gang's all here," he says jovially, but too loud. He opens his arms wide and before anyone can stop him, he wraps Travis Parker in a giant bro hug, complete with a double back pat.

Oh God.

I'm mortified, but Travis Parker rolls with it. "Hey, man," he says, clapping Pop on the shoulder like they go way back. "You must be Mr. Salvatore himself."

"The one and only," says Pop. He's way too happy. I've only ever seen him like this one other time at Uncle Tony's wedding. I think—I think he's *drunk.*

Oh my God. This CANNOT be happening.

Ma pulls Pop back by the crook of his left arm. Her face is plastered in a Dazzlingly Bright smile, which I know is masking the rage and embarrassment burning just beneath the surface. "Yes, my husband, Gio." She laughs. "I'm so sorry. We're real huggers in this family."

Pop pulls out of Ma's grip. Her fingers reach for him, like he's about to fall off a cliff, but he wiggles away from her. "Eh, I'm a good guy. I'm good guy. Right, babe?"

That does Ma in. Ice creeps into her voice. "Gio, can you get the oven started in the kitchen? We'll open soon."

"Don't think you're gonna hog all the spotlight, Christine," he says, shrugging her off again. "I own this restaurant too, you know."

They can't get any more of this on camera. This is exactly what Ma was afraid of—getting the too-personal side of our family. If Pop keeps this up, Ma will pull the plug on the whole show. I step in. "Come on, Pop. Let's get ready."

"I'm not going anywhere," he says, his punchy mood slipping away.

Fortunately, Candace clears her throat and says, "You know, I think we've got what we need. Why don't we call it a night?" She twirls a finger in the air, signaling to the crew. The cameramen shift their equipment off their shoulders.

"Yeah," Travis Parker says, yawning, "I'm pretty wiped. Great first day, gang. Candace, what time are we starting in the a.m.?"

They trail a finger down their iPad screen. "Not until ten. We'll go on a shopping trip with Christine—Mr. Salvatore too, if he's up to it, then some one-on-one time with Luca."

That slows the Embarrassment Express choo-chooing in my head. "Wait. Me?"

Travis Parker smiles. "I wanna get to know the future master chef. That okay with you?"

"Absolutely." *Omgomgomgomg.*

"Good," he says, and gives me a fist bump. Then he nods his chin at Ma and Pop. "Good luck with service tonight. Pleasure to meet you all."

He and Candace leave, and I'm so relieved because the tension building between Ma and Pop is like a shaken can of soda. Soon as the camera crew pack up their stuff and get out, we're gonna have an explosion on our hands.

But when they leave, Ma doesn't yell at Pop. She just points at the door. "Gio, I can't do this right now." I've never heard her sound so defeated. "Please. Just go."

"Kicking me out again?" Pop says. "That's what you do best."

"Gio, *please*." A hard edge sharpens her words. "Out. Now."

Pop is about to protest, but I gently grab his wrist. He flinches, like he didn't notice me standing right next to him until I touched him. "Please, Pop," I say. "Go home."

That sobers him up. His scruffy face wrinkles. He nods several times in quick succession. "Yeah, okay. Yeah." He looks at Ma, like he woke up from a dream. "I'm sorry, Christine. I—"

"Tomorrow, Gio," she says. "I've got a restaurant to run."

Ma retreats to the kitchen. Pop squeezes my shoulder, tells me he's sorry, and leaves. And the worst thing is, I don't wish he'd come back.

Chapter 25

"Tell us everything," June says at my locker on Monday morning. She bounces on the tips of her toes. Her squishy octopus key chain flops on her backpack zipper. "Is he everything you'd dreamed he'd be?"

Will sways energetically behind her. "Did he try your pizza yet?"

I grab a folder, close the door, and spin the lock. "Better than my dreams. And no pizza sampling yet. Just introductions and basic stuff last night. But TP and I are filming together this afternoon. Maybe then?"

"*TP?*" June says, looking impressed. "Already using nicknames?"

Will chuckles. "TP. Like . . . toilet paper."

"OMG. NO." I laugh, shoving him away. "Now every time I look at Travis Parker, I'm going to think about poop." I mock cry. "Look what you've done! You've ruined my idol!"

"Oh please," says June. "Nothing could ruin Travis Parker for you. He's like a god. You can't ruin perfection."

I shut my locker and spin the lock. "Him hating my pizza would ruin things."

"Dude, he's gonna *love* your pizza," says Will. "Are you gonna make him the buffalo chicken one?"

"I like the one with bacon, dates, and goat cheese better," says June. "I bet he'd let you take over the whole show if he tasted that one."

My cheeks burn. "You guys, cool it. It's too early for all this praise." I hug my binders to my chest. "But no, I'm not gonna make him either of those." I pull them in closer with a whisper. "I've got something brand-new cooking up for him."

"Omg. Tell us what it is!" June squeaks. "We can totally workshop it with you."

Will shrugs. "I'll just eat it. You've never made anything I didn't like."

"Nah, it's staying a secret." I'm trying to keep it cool, but whenever Will says nice things about me, I get all blushy, so I change the subject. "How's the band going? You guys get a chance to practice that song I asked about?"

Brrrring! The first period warning bell blares.

"We've almost got it," says Will. "June's really crushing the vocals. She hit an F at practice on Saturday."

I'm not sure what that means, but I say, "Whoa."

She tosses her hair over her shoulder. "It wasn't *that* big a deal."

"Well, I was impressed," Will says, tucking his thumbs in the pockets of his track pants.

A jealous gurgle turns in my intestines. Which is stupid. Them getting along is making everything better. And June *is* impressive. But I want him to be more impressed by me, and it's all worse because I know she has a crush on him.

I was kidding myself if I thought I was going to be able to pay any real attention to school stuff today. I'm supposed to be bisecting or dissecting shapes or whatever in math, but I keep imagining Ma chatting with Travis Parker at our local grocery. Filming B-roll up and down the aisles. Sniffing tomatoes and onions to see if they're ripe. Laughing at food puns. And I'm not there for any of it. I'm missing more of our foundational scenes and some of that saucy middle part of the episode. I don't want to miss the heart-to-heart he always has either.

Visions of Pop making a fool of himself invade my daydreams. The smell of his breath. The way his lips and tongue weren't quite in sync. How words came out with fuzzy edges. It kills me that that was the first impression Travis Parker got of my dad. Pop's not like that in real life. Sloppy. Drunk. He was just upset. I mean, at least, I think? What if there're things I don't know? What if Ma and Pop have been putting on more of a show than I even realized?

No. There's no way. I know my parents. I know my family. That's not Pop. But you can't toss out a first impression. It's not like a burned pizza. You don't get to remake it. It's permanent.

When I check my phone at lunch, I've got a bunch of notifications. Texts from Ma and Pop, but not in the same thread.

Ma: Hi, baby. Come straight to the restaurant after
school. Gramma Salvatore will pick up Nina and
Elio so you can film with TP. Love you.

Much as I obsess over food, I'm too excited to eat anything now. I send back a quick okay message. Then I read Pop's text. I get queasy.

Pop: Luca, hey.

Pop: About last night, I'm really sorry.

Pop: No. Sorry doesn't even begin to cut it. I was way
out of line. I promise that won't happen again. I
swear.

Pop: I apologized to your mom too. Just FYI.

Pop: Sorry for all the texts. I know you're at school.
I'll talk to you later. Love you, kiddo.

I don't respond to Pop. I'm glad he's sorry, but a text apology? C'mon. That's not enough. Not after embarrassing me in front of TRAVIS PARKER. He knows how much this means to me. How much *we* need this.

Soon as school lets out, I hoof it to Mamma Gianna's.

Even though I already spent time with Travis Parker and the film crew last night, I'm a tangle of cold spaghetti all over again.

Travis Parker himself holds the front door of the restaurant open in greeting. He's wearing a different striped button-down today—yellow and black. My inner noodles unwind, warmed by his genuine smile.

"Luca! I've been waiting all day for this." He ushers me in, taking my backpack off my shoulders, and handing it to Candace Goodwater. They take it from him without even looking up from whoever they're texting. He goes on, "Don't get me wrong, I had a great day with your mom. But you—you remind me of myself when I was your age."

My ears heat up. "Really?"

"Hey!" Candace wags a finger at us. "Save the charming moments for the camera." She calls to the crew, who are sipping sodas in a booth near the back. They hop up, shoulder their equipment, and start recording (I think).

"I was thinking," Travis says in the same warm tone. "How about you and me throw a pizza together. You give me some tips, and I'll share a few tricks of the trade?"

I beam. *Is this our heart-to-heart? The moment I gain some inspired words of wisdom from my icon?* I swallow, trying to wet my suddenly dry mouth. "That would be amazing."

How is this my ACTUAL LIFE?!

We head into the kitchen, where I give Ma a squeeze,

wave to Cesar, and wash my hands. Then Travis Parker and I toss on aprons, and all of a sudden, he's watching me mix a fresh batch of our signature dough.

"Potatoes, huh?" he says. "Can't say I've seen too many recipes stray from the typical ingredients. Most chefs mess with the toppings or the sauce."

"This is how we've always done it," I say, kneading by hand. "Traditions are important in our family. We're keeping my great-grandma's legacy alive."

"You're really honoring her memory." Travis Parker pokes the dough with a finger. "Look at that squish. Perfect texture, and that golden-honey color is exquisite." He wags his fingers at the camera man. "Get in there, dude. Take a good look at that!"

I reach for the rolling pin, but Travis Parker stops me. "You don't toss your pizzas?"

"Grandma used to, but I never learned," I say sheepishly.

He shoves his sleeves past his elbows. "Well, today's your lucky day."

For the next thirty minutes, I'm living in an alternative pizza reality. My celebrity idol demonstrates how to pad out the dough in his palm, spinning out a puck of gold until it gets wider and wider, stretching into a perfect wheel. I watch, totally in awe. When it's my turn to try, the dough hits the floor. I'm horrified, but Travis Parker laughs, pats me on the shoulder, and tells me to try again. He fixes my wrist. Helps me find my balance. I lose count of how many times the dough falls from my fingers, but every time it does, he encourages me to pick it back up. To try again. Like he really believes in me.

And then it happens. The dough spins over my head, twirling faster and faster. I don't blink, afraid I'll lose the magic of the moment, of finally finding the right rhythm. When I let the dough land, it's not a perfect circle, but it's pretty darn close. *God, this footage is gonna be SO COOL when it airs. I'm gonna look like a total boss.*

"Mamma mia!" Travis Parker shouts. "Look at that! One afternoon and you're already better than half the chefs I've trained."

"You really think so?" I say, flattening a lumpier spot in my crust.

He raises an eyebrow. "You've watched my show, right? Don't you think I know what I'm talking about?"

I laugh nervously. "I mean, yeah. I've watched every episode of *Pizza Perfect* like a million times. Of course, you do."

"Then you can trust I'm telling you the truth," he says.

We dress the dough in tomato sauce, cheese, our home-made Italian sausage, and our house seasonings. While it bakes in the oven, Travis Parker and I sit across from each other in a booth. Ma joins us, taking the spot next to me. The camera crew are on break, so it's just us. Travis Parker's shoulders sink a little as he rests into the booth.

"It's only been a day, but I gotta say: I'm impressed." Travis Parker's eyes travel the wall murals. "I know you all have been having some challenges, though. Tell me more about that."

Ma sighs. "Money's been tight. Keeping Mamma Gianna's running, especially with more chains and trendier pizza places opening, has been difficult. We do our best to keep our family recipe alive, but I'm worried we're not keeping up with the times. That we'll get beat out by the shiny new guys."

Travis Parker frowns. "You've got a solid establishment. Great za. Trust yourself."

Ma's lips pinch together. "I wish it were that simple. Running the restaurant, hustling a side business, managing a family—it's been hard on all of us."

"Juggling business and family is never easy. I get it." He scratches his goatee. "My first restaurant went under in a year. Took a major toll on my relationship with my partner."

I glance at Ma. I can't help but think about her and Pop. All their problems. But she doesn't meet my gaze. She's nodding, staring at her hands cradled on the table.

"Sometimes I wonder who, or *what*, I'm really married to." Ma sort of laughs. She waves her hands at the walls. "My husband or this place."

My husband. That's a surprise. I can't remember the last

time I heard Ma call Pop her "husband." She's referred to him as "that guy" or "your father" for months now, like he's not attached to her at all. I wonder if she's just saying that because of Travis Parker.

Travis Parker shakes his head. "I used to feel that way too. Between the show, writing cookbooks, celebrity events, and running restaurants in San Francisco and New York, I kept missing being there for my husband. We almost called it quits a couple times."

I do a double take. Everyone knows Travis Parker is gay, but he never talks about his personal life on camera. Like *never*. I lean forward. Not only is Travis Parker everything I want to be, but he's like me in *so* many ways. This feels like a surprise gift—getting to hear from the real Travis Parker. The one the camera doesn't show.

"Parallel lives," Ma snort-laughs, stealing the words right out of my brain. "Well, minus the show, obviously." She flips her watch up. "Your pizza should be done. I'll go grab it from the oven. Be right back."

As soon as she scootches out, I fold my hands on the table, and ask, "How did you make it work? With your husband?"

Travis Parker pushes back into the cushioned booth with a sigh. "I had to think long and hard about what I was really living for: my work or my family. It hit me not all that long ago when we were home one night cooking. It was the same meal I'd made him on our first date. I realized something had to go from my life, and it couldn't be him." He twists the ring on his finger. He smiles. "Honestly, that's why this is the last season of *Pizza Perfect*. It was all too much for us. I'm choosing my husband, and our chance to start a family, over the show." He laughs. "And I've never been happier. Luca, whatever you do to chase your pizza dreams, don't forget what matters most."

I nod. "I—I won't."

His words marinate in my gray matter. I think a little about Will, and even June. I think *a lot* about Ma and Pop. The kind of love they must have had once upon a time. All the things they must have forgotten since having kids and taking over the restaurant. Which makes me a little less angry at them.

Then Ma is standing at the end of the table, pizza pan in one hand and a stand in the other. She sets the steaming pie in front of us. My mouth waters. Travis Parker's eyes take in the caramelized cheese and hills of browned sausage. Ma serves him a slice, warning him that it's hot. But he shoves the tip of the triangle into his mouth anyway, instantly making the most blissed-out moan I've ever heard him make. (And I've seen him eat a TON of pizza).

"Dude." He swallows his bite, smiling brighter than sunshine. "DUDE. THIS is where IT. IS. AT. Hello, Mamma Gianna's." He beams at me. "Luca, you've got the magic touch."

Welp. There it is. I can officially die happy now.

But the best part is that he hasn't even tasted my greatest-of-all-time pizza creation yet.

First, though, I've got another recipe to execute—putting Ma and Pop back together. And now I think I know just what to do.

Chapter 26

While Ma and Pop film with TP Tuesday evening, I pull
Nina and Elio into my bedroom so Gramma Salvatore can't
hear us scheming.

"Look," I say, "Ma and Pop are getting worse by the minute. If we wait for their anniversary to spring our surprise,
it might be too late."

What I don't tell them: I overheard Ma on the phone
with Nonna Zaza last night. She was talking about Pop.
About lawyers. She even said the D word. But I don't
want Nina and Elio to worry *that* much, so I keep that to
myself.

Elio frowns. "Then what do we do?"

"Well, if we wanna go *big*, there's nothing bigger than
Travis Parker." I crack my knuckles. "I say we move our plan
up to this week. Get the PP crew to film the whole thing!"

Nina looks like she smells something rotten. "But, like,
didn't Ma say we had to keep family stuff out of the show?
Like, isn't that the exact *opposite* of what she wants?"

I wave my hands. "No, no. She doesn't want any *fighting* on camera—this would be all lovey-dovey, ooey-gooey. No drama." I've played the scene over in my head a million times. Our parents seeing what we put together. Ma bursting into tears of joy. Pop patting me on the back, all proud. The five of us group hugging on camera. TP and Candace patting their eyes dry. It'll be GOLD.

"I don't know, Luca. This seems—"

"Trust me, Nina," I say. "I've gotten Ma and Pop through all sorts of fights. I know what I'm doing."

Elio inches closer to her on the bed. "It's *Luca*. He always knows what he's doing."

My chest puffs. Elio's never said anything like that about me. "Then we're a go?"

Elio and I stare at Nina. She shrugs. "Fine." A smile curls on her lips. "Let's do this."

While we're filming Wednesday afternoon, I tell Travis Parker I want to surprise my parents with something special: a family dinner for just us Salvatores, prepared by yours truly, held in the restaurant. I tell him it's my way of saying thank-you to Ma and Pop for everything they do for me and the twins. Perfect for the 'Dough' segment about the foundations of our restaurant, right? I convince him that it *has* to be a secret from my parents. The best news? He's all about it. Says he'll loop in Candace and the crew and offers me Friday night, the second-to-last day he and

246

the *Pizza Perfect* crew will be here. (Saturday is reserved for filming the "Pizza Perfect Challenge"—I'm still trying to convince Ma to let me decide which pizza we'll serve Travis Parker, but she won't budge on Great-Grandma Gianna's signature Italian sausage and peppers pan pizza.) Anyway, we shake on our secret mission, and I only feel a little guilty about lying to him about what we're *really* planning.

The only people who know the truth are Elio, Nina, June, and Will. I start thinking of them as my own personal crew. My "Parent Perfect" dream team.

When school gets out on Friday, I pick up Nina and Elio. We make our way to Mamma Gianna's. The restaurant is empty aside from Cesar, who's prepping for service that night, and Candace, who's helping us set up. Ma and Pop just so happen to be with Travis Parker on a "surprise" trip to purchase a new refrigerator, compliments of *Pizza Perfect*. Yeah, he was *that* horrified by our rattling, metal monster. (Fingers crossed that's not *all* we're getting out of this experience.)

With the door locked behind us, we only have a little over an hour to prepare everything before Ma and Pop get back; our surprise has gotta happen in time for us to open. First thing we do is rearrange the dining room, make it look exactly the same as it did fifteen years ago. We've got a creased photograph to base everything off of—Nina swiped it from Ma's bedroom. We haul the broken jukebox up front. We shimmy Mr. Chef back where he used to be by the register.

June and Will arrive just before I head into the kitchen. They look amazing. June is in a black dress with ruffles. Her hair is curled and held back with a glitzy headband. She's pretty, *of course*. Will is in black slacks, a gray button-down shirt, and a black skinny tie. His guitar case is strapped across his back. He looks pretty amazing too.

"Do you mind if we practice a little before they get here?" June asks. "I haven't warmed up enough today."

"Of course," I say. "By the jukebox is fine, but hide when my parents get here."

"Duh," says Will. He tosses his hair dramatically. "We're part of the *surprise*."

Nina runs up and tugs my arm. "Should we get changed? I want to put on my dress too."

I glance at the wall clock behind the register. Only about thirty minutes before Ma and Pop get back. "Sure, just don't get dirty. Okay? Elio, you get changed too."

He groans. "I hate dress clothes. The collars are always too tight."

"You don't have to wear it long," I say. "And remember— it'll be worth it. We're doing this for Ma and Pop. For our family."

Elio scuffs his shoe on the floor. It squeaks. "It better work."

I grab him by the shoulders. "It'll work. Now go. I've gotta finish my part of the plan."

While Will tunes his guitar, June hums scales, and the twins change clothes, I make my way to the kitchen. Time to make the most important pizza of my life. The one that's gonna save my family.

Twenty minutes later, when my masterpiece *za* is in the oven, Candace steps into the kitchen. "TP just texted. He and your parents are en route. T-minus ten!"

I yell thanks, and she disappears. I'm sweaty and gross, but I can't stop now. I run to our teeny supply closet, grab an ancient, dusty candle from a box on the top shelf, a clouded-glass holder, and some matches. Then I march to the dining room to conduct my final check.

Elio and Nina are dutifully waiting near the register. Elio is wearing black pants, a white dress shirt, and a red bowtie that he got for one of our cousin's weddings. Nina is in a velvety emerald dress and patent leather shoes.

"Don't you two clean up nice," I say. I hand them each a cloth napkin. "Drape this over your arm when you serve the beverages. Okay?"

I make my way to the table we set up with a red-and-white-checkered tablecloth. I nest the candle at the center and light it. Elio and Nina already placed cloth napkins, plates, and cutlery. I beam. It's PERFECT.

"Nina," I say. "When Ma and Pop get here, I want you to

show them to the table. Elio, don't forget to pull the chair out for Ma."

"We *know*," says Nina. "You've told us four hundred times!"

Candace covers their snicker with a smile. Then they glance out the window. "They're pulling up. Places, people!"

I bolt back to the kitchen, taking June and Will with me.

"You guys remember the plan?" I ask.

Will smirks. "Like Nina said—you've told us four hundred million bajillion times."

"We won't mess up." June rubs my arm. "We know how important this is."

"Thanks," I say, trying not to get emotional. "Time to get the pizza out of the oven."

Moments later, the front door creaks. Ma gasps. She asks what's going on. Her voice doesn't sound upset, though. More excited. Surprised. I grin. This is totally going to work.

When I come out of the kitchen, steaming pan in my hand, I find Ma and Pop seated across from each other. Nina and Elio stand on the far side of the table, pouring sparkling water into stemmed glasses. The film crew is positioned around our parents. Travis Parker and Candace watch from a distance, near the front door, grinning at each other. I can't stop smiling—this is *exactly* how I pictured it.

Ma and Pop silently ask me what's going on with buggy eyes, but I just say, "Welcome to Mamma Gianna's. Tonight, *we* are serving *you*." I set the pizza between them.

Ma's hand covers the surprise on her lips. "Oh, Luca . . ."

The pizza is baked in the shape of a heart, spotted in heart-shaped pepperoni. Her head shakes. I can't tell if it's disbelief or joy or shock or disgust. My eyes flit to Pop. His eyebrows are nearly in his thinning hairline.

I proceed with the speech I rehearsed a billion times. "Nina, Elio, and I know things have been hard lately. Life is stressful. I mean, I get it—I'm in middle school after all."

Pop snort-laughs. I ignore his interruption, nodding at the twins, and say, "Me, Nina, Elio—we love you. A lot. We love our family. And we know you love us." I pause, making sure they're both looking at me. "But it feels like you've forgotten that you love each other."

Ma's head stops shaking. She glances at the cameras trained on her. Her body goes rigid. "Luca, I—"

But I don't let her cut me off. This moment is going to be magic. It's going to work. I just know it. "*So* we thought we'd remind you by doing something special. We were going to wait for your anniversary, but what better way to celebrate than with *Pizza Perfect*? Thanks to Travis Parker, we were able to make our surprise *extra* special."

I glance at my idol, but now he's not grinning so much. In fact, he looks confused. So does Candace. I mean, clearly this isn't the family dinner I promised them. A worm of doubt wriggles against my bladder, but I can't stop now. *This will work. This* will *work.* I take out the photograph from my back pocket and slide it between Ma and Pop. Candlelight flickers on the glossy finish. Younger versions of Ma and Pop sit in this very same spot at Mamma Gianna's. Her hair is bigger, curlier. His body is thinner. But they're both smiling. Big and real and true. Between them is a heart-shaped pizza, just like the one I made tonight.

"Kiddo, I don't—" Pop starts.

But I don't let him go on. "We re-created your first date because you need to remember how much you love each other. Life isn't easy, but look at all of this. This restaurant. Your kids. You can't give up on Mamma Gianna's. On Nina and Elio. On me. You can't give up on each other." My voice cracks. "Not on our family." Nina and Elio sidle up next to me. I wrap my arms around them. "We love you. But we aren't complete unless you love each other too."

At the exact right moment, June and Will emerge from the kitchen. Will strums on his guitar. June sings the opening lyrics of Norah Jones's "Come Away with Me." Her voice is rich and soothing. The strum of the guitar strings is warm. Ma's and Pop's chairs screech against the floor at the sound of the music.

"Our song," Ma whispers. Her eyes are wet pebbles. Her lower lip trembles.

Almost like instinct, Pop reaches across the table for her hand.

She looks at it. She nibbles her lower lip. Slowly, she reaches for it.

IT'S WORKING! It's like I'm outside my body, watching everything I so carefully planned come to fruition. I feel like I swallowed the sun.

And then Ma pulls her hand back. Her chest shudders. She bursts into tears, shoving her chair out from under the table. She heaves a sob. "Luca, I—I'm so sorry."

Will stops playing. June stops singing. I plummet back into myself with a sudden, painful heaviness. "Ma, wait!"

She shoves her hand at my face like a crossing guard holding up a stop sign. She keeps walking. Travis Parker and Candace sidestep as Ma bursts out the front door, hiding her face with both hands. The crew lower their cameras, looking at Travis Parker and Candace for guidance, but they're both blank-faced.

Oh God. I'm gonna be sick. What just happened? How did it all turn rotten so quickly?

My head whirls to Pop. He's just sitting there. Like a freaking dope. Why the heck isn't he moving? Why isn't he chasing after Ma like they do in the movies? That pisses me off. I can feel myself turning red. "What are you doing?" I shout. "Go after her!"

"Luca," he whispers. "That's not what she wants."

"What are you talking about?"

Pop hauls himself slowly off his seat. "You meant well,

Luca." He pulls Nina and Elio to him. "Why don't I take you kids home?"

My skin is flaming hot. "That's all you're good for, isn't it? Running away. Abandoning us. But not me. I'm better than that. I'm *staying*."

"Luca, come on," Pop calls after me. "Let's talk about this."

But I'm done. I spin around. Words blowtorch from my mouth. "If you wanna go, then PISS OFF!"

The syllables sear my lips. I've gone too far. But I don't freaking care.

Pop shouts my name. He demands I come back this instant, but I don't.

I stomp into the kitchen, ignoring everyone and everything.

Chapter 27

When I get angry—like *really* freaking pissed off—I lose control. It's been that way my whole life. My parents have tried to convince me to talk to a therapist, but I can manage my own feelings. Ma calls the explosions my Rage Mode. Sort of like the Hulk, except I don't turn green and muscular. My transformation is way less cool. My hands shake. My knees quiver. My vision narrows. I'm like those horses they drive around the city with blinders on; all I can see is what's right in front of me. My heart feels like it's trying to jump ship from my body. The rest of me goes on autopilot. I don't realize what I'm doing. My hands, my feet—they do whatever they want. I'll come out of Rage Mode and be in the middle of doing something random: throwing socks out of my drawer, tearing tissues into confetti.

I'm only vaguely aware that I'm rage-making a pizza. Well, not really *making* a pizza. I'm pulverizing dough on the counter. Over and over my fists drive into the yellow goop.

The sticky pile of flour and water and potatoes wheezes with each punch. I don't stop torturing the dough until I feel a hand on my shoulder. I flinch at the touch. "WHAT?"

Travis Parker recoils. "Hey. Sorry." His hands are up in surrender. *Ohgodohgodohgod.* He shrinks back a step. "Just it, uh, looks like that dough can't take much more. You know?"

Please, patron saint of nightmares—tell me this isn't reality. That I didn't just shout at Travis Parker. I'm horrified. Rage Mode deactivates. "Oh my God." My fists unclench. "I'm so, *so* sorry. I didn't realize it was you."

He thumbs his nose. "What, uh . . . what happened back there? With your parents? That's not exactly the scenario you and I agreed on."

My embarrassment doubles. My eyes fall to the floor. "I thought . . . I thought I was doing the right thing. Getting Ma and Pop back together."

Travis Parker nods. His fingers ripple on the counter like he's playing invisible piano keys. "My parents divorced when I was little older than you. Hurt like hell when they told me."

"My parents aren't getting divorced," I say. "They're *separated.* They're gonna work it out. They just need to remember. It's my job to help them."

Travis Parker exhales a low whistle. "Your job? Mighty tall order for a kid."

"It's always been my job to fix things," I explain.

"Whenever Ma and Pop have a problem, they come to me. I listen, I tell them what to do. Same thing for Elio and Nina. Even my friends. June and Will"—I point in the direction of the dining room—"they didn't get along until a couple weeks ago. Without me, everyone in my life falls apart."

"That's a lot of pressure," he says. "Especially when it doesn't work out the way you thought it would."

"If they'd *listen*, it would. If they'd just *trust* me." I bash the dough again. "Everything would work out fine. I know what I'm talking about."

Travis Parker leans against the wall. "You know a lot for a kid. I'll give you that. But marriages, relationships—those aren't things an eleven-year-old—"

"I'm *twelve*. And I'll be thirteen in June."

He laughs. "Okay, those aren't things even a *twelve*-year-old can know the answers to. You're a kid. You have a right to be just that. Running a restaurant, being married, raising kids—that's a lot. I'm sure your parents rely on you the same way mine used to rely on me. But that doesn't make it right. You shouldn't have to be responsible for anything more than just being you. Being a kid."

"But if I don't fix everything, who will?"

"*They* will—your parents," he says, hands flying up. He doesn't sound mad, just passionate. "But if you don't give people the chance to solve their own problems, they'll never learn. You can't control everything, Luca. You can't decide those things for someone, much as you think you know what's best for them."

"But what if they're wrong?" My fists clench again. "What if they hurt people because they choose the wrong thing?"

"Then they'll learn from their mistakes," he says. "They'll try again. But if you're always orchestrating everything, your parents' marriage, your siblings' relationship, even your friends' friendships—those things won't belong to them. They'll belong to *you*. Would you want someone else owning your relationships?"

"No." I hate this. This doesn't sound like the heart-to-heart version of Travis Parker I watch on TV. He sounds *real*. I'm not sure I like it. Why isn't he just making me feel better?

"That's what I thought, but don't get me wrong," Travis Parker goes on. "What you're doing comes from a place of love. But if you *really* love people, you've gotta let them live their own lives. Even when it hurts."

"But what if they get it wrong?"

Travis Parker grins. "People are allowed to be wrong. Do *you* get everything right?"

I snort laugh. "Obviously not."

"Right. You were *allowed* to make a choice. It didn't work, but it was *your* choice. Your parents, your brother and sister, your friends—they deserve the chance to get things wrong too."

What he's saying makes sense, but I hate that it makes sense. That means *I've* been wrong about a lot of things. I narrow my eyes at him. "Were you like a therapist in another life?"

He belly laughs. "Doubtful. But I've got a great one. Everyone should try therapy."

I sigh, looking at the sad, flappy dough I used as a punching bag. "I really screwed things up, didn't I?"

"What's done is done," he says. "All you can do is move forward knowing what you know now." He scratches his chin. "Let's say running other people's lives isn't your top priority. What would you be doing with your time?"

"I don't know." My gaze drifts to the oven. "Making pizza?"

Travis Parker grins. "Now *that's* what I'm talking about. All that energy and time you pour into thinking about what other people should be doing, dump it into your baking. Do what you love." His grin stretches. "What do you say? How about you make me some za?"

"Right NOW?" That's a terrible idea. I'm still all discombobulated. Anything I make will taste like Oscar the Grouch baked it.

He shrugs. "Why not? If the kitchen is where you go when you're angry, maybe it's the place where you can heal too."

My lips twist. I chew on his suggestion. My fingers *are* itching to do something. "Maybe it's not the worst idea."

He claps his hands together triumphantly. "Then get to it, chef. I'll hunt down your mom. We'll get the restaurant open, since your dad took Nina and Elio home. When I come back, I wanna taste a Luca special. Capisce?"

I nod. "Capasce."

Soon as he's gone, I dump out the dough I obliterated. I grab a fresh ball and roll it out. My hands reach for ingredients. I sauté. I blend. I scoop and mix and toss. At some point—I'm not sure when—one of the camera crews is standing behind me, filming my process. I ignore them, determined to put all my energy into this pizza. Sixty-something minutes later, I pop a pie into the oven that feels like my heart in food form. It comes out twenty minutes later. I call Travis Parker into the kitchen.

His eyes bulge when he sees the deep-dish pan. "Luca, what did you do?"

I swipe the sweat from my forehead with the back of my arm. "You asked for the Luca special, so you got it. This is my never-before-made arancini pizza. I took our traditional crust and brushed it with garlic butter. The sauce is our house specialty topped with a blend of Italian cheeses, sprinklings of crushed meatballs, sauteed mushrooms, and fresh spinach. I topped that in a crust of saffron-flavored arancini rice that I dusted with breadcrumbs and grated cheese. It's finished with a drizzle of balsamic reduction and garnished with fresh parsley."

"Mamma *mia*." All his shiny, white teeth have come out to smile at what I've done. "Can I taste it?"

"Please." I cut him a triangle. Strings of cheese ooze from the sides as I pull it from the pan. I plop the gooey, steaming wedge on a plate and hand it over. He doesn't waste a second blowing on his forkful to cool it down. The instant it hits his tongue, he dances around the kitchen, fist-pumping his fork in the air. He manges, giggling like a kid. The cameras catch all of it. All I can do is smile. *If only this were the Pizza Perfect Challenge*, I think. *If only Ma believed in me.*

At last, he swallows his bite and says, "Luca Salvatore. This is outstanding. Seriously. You're nearly thirteen years old, and you just made one of the best bites of my life. Congratulations, sir. This right here—this is pizza perfect."

I'm pretty sure I melt right into the floor.

When I drive home with Ma that night, I'm still buzzing. Even though she looks like a zombie and won't really talk to me about what I did to her and Pop with the surprise date, nothing can take away from what happened in that kitchen with Travis Parker. It was a dream come true. I go to sleep replaying him taking the first bite over and over and over.

At some point, though, nightmares replace my dreamy moment. Flashes of Ma and Pop take over. Her walking out. Pop sitting there. Nina and Elio watching with tears gushing down their faces. June and Will embarrassed and awkward, pointing at me, telling me everything is my fault. Then I'm surrounded by my family, and they're saying the same thing. *This is your fault. Your fault. Your fault. Your fault.* Travis Parker and Candace join in. It builds and builds until I'm trapped in a circle of giant, pointing fingers. I wake up in a sweat. I feel like throwing up.

I try to shake it off Saturday morning because this is our last day of filming with Travis Parker and the *Pizza Perfect* crew. All our filming and trying to impress Travis Parker ends with today's Pizza Perfect Challenge. Today decides whether or not Mamma Gianna's has a future. After last night's disaster, I'm not too hopeful.

Around nine, bleary-eyed and in desperate need of an espresso, Ma, Nina, Elio, and I make our way to the restaurant. Pop is waiting in the parking lot with his thumbs in his belt loops. He looks about as ragged as we do. TP and the crew have evening flights out, so we've gotta film early today, which feels like an extra helping of hurt.

"Please, Ma," I say, following her into the kitchen. "Travis Parker *loved* my pizza last night. We should use it for the Pizza Perfect Challenge. *Please.*"

Ma exhales through her nose. "Luca. NO. No more stunts. Last night, you specifically went against my wishes. You *knew* I didn't want our private life out there."

"But—"

"Basta!" Her palm cuts me off. "You've done *enough*.

We're serving Great-Grandma Gianna's signature pizza. End of story."

I want to scream. I want to cry. But I'm so tired, I'm so over fighting with her and for her, for this place, for something no one other than me seems to want, that I go quiet.

I can barely watch as Travis Parker eats the bready wedge of sausage pizza. When they edit this footage, they'll add a graphic of all the pizzas he's ever tried. Travis Parker's voice-over will explain what he loves and what he doesn't about our za and how it stacks up against other restaurants. (I'm freaking glad they spare us in the moment—I don't think I could handle it in real time.) Don't get me wrong, Great-Grandma Gianna knew what she was doing, but that pizza isn't *me*. It's not why Travis Parker is here. It's Mamma Gianna's past, which hasn't been going so hot lately. It's not her future. I'm not sure what he's eating will stand out from the rest.

Ma and Pop can't even look at each other. They force the twins and I to stand between them as Candace and the crew get us into position for the final moment we're going to film with Travis Parker.

"Remember," Candace told us ahead of time. "No matter what you're gifted from TP, keep your faces up. It could be nothing, it could be 10K. He doesn't even tell *us* what he's going to give guests until we're filming. I know how much this means to all of you, but I—I just want to manage your expectations."

"Thank you for everything you've done," Ma said, taking Candace's hand in hers.

Candace squeezed Ma's with their free one. "It's truly been my pleasure. You really do have something special here." They winked at me when they said that.

An eternity passes as Travis Parker eats the pizza. Cameras are rolling. He takes notes on a pad of paper. He hums to himself. He takes another bite. Meanwhile, Ma, Pop, Nina, Elio, and I stand in front of our mural, waiting for the judge to give his final verdict. I swallow back my nausea.

"Well, Salvatores," Travis Parker says at freaking last. "It's been an outstanding week getting to know all of you. I've loved hearing about your family's history, and how this restaurant came to be. A real labor of love nurtured generation after generation. Even with the massive variety of pizza joints in Chicago, your restaurant holds its own. What's impressed me more than anything, though, is this guy right here." He takes a step forward, pointing at me. "Luca Salvatore, you're the real MVP of Mamma Gianna's. Your passion for pizza is infectious. Your earnest desire to help your family is unparalleled. And your creativity and ingenuity with recipes—it's out-of-this-world amazing."

I'm pretty much hyperventilating at this point. I can't believe he's saying all these nice things about *me*. ME. I must be close to falling apart with joy because Pop's hand clamps on my shoulder like he's trying to keep me steady.

Travis Parker goes on. "This pizza here, it's good. And normally, I'd judge a restaurant based on the pie they present for the final challenge, but, Luca, that pizza you made last night—that was sincerely one of the best things I've ever eaten, and I've eaten *a lot* of food. I have no doubt that if you keep chasing *your* passions and *your* dreams, you'll achieve true greatness."

He punches "your" so much, I know he's not just talking about the pizza. He's saying-without-saying that he wants me to focus on *me* and not other people. I'm like, *I get it, I get it!* But I can't say that.

Travis Parker's eyes lift from me to my parents. "Gio, Christine. You've got so much to be proud of. What an incredible restaurant. But even more important, what incredible kids you're raising. I've been so impressed with you all, and I believe so much in what you're doing here that I'm ecstatic to share that I'm giving you all"—he pulls an envelope from his back pocket—"$50,000 to expand Mamma Gianna's however you see fit."

Time freezes.

Fifty.

Thousand.

Dollars.

My mind can't quite make sense of a number that large. *HOLY. FREAKING. CRAP.*

Time picks up again. We explode. Nina and Elio jump

around. We shout. We scream. Ma bursts into tears. Pop yelps in surprise, then covers his mouth.

Then the most shocking thing happens: Ma grabs Pop's face and plants a kiss right on his lips. A REAL KISS. I haven't seen them do that in MONTHS. Most kids would throw up in their mouths watching their parents lock lips, but I start crying. Like a big freaking baby. I can't believe it. It worked. My parents are *kissing*. Our family business is going to make it.

We're going to make it.

A fat, hot gusher spills down my cheek.

Travis Parker looks like he's going to say something else to the camera, but I can't help myself. I wrap him in a hug.

And he hugs me back.

Chapter 28

Travis Parker, Candace Goodwater, and the *Pizza Perfect* crew hightail it out of Mamma Gianna's around three in the afternoon to make their flight back to LA. When the door closes behind them, Ma, Pop, Nina, Elio, and I exhale at the same time. Residual static tickles my skin from winning all that money, but now I'm totally stunod. I reached the peak of Mount Vesuvius after sprinting the whole way with two donkeys on my back. I didn't realize just how much energy I'd poured into filming until I didn't have to be on anymore. I could take a yearlong nap and that still wouldn't be enough.

Pop uncorks the bottle of sparkling grape juice Candace left us. He splashes the amber liquid into five glasses. We wriggle into a booth near the window, liquid gold sloshing. Me next to Ma. Pop wedged between Nina and Elio across from us.

Ma raises a glass. "To Luca, for saving Mamma Gianna's. Salute!"

I smile, studying the scratches in the table. I raise my glass alongside the rest of my family. We shout together, "Salute!" *Clink, clink, clink!*

But Travis Parker's words echo in my brain. I can't let my family think this was all *my* doing. "No. *We* did this." I raise my glass again. "Here's to the Salvatores. For showing the world what the best family in the world can do. Salute!"

"SALUTE!" *Clink, clink, clink!*

We lounge around, and even Ma and I laugh about our favorite filming moments until just before we open. She and I are usually the first to end a party early in the name of business, but not today. For once, she isn't in a hurry to leave the celebration behind. I follow her lead, thinking maybe we've finally earned this moment. But eventually, the party ends because hungry mouths will be knocking on our door in fifteen minutes. Pop takes Elio and Nina home. Ma and I muster enough energy (with the help of espresso) to get through service.

And Madonna mia, what a service it is! Word got around town faster than a tornado that Travis Parker was here. It was supposed to be hush-hush, but how could folks not notice him and his crew setting up shop all week? By seven o'clock, we're at capacity and have an actual waiting list for dine-in. We've even gotta call Pop to come back and help. While the three of us and Cesar tackle this and that, we all agree that, with our new influx of dough, it's time we hire some extra help.

At close, things get a little . . . awkward. The rush of excitement from winning all that money seems to be fading. Ma and Pop sort of hug, but they don't kiss again. I'm tempted to start singing "Kiss the Girl" from *The Little Mermaid*, but no one wants to hear me sing. (Not even me.)

So they don't. Which is disappointing. But I start to wonder if their kiss in front of Travis Parker was old habits dying hard, like that night at the hospital when Pop kissed the top of Ma's head. Or if maybe it was just for show. For *the* show. I wonder how much we all perform for each other, even when the cameras aren't rolling, trying to do what we *think* people want instead of showing what's really going on. I think about how Travis Parker's voice changed when he was talking to me without the cameras. How Ma only wears her Dazzlingly Bright smile for customers. How I always tell people I'm fine when I'm not. I think about all the confusion and hurt living like you're on a reality show can cause. How much hurt and confusion it's caused *me*. Now that we've been on TV and taken performance to the extreme, I wonder if it's time to put that aside—to just be . . . *real*. Even if it hurts.

Pop gets in his car and heads for his apartment. Ma and I get in our minivan. She turns the key in the ignition, but instead of backing out, she looks at me. "Luca, can we talk?"

My stomach gurgles. "About what?"

"What you did, getting us on the show, finding a way to save the restaurant," she says, fidgeting with her necklace, "it means the world to me. You gave our legacy a fighting chance. You gave our *family* a fighting chance." The gold chain twists around her index finger. "But I know saving the restaurant wasn't your *only* goal. You're upset about me and your father. The separation."

I'm tempted to shrug it off. Tell her I'm fine. Play the stoic role of oldest son and confidant, but I'm so tired. I don't want to be strong. I want to be honest.

"Yeah," I say. "It sucks. I hate what's happening to you and Pop."

Her hand slips to the gearshift, but she doesn't move it. "It really does. Trust me, the separation—it isn't easy on us either. But about what happened last night. That . . . *date*. What you did for me and your father. You meant well, I know, but—baby, your father and I have a lot of problems. Our marriage, well—you've seen a lot. Heard a lot. Too much probably. I just—I don't want you thinking there's hope where there might not be. That you could do something to save our marriage the way you saved the restaurant."

I turn my head away from her. *You can't control everything.* I can't get Travis Parker out of my head. Who'd've thought I'd ever see that as a problem?

I sniff. The yellow streetlights out the passenger window blur. "I know I can't save your marriage, but you and Pop—you *kissed*. When Travis Parker told us we won the money."

I hear the *squeak* of her fingers tightening around the leather steering wheel. "I was worried you'd get the wrong impression."

My jaw clenches. "Wrong impression? So you *didn't* mean to kiss Pop?"

"I'm saying it's complicated. Your father and I, we've been together a long time. Sometimes a kiss means something, and sometimes a kiss is just a kiss."

"That's stupid. A kiss *does* mean something." I haven't had my first kiss yet, but I know it'll mean something. That *every* kiss I have will mean something. "You and Pop must still love each other."

Ma is slower to respond. "You're right. We will always love each other because we made the three most important things in our lives together: you, Elio, and Nina. But that doesn't mean we should stay married."

"But you *kissed*."

"I know, baby. I'm sorry that confused you."

Under my breath, I say, "*I'm* not the one who's confused."

Ma sighs. "I know it's hard, Luca. I'm sorry. Really."

I don't respond. If I do, I'll start crying and I don't want to cry. That'll mean I'm not in control, not just of the situation but of *me*. I can't let go of *that* much, sheesh!

"I'm sorry too," I finally say.

She reaches over and squeezes my knee. "I'm sorry this is hard, but we're gonna get through this. We will." She pulls her hand back, shifts into reverse, and starts to drive home. "I want to talk about something else too."

Patron saint of mother-son relationships and car rides, please let this be something good. My fingers lace together in my lap. "What?"

"I—I owe you an apology," she says.

I double take. "Mi scusi?"

Her eyes shimmer in the streetlights. "All this time, you've been trying to get me to taste your pizza, to recognize what a genius you are in the kitchen, and I've let you down." She shakes her head. "Worse than that, I've neglected you. Your talent. Your heart. It was *you* and *your* pizza that got us that money. Not me. Not Great-Grandma Gianna's pizza. *You*, Luca. And I'm done ignoring what's right in front of me because I'm—I'm scared of change. From now on, your pizzas will be on the menu."

I gasp. "Are you—are you *serious*?"

"As Gramma Salvatore at Good Friday Mass," she says. "I mean it, Luca. I should have been taking you seriously eons ago. I'm so sorry it took me this long. Can you forgive me?"

"Of course!" I fling my body across the car and squeeze her.

She shriek-laughs, grasping for the steering wheel. "Watch out! The menu won't change if we end up in a ditch."

I release her, heart racing. *I'm ON THE MENU!* All the pizza possibilities stack up in my mind. *Which one will I do* *first? The buffalo chicken that Will loves so much? The fig and prosciutto that's June's favorite? Or the arancini pizza that won us $50,000 from Travis Parker?*

"You're happy?" Ma asks as we pull into the driveway.

"Are you kidding me? Of course, I'm ha—" But I stop. Happy isn't right. That's just what's sitting on top. I'm still sad about her and Pop. About June crushing on Will. And I'm overwhelmed from a week of filming. "I'm a lot."

She laughs. "Me too. A lot, a lot. I'm glad we can be a lot together. I love you, Luca."

"I love you too," I say.

And for the first time in a long time—maybe for the first time ever—I feel like my mom sees me. All of me. Not just the son who gets stuff done. Or the reliable big brother. Or the kid who's always fine when everything else is falling apart.

She finally sees the whole pie, not just the slice I'm serving her.

Chapter 29

Getting back into the normal swing of things is rough. I mean, how do you go back to "normal" after a week of chilling with your culinary idol? Since my body is beat, I start off by sleeping most of Sunday, and then it's back to school on Monday even though I'm pretty sure I've earned a whole month of vacation. Ma and Pop say my education can't come at the cost of our restaurant, so it's back to Riverfront Junior High despite my best efforts.

It's good to see my friends, but Will and June are all questions. *What happened after the date? Are your parents mad? What happened with Travis Parker? How did the Perfect Pie Challenge go? What did you serve him? Did he like your pizza? Did he give you get a million billion trillion dollars?*

When I tell them how much money he gave us, their eyes frog out of their heads. "Not quite a million," I say, "but it's the most anyone on the show has ever gotten. I looked it up."

"Dude," says Will. "DUDE. That's EPIC."

"I knew you'd impress him," June says.

"I couldn't have done it without you guys." I throw my arms around their shoulders. "Thank you."

"Anything for you." June grins.

Will twists under my arm, until he's looking me in the eyes. "You're totally welcome, but, like, we still get free pizza, right?"

I laugh, pulling my arm back because being that close . . . is a lot. And I'm still . . . *a lot*. A lot of feelings. About Will. About June. About Will *and* June. A lot I don't know what to do with. But I try to play it cool. "I'll get you both free pizza until you're good and constipated."

June groans. "Ew!"

But Will giggles. "You're such a weirdo."

I shrug. "Takes one to know one."

It feels good being back with them, but we still don't get to hang out all week. Ma and I spend afternoons trying out recipes and deciding which of my pizzas to add to the menu. After several taste-testers served to Elio and Nina, we go with the chicken piccata pizza I made when Candace was scouting us. I'm beyond stoked.

Meanwhile, Will and June are in their last week of practicing for the Battle of the Bands competition. (Thank GOD. I'm so over them having all this alone time and listening to them go on and on about rehearsals.) It feels like they're ditching me every day after school, but when I make a joke of it to June, she pouts and says that *I* ditched them last week to hang out with Travis Parker. I *kinda* get it, but ALSO: I was filming a TV SHOW with a CELEBRITY chef to save my family's restaurant from FINANCIAL COLLAPSE and my parents' marriage from certain DOOM . . . and they're practicing for a junior high band concert, but . . . *whatever.*

Totally the same. (EYE ROLL EMOJI.)

You'd think by now I'd be over them spending all this time together, except every day in advisory I hear this announcement: "The spring dance is a little over a week away! Get your tickets before it's too late—and don't forget to ask your date!"

Ask your date.

I'm not really interested in *dating* (at least . . . I don't think so?), but the idea of going to a dance with someone doesn't sound *so* bad. I catch myself daydreaming about it while I'm eating breakfast cereal and on the walk to school and when I high-five Will in the hallway and before I go to sleep. Every time I do, I imagine myself in the cafetorium, lights dimmed, colored strobes flashing, music blasting out of the overhead speakers, and I see myself swaying to the beat across from one very specific person.

Will White.

GULP.

Because I'm a total weirdo, I picture him in a full tuxedo

with tails and slicked back hair. Like he's the Duke of Chestertonworthingbury Abbey Castle. Or something. I get hot and tingly all over, and it's WEIRD.

But here's the thing: even if Will *did* like me, I *can't* ask him to the dance because June is dying for him to ask her. What kind of a friend would I be if I did that? Not a good one. Definitely not a *best* one. And she keeps texting me asking if he's said anything about asking her to the dance. Fortunately, he hasn't, but her asking all the time is getting on my nerves.

So, yeah, I've been dreading Friday night. But now here I am, sitting in the Riverfront Junior High cafetorium— *alone*—watching my best friend and my friend/crush jamming out to Kelly Clarkson's "Since U Been Gone." Will is shredding (that's what band people say, right?) the guitar. He's wearing a white T-shirt with the sleeves rolled up. It makes his pasty arms seem extra long. He's got a red bandanna tied around his forehead. His head rocks with each ferocious strum. He looks so freaking cool. June is center stage holding the microphone in two hands, the foam cover pressed to her lips. She's wearing skinny jeans with jagged tears in the knees. Her silver sequined shirt is torn too. She looks like she got attacked by a velociraptor. Which is cool, I *guess*. But her voice is strong. It's impossible not to be impressed by how grown-up she sounds.

As they perform, I catch them making eye contact with

each other. I tell myself they're just keeping each other on beat. But that twinkle in June's glances—it's obvious they've reached telepathic levels of understanding. There's something more between them. Something I helped them find. Something Will and I don't have. Something we'll never have.

When they finish the song, the crowd throws their hands up and screams. We were told by Mr. Lewis, the band teacher running the competition, that applause and cheering will determine the winning band. I add my voice to the mix, but it hurts. Not because I'm tearing up my vocal cords to make sure they come in first, but because I feel like I'm rooting for June and Will—as a couple, not bandmates.

After the fifth and final band wraps up their last song (to meager applause—practically golf claps), Mr. Lewis calls all the bands onto the stage. Will, June, and the rest of their band grip each other's hands. I laser focus on Will's and June's laced fingers. I'm so lost in their hand-holding that I miss when Mr. Lewis announces that they won. They scream and jump around the same way Elio and Nina did a few days ago when Travis Parker told us we were getting $50,000 for the restaurant. June throws her arms around Will. She spins him around, her chin buried in his neck. He hugs her back.

A lightning bolt flash of Ma kissing Pop at Mamma Gianna's strikes me. A nasty medley of feelings simmers in my stockpot body. Frustration. Sadness. Anger. Worry. Jealousy. Hope. It's A LOT, and I feel like I'm gonna bubble over.

But the sensation fades the more I think about it, because as much as *this* sucks, maybe there's a silver lining. Maybe I'm more of a matchmaker than I gave myself credit for. Maybe Travis Parker was wrong about me. Will and June didn't like each other at all. Then I intervened. They became friends. Now June *like*-likes Will. Because of what *I* did.

If I could bring Will and June together when it seemed completely impossible, why couldn't I still do that for Ma and Pop?

Chapter 30

June's and Will's clasped hands circle my head like cartoon cuckoo birds. Instead of letting myself get dazed like I've been bashed by an oversized sledgehammer, I daydream ways to get Ma and Pop back together.

On Sunday, even though the twins and I *don't* need her, Gramma Salvatore babysits while our parents tackle loan repayment plans at the restaurant. Nina and Elio don't fight like they used to, and now that I don't have to worry about the restaurant so much, I can join Nina and Elio on the couch to watch cartoons. And it's not like Gramma Salvatore makes a difference being here—she's in the guest room talking to "one of the girls."

Nina and Elio are sprawled on either side of me, their feet kicked against my thighs. (Turns out I was born to be a toe barrier.) While we watch, my red notebook is open to a fresh page with "Save Ma and Pop: Take Two" underlined at the top. I tap my pencil against it, but no matter what I do, I can't get my brain to work.

Nina nudges me with her big toe. "I'm bored."

"We can watch something else," I say, chewing my eraser.

Elio flops onto his stomach. "I'm tired of watching. Let's *do* something."

"We should build a fort," Nina says, sitting up. "Remember how we used to, Luca? When we were little. You'd make secret rooms with the blankets and kitchen chairs and pillows. That was fun."

"I wish you'd play with us again," says Elio.

Normally I'd tell them I'm busy, that I have too much to worry about, that they can play on their own—but I can't remember the last time I played with them either. When was the last time I was their brother, not their babysitter or parent? Fort building used to be one of *my* favorite things. Suddenly, I want that feeling again. To just be a kid.

I close my notebook. "Let's do it."

Elio nearly falls off the couch. "What? Really?"

"Did I stutter? Andiamo!" I say. "You two, bring in the kitchen chairs. I'll grab the blankets."

Elio bolts, shouting, "This is gonna be the best fort ever!"

Nina takes her time following him. Right before she disappears into the kitchen, she turns her head and says, "I like this version of you a lot better."

I smirk. This *version of me*. Does she mean someone who does what she wants because that's *very* Nina? Or does she mean she likes me better when I'm not stressing? I pull old throw blankets from the closet. Honestly, with Nina, it could go either way.

I'd ask her, but we get to it, lining up chairs in front of the couch, creating the skeleton for our fort. We pull off cushions and build out walls, and then we drape layers of blankets until we've got a large open space in the middle, two smaller "rooms" and several "secret" entrances. We goof with each other as we build, pretending we're explorers on a strange planet setting up our base camp. And even when Nina and Elio disagree about where the main entrance should be, they don't get into a fight. Which is weird. Nina goes with Elio's idea, which, if you ask me, is the better option. Maybe we're all growing up a little. I almost applaud Nina for being so willing to let Elio have a say, but I don't want to jinx it. As we're adding the finishing touches with throw pillows, my phone buzzes.

Will: hey

Me: hey.

Will: whats up

Me: Babysitting.

I delete that text and retype it.

Me: Hanging out with my sibs. We built a lit fort. I'll
    send you a pic.

Me: hbu

It's weird, wanting to talk to someone and not wanting to talk to them at the same time. I mean, I'd jump at the chance to hang with Will the way it was before June knew he and I were friends. When it was just the two of us. But it would be really crappy of me now that he and June are "bandmates" (and since she's got a crush on him). We can never go back to that. I put them together. I can't undo that.

Will: just chillin

Will: I want to ask you a question tho

A question. Madonna Mia. My heart is a pancake, flattened and flipping on a hot skillet. I lean against the doorframe. I have a feeling I know where this is going, and I hate it.

Me: Ask away.

Will: the spring dance is next week

Called it. I knew he was gonna bring up the dance.

Will: and I was thinking of asking someone

My brain cracks open. Runny gray yolk scrambles and shoves my pancake heart out of the frying pan. I freaking called it. Of course he's coming to June's best friend with this. Better to make our conversation as short and quick as possible. I get right to the point.

Me: You should just ask them.

Will: but what if they don't like me like that?

Salt in the eggs, salt in the wound. He's really gonna make me say it, isn't he? I can't believe I've gotta coach my crush on how to ask my best friend to the spring dance. This SUCKS.

"Luca, come play!" Nina's head pokes from under a flap of yellow blanket. "Elio plugged in his kaleidoscope light—it looks like a crystal cavern!"

"Cool. Gimme a sec."

Elio's head groundhogs from the "roof." "You're not ditching us, are you?"

"No, no, I just—" My fingers fly across my phone screen. There's no point in fighting it.

Me: Look. June likes you. She told me so.

Me: You should just ask her. She'll say yes.

Three dots bubble on the screen. They disappear. Then:

Will: oh

Will: wait

Will: you want me to ask her

Of course, I *don't* want him to. Is he *that* clueless? But I can't hurt June again and tell Will *I* like him, which doesn't even matter, because Will is *clearly* into her and me telling him the truth will only take us to AWKWARD CENTRAL, so:

Me: Of course. She'll be so happy.

Will: oh

Will: ok

When he doesn't text me back, I shove my phone under my thigh. I don't have anything else to say. But at least he and June will be happy.

* * *

On my way out of Riverfront Junior High on Monday afternoon, June shoulders up to me. She's full-tooth grinning and her cheeks are bubblegum pink.

"Guess what," she whispers. She bounces on the tips of her toes. Her squishy key chains on her backpack zippers flop behind her.

Ugh. I can smell it on her. IT happened. But I play along, asking, "What?"

Before I can get the word out, she squeaks, "I got asked to the dance!"

For half a heartbeat I let myself believe someone other than Will got to her. That she said yes. That there's still a chance I had it all wrong. That Will and June don't like each other. That I'm someone Will could like. That I could have a shot at a date to the spring dance too.

Instead of torturing myself, I plunge into the ice-cold waters of my own making. "Will asked you?"

She stops bouncing. "How did you know?"

Mamma mia, I hate this. "He texted me last night. Asked if he should ask you. Look, I—"

She gasps, "Omg. Did he really? Tell me exactly what he said. Does this mean he really, like . . . *like*-likes me?"

I side-eye her. "I thought you didn't want a boyfriend."

She fidgets with the zipper on her pink windbreaker. "I mean, I don't—or I didn't, but then I met Will, and, well, we're pretty much eighth graders, and he's cooler than I thought. And then there's the band and everything. Maybe I changed my mind. *Maybe*. I mean, I'm not ready for a *boyfriend*, but I still like that he likes me."

INTERNAL FACEPALM. My best friend and I are the same person. She's saying everything I've been thinking and feeling. How did this happen?

Oh, right. ME. (GAAAAUUUHHHHHHHH!!!)

"Well," I say, "I can confirm that he likes you." An unintentional edge sharpens my tone. My fingers clench. My disappointment curdles into frustration. I need this conversation to end before I get angry.

"But like, is that what he *really* said?" she asks. "Show me the texts!"

I shrug away from her. The olive oil in my pan is about to reach scalding temperatures. "Not right now. I've gotta get to Mamma Gianna's."

She pouts. "Fine. But you *swear* he said he likes me?"

I keep walking. "I'll talk to you later, okay?"

"Wait!" She grabs my shoulder. "I don't want to be alone at the dance with him. You've *gotta* go with us!"

Knife! Stomach! TWIST! "Uh, I don't know. Maybe. I, uh—I gotta go."

I book it out the front doors before she has a chance to say more.

Pop is setting up the new fridge Travis Parker bought us when I get to Mamma Gianna's with Nina and Elio. It's a weirdly warm spring day, even for late April. So warm I'm sweating, though that might be more about me freaking out about June and Will than the weather.

"Hey, kiddos," Pop says. He pats the side of the silver beast. "What do you think of this stainless-steel beauty?"

Elio jumps in place, tipping his head back like he's trying to see the top. "It's HUGE. We could fit a whole cow in there!"

Pop laughs. "Not quite, but it's a solid upgrade from that old clanker. We're gonna need the space too. I've got a feeling business is about to boom." He points at me. "Speaking of . . . We just got a massive order from Riverfront Junior High for Friday night. *Someone* forgot to mention he has a school dance coming up."

I avoid his can-opener eyes. "I'm not going."

"What?" Pop says. "You gotta go. Dances are fun."

Nina wiggles her butt. "Can I go? I wanna dance!"

"Heck no." I breathe—my temperature's rising again, and I don't want to snap on my family. Not with how good things have been. "I just don't feel like going, okay?"

Pop wipes his greasy hands on an old rag. "Well, I already volunteered to help at the dance since I'm bringing the goods. Would be kinda weird to be at your school dance without you, Luca. How about you help me run the food station? Maybe you'll decide you want to get your groove on once you're there." He does the John Travolta finger point. *ERMAGERD, NO.*

I drag my hand down my face. "Madonna mia, Pop. No one says 'get your groove on.' You sound like a dinosaur."

"Hey!" he shouts playfully. "I'm not *that* old."

Elio giggles. "Yes, you are. Look at all those gray hairs!"

Pop raises his arms. "You think I'm a dinosaur? Fine. I'll velociraptor your behind, you little punk." He makes a clacking-hissing sound like one of the dinosaurs from *Jurassic Park*, his fingers hooking into claws. He high-knee runs at Elio and scoops him up. He shoves his face into Elio's stomach like he's eating him while he tickles his sides. Elio shrieks, cackling. "Stop! Stop!"

Pop stops. "Still think I'm a dinosaur?"

"No, no!" Elio inhales. "Put me down."

Pop sets Elio back on the floor. He adjusts his shirt, which rode up his back when he was chasing my brother. Then he looks at me. "So, I can count on you to be my helper Friday night?"

I don't want to, but it doesn't feel like a choice. But at least it'll mean I don't have to be around Will and June. I don't have to watch them dance and turn into heart-eye emojis over each other. I'll be where I'm supposed to be— with my pizzas.

"Fine," I say. "You've got yourself a deal."

Chapter 31

The rest of the week, every time June or Will bring up the dance, I've conveniently gotta leave or I serve up a different subject. They get on me about why I'm not going to the dance like everyone else, why I've gotta be in charge of pizza, but I grapevine away from their badgering each time. ("I'm already committed to helping Pop." "This'll be good for business." "I don't really like dances anyway.")

The spring dance is at four thirty on Friday afternoon, just long enough after the end of school for student council to get the cafetorium decked out in balloons and streamers. Pop and I arrive at five with thirty-five pizzas ranging from cheese to pepperoni to veggie. A little something for everyone. My classmates are shuffling side-to-side under spinning, rainbow lights when we walk in hefting cardboard boxes and bags of paper plates and napkins. I scope out the scene as we set up. Some kids got all dressed up, and a few went all-out with their makeup and hair. A whole bunch are in regular old street clothes. Pop and I are both wearing Mamma Gianna's T-shirts and jeans, so we really stand out.

Pop positions a stack of cardboard pizza boxes at the edge of a long table. "You sure you don't wanna go out there?" He places a table tent in front of them that says, "Mamma Gianna's Italian Sausage Pizza."

"Look at all these hungry mouths." I wave my hand at the swarm of students already lining up for complimentary slices. "You can't keep the hoard at bay on your own."

"Believe it or not," Pop chuckles, "I've taken on bigger challenges. If you change your mind, just know it's fine by me."

I hand an eighth grader a plate with two slices of extra cheese and direct her to the Parmesan and red pepper flakes at the end of the table. "I'm not changing my mind. This is way better than dancing."

But even as I say it, my head involuntarily gazes over the swaying bodies and helium laughter. The exact opposite of what I should do. Seeing June and Will together will send me spiraling. But the patron saint of junior high dances must be looking out for me because I don't spot them in the crowd.

But that protection is short-lived; Will and June appear in the pizza line a whopping two minutes after I convince myself I can get through the whole dance without coming face-to-face with them.

"Luca!" June's blond ringlets bounce as she bops to the beat. She's wearing eyeliner and shiny pink lip gloss. Instead of a dress, she's in a striped blouse with silver threads running through it, a purple skirt, and tights. "When did you get here? I didn't see you come in!"

That was the idea. "Just a little bit ago. We've been busy with the pizza."

Pop waves hello next to me.

"You should come hang with us," says Will. I've been carefully avoiding looking at him, but now it would be weird if I didn't. Seeing him next to June in his black T-shirt and jeans, his hair even more perfect than usual, I get as weird and squirmy as uncooked calamari.

Pop hands June a plate of pepperoni pizza. "I keep telling him he ca—"

"We're really busy," I say, cutting him off before he accidently forces me onto the dance floor and into the most awkward situation of my life. "You guys have fun, though."

"You sure?" June asks, lifting a slice to her mouth.

Will cocks his head, trying to catch my eye. "We're with a group of theater and band kids over there." He points toward the stage. "It's not like we're all, uh, couples or anything."

June swoops her arm under his and yanks him close to her, grinning. "Right. Not *everyone* is."

GAG. But I keep my upchuck down and pass Will a

plate—one slice of cheese, one slice of sausage. "Yeah, no. I'm good. I'll talk to you guys later, okay?"

"Suit yourself," says June. She yanks Will away, and he sort of fumbles, glancing back at me with a question-mark face. I ignore it, and he eventually gives up and follows June.

"You okay?" Pop asks as he opens a fresh box of cheese pizza.

"What? Yeah, I'm fine." I flash some teeth, then I serve the next kid in line. I don't want to talk about Will and June with Pop. It's embarrassing. I feel stupid that he can tell something's wrong with me. *I'm* not supposed to have problems. I'm supposed to have it together.

Pop doesn't push it, thank God, but I suspect it's mostly because we've got an endless line of chirping baby birds wanting more, more, more. We fall into a rhythm of taking orders and dishing out our famous (or soon-to-be famous) pizza.

Out of the corner of my eye, though, I can't help but keep tabs on June and Will. Turns out he was telling the truth; a big circle of artsy-fartsy kids dance near the front of the stage. No one dances *with* anyone in particular, not even Will and June. That makes me feel a little better.

It's like that for such a long time that I'm almost convinced I've got nothing to worry about. Maybe June and Will won't get couple-y or sappy. They're just two *friends* dancing.

No. Big. DEAL.

And then—BA DUM: a slow dance. The epitome of COUPLING. Peak ROMANCE vibes. My cold spaghetti tummy stirs. *No. No. NO.* I almost drop the plate of sausage pizza I'm handing to an eighth grader. My pulse speeds up as a few kids slowly, awkwardly pair up. A few sway near-but-not-*too*-near each other, like there's an invisible balloon between them. Fewer still put hands on shoulders. And a whole bunch more use this song as an excuse to check out the games set up in the gym.

But with fewer kids on the dance floor, I've got an even better view of June and Will. They didn't leave for the gym. They also ignore the invisible balloon rule, their hands draped over each other's shoulders. I want to look away, but I can't. My chest hurts. Will and June *do* like each other. I never had a shot at dancing with him the way June is right now. I fidget with the corner of an empty cardboard pizza box. They talk as they dance. It looks serious. Like they're telling each other about how they really feel. I look away, busying myself by breaking down a stack of empty boxes.

Smashing cardboard feels good. Really good.

After what feels like an eternity, the stupid song ends. June gives Will a quick hug, and then, as an upbeat, synthy song picks up, she lets him go and walks toward the gym. But he doesn't follow. Something isn't right. I toss a pummeled pizza box into the trash. Even in the dim lights and from a distance, I can tell June's upset. The way her head hangs, the slow gait of her walk. *Uh-oh*. If Will hurt her, I'm gonna go full Rage Mode. I don't care if I've got a crush on him. No one hurts my best friend.

But then Will is walking toward *me*. A dash of curiosity simmers into my anger. Ignoring the line of kids asking for seconds (or thirds), Will pokes his head between two girls and says, "Luca, can I, uh, talk to you?"

I zero in on the task at hand. Pizza to plate to kid. "I'm kinda busy right now."

"It won't take long," he says. Even with music blaring, I can tell his voice is kind of shaky. "It's important."

I glance at the cafetorium exit, wondering if June will reappear. She doesn't. "Is this about June?"

Will wiggles like he's gotta pee. "Just—can we talk over there?" He nods his chin toward the hallway.

I'm about to tell him no, but Pop takes the plate from my hand. "Go," he says. "I got this. Talk to your friend."

"But—"

"Luca, go. Be a kid."

I feel a flash of anger, but it's a different flavor. *Be a kid?* Pop (and Ma) are always asking me to act grown-up. I have. I do. So why does he get to decide when I get to "be a kid"? I don't want to be a kid. Not anymore. Being a kid is scary. Crushes and dances and not knowing what your friends are really thinking. I know pizza. I know how to help Pop. But

I don't know what to do about Will and June, especially if they're mad at each other again. What if I have to make a choice between the two of them? I won't do that. I *can't*.

But Pop literally shoves me away from the table, and I'm forced to follow Will out of the cafetorium to a bench by the locker banks. He sits down. I sit next to him. His knees angle toward me. Mine angle toward his. There's a triangle of air between us.

"So, what's up?" I ask, staring at my hands. "Did something happen with June?"

Will's left knee bounces. "No, I—I mean, kind of. It's—it's complicated. I, uh, I need to tell you something."

"I saw her leave," I say. "Do you not like her anymore?"

His knee bounces faster. "Not exactly." He takes a deep breath. "I like someone else. I mean, I've *always* liked someone else. Don't get me wrong, June's great, but I just went along with asking her to the dance because that's what she wanted . . . and that's what I thought *you* wanted."

"When did I ever say I wanted you to go to the dance with June?"

He rolls his eyes at me. "When I texted you about the dance. I was trying to tell you who I wanted to ask, but you cut me off and made it this whole thing. I didn't know what to do, so I went with it because . . ."

My hands grip the edge of the bench. "Because?"

"Because I was gonna ask *you*, you dork!"

My head snaps up. My heart stutters. Both eyebrows rise. I must've forgotten to clean my ears out this morning. "You were gonna ask *me*?"

He sits on his hands. "Yeah, you. I was thinking about it for weeks. About *you*. You're funny and smart and talented. You care about people more than anyone I've ever met. Other than my mom and Uncle Leon, no one has cared about me the way you do. Like, I don't come from a big family, but you welcomed me right into yours. You made me feel like I belong." His fingers comb through his hair. "I've liked you for a while now, but I didn't know how to tell you.

"When I texted you the other night, I was trying to figure out if you'd even want me to ask you, if you liked me like that, but then you hijacked the conversation and took it in a totally different direction, and I felt like I didn't have a choice but to ask June. I mean, after she got all weird about you and me hanging out, I only tried to be her friend because she matters to *you*. But then she and I became real friends, and things with her kept getting more . . . intense. At least for her. So during the slow dance, I told her the truth about how I feel about you."

"That's why she left," I say, starting to realize what an idiot I've been. *I* put Will in that terrible position. *I* got June hurt. "This is all my fault."

"Luca, don't do that. You're always blaming yourself for

things. It's not your fault." He scoots closer. "Look, June was sad, not mad. But this isn't about her right now. One of my favorite things about you is how much you care, but you almost care too much. In cooking class, with me and June, even with your family. I've seen you do it. Sometimes I wonder—I don't know—if you, like, need to take better care of yourself. You know? And maybe—maybe let other people care about you. I want to do that, if you'll let me."

My ears ignite. *I need to take better care of myself.* Ugh. I think he's right. I hardly ever think about what will make me happy. Not really. Getting on *Pizza Perfect*, meeting Travis Parker—all that made me happy, but it wasn't for me. It was for my family. For the restaurant. But what *do* I want? What's just for me?

Will makes me feel brave and that makes me feel safe. Safe enough to finally say the truth I buried inside. I take a deep breath. "You're right. I wanted to go to the dance with you. I've liked you for a long, *long* time. And I—" Wow, saying this is hard. "I *do* need to take better care of myself. And I'm not very good at letting people take care of me. But I'd like you to try."

Will scoots closer. "Really?"

"Really." I smile, tingling from the back of my neck down to my toes.

He grins. He eyes the spiral of yellow-green-blue lights coming from the cafetorium. "The dance isn't over yet."

"But I've got the pizza—"

Will leaps up. "Luca, stop! Your dad's fine. Dance with me. It doesn't have to be a *thing*, but, like . . ."

I taste-test the idea. I imagine us dancing together. An espresso shot of adrenaline and warmth rockets through me. He's right. Pop will be fine. I *do* want to dance. And I'm tired of telling myself no.

I push myself off the bench. "One song."

He grins. "Really? Okay!"

I follow him past the pizza table (totally avoiding Pop's stare) to the front of the cafetorium near the stage, where the theater and band kids are dancing in a big circle. June's next to Anya and some other kids from the musical. I'm nervous she'll be mad, seeing me with Will, but she smiles. I smile back. Slowly, I dance to the beat, one foot at a time, until my whole body is grooving and shaking and swaying along with everyone else. Someone starts that scuba-diving move and then we're all pushing shopping carts and flashing cat's eyes. We look ridiculous, but it's fun. Will and I dance closer to each other. His black eyes sparkle in the yellow, green, blue lights. I think about what he said on the bench. How he's shown up for me when I needed help at the restaurant. The way he reminds me to just have fun and play video games. How he really hears what I'm saying. *I wonder if you need to take better care of yourself.* He sees me in a way other people don't. Not even my own parents or my best friend have ever called me out on caring too much. They all rely on me to do exactly that. But maybe Will's right. Maybe I should care a little less about other people and a little more about me.

As our one agreed-upon song ends and another begins, I don't stop dancing. I don't want to. This feels like caring about me. Not Pop. Not the pizza station. I'm having fun dancing with a boy I've had a crush on for MONTHS. This is just for me. Not for my family. Not for Mamma Gianna's. Not even for Will, if I'm being honest. And this almost didn't happen because *I* got in my own way. I tried to make my friends happy, but I just made everything worse for all of us.

And I realize . . . I've been doing this my whole life. And, maybe, I've been keeping myself and others from being truly happy because I thought I knew what was right when maybe I *don't*. *Oh God*. That's an awful thought.

But maybe that's the truth about relationships that are like triangles: they don't work. One person can't control what happens with or for other people because one person *can't* have ALL the answers. We've all gotta decide what we want and need for ourselves, even if it seems, at first, like someone might get hurt because of what they choose to do.

Will shimmies closer to me with a finger in his mouth like a fishhook. I reel him in. He looks like a total dope, but I probably do too. (Scratch that. I *definitely* do.) But I don't care because we're laughing, and this is fun. It's not work. It's not saving my family or my parents' marriage or the business. It's light and good and easy. It's what I imagine being a kid is supposed to be like. It's a feeling I forgot, or maybe never really let myself feel because I've always been the oldest kid, the reliable one, the Salvatore who gets stuff done.

But I like this feeling. It's a slice of bliss, and now that I've tasted it, I don't ever want to let it go.

Chapter 32

The thing about slices is that they end much too quickly. You wanna gobble up another one, but if you eat a whole pizza's worth of anything, you're gonna upchuck all over your sneakers. As much as it sucks when they announce the final song of the dance, I'm not heartbroken. This was enough of a taste of being just me, just a kid, to realize what I've been missing. But I can't let myself feel this good without fixing a problem I made first.

When the rainbow lights go dark and the harsh fluorescents come on, I pull June aside. We'd danced around each other like I didn't ruin her night, but invisible tension presses between us like we're magnets with the same charge. I can't let her leave without one-on-one BFC time. Before she can talk, I blurt, "I owe you an apology. I messed up big-time with Will. I'm really, *really* sorry."

Her arms cross. Her nose wrinkles. She nods. "Not gonna lie, tonight kind of sucked. I mean, I'm not like *devastated* because I won't let a boy do that to me, but it's still, you know, disappointing." She huffs, arms falling to her sides. "Honestly, it's not even Will I'm most upset about. It's you. It's *me*."

I make a what-the-what face and hold up a hand. "*You* didn't do anything wrong. *I'm* the one who told Will to ask you to the dance. I should've told him how I really feel."

"And *I* should've realized you liked him," June says with a sigh. "I mean, it was obvious you had a crush, but I ignored it because I had a crush on him too." She twists uncomfortably on her left leg. "And I hate to admit this but part of me thought, because I'm a girl, that of course he'd like *me* instead of you. Which is awful. Even homophobic, now that I say it out loud, which makes me legit sick to my stomach. I guess what I'm saying is, I should've asked how *you* were feeling. I shouldn't have assumed, especially since he was your friend first. I'm really sorry, Luca."

UM, plot twist! I wasn't expecting *my* apology to turn into *getting* an apology. I hadn't even thought about it that way, but HELLO, LUCA. This is exactly what Will (and Travis Parker) are saying. Other people's happiness always comes first, so I don't even realize it when my best friend isn't being the best friend she can be to me.

"Obviously I forgive you," I say quickly. "But I'm still sorry too. This whole thing turned into a big mess. You're my best friend. I never want to hurt you. Can we promise we'll tell each other the truth from now on, even if it might hurt?"

"You're my best friend too." She sniffs. "Yeah. Only the truth from now on."

I give her small smile. "Hug?"

She cocoons me in her arms. I sink my chin into her neck. We squeeze each other. Then we say goodbye because I still gotta help Pop clean up and I want to say goodbye to Will.

He waits for me by the water fountains. "Is June okay?"

"Yeah," I say. "We had a good talk. Are you okay?"

Will scuffs his shoe on the linoleum. "I feel a little bad, but I'm all right." Then he smiles. "Actually, I'm great. I didn't think I'd get to dance with you."

Marshmallowy joy heaps in my chest. "Me either."

"Is it weird if I hug you?"

"Not weird."

I hug him. A two-arm, chest-to-chest, five-four-three-two-one hug that leaves me a little breathless. Then we say goodbye, and I hightail it back to Pop while Will heads out to find his mom's car in the pickup line.

Pop smirks, eyebrows wiggling. "Soooooooooooooo . . . You have a good time?"

"Oh my GOD, don't EVEN," I say, trying to play it cool and totally failing because I'm sure I'm a cherry tomato. Obviously Pop saw everything. *Madonna mia, this is embarrassing.*

We quickly pack up, and the whole time I avoid looking Pop in the eye because I'm reliving every moment I was on the dance floor with Will. Relishing that electric buzz. The pulse of the music. No matter how I try to control my face, I can't keep from smiling, and I know Pop'll notice. I'm such a dork.

When we're back in our minivan, though, there *is* something I want to talk to Pop about. "Can I ask you something? About Ma?"

He sits up a little taller. "Uh, sure."

"Are you . . . happier not being around her all the time?" I ask.

Pop scratches the back of his head. He squints out the rear window as he backs out of the parking space. "It's complicated, Luca. I—I'm not sure."

I nod. "I want you to be happy. Ma too. I've been pretty upset about the separation, you moving out and all that. It sucks."

"I know, bud," says Pop, switching the gearshift into drive. "I'm really sorry."

I pull my left leg under my butt, so I'm a little taller in the passenger seat. "I really am sorry I sprang that date on you and Ma while Travis Parker was here." Travis Parker's voice echoes in my brain. "I thought I was helping, but I—I can't control what happens with you and Ma. I hate that I can't keep you together."

Pop brakes at a red light. "Keep us together? Kiddo, did you think you could do that?"

"For a while." I shrug. "Yeah."

Pop shakes his head. "I'm sorry. I—I didn't realize just how much this was affecting you. You're always so stoic. I feel like an idiot. *Of course* it's affecting you." He reaches over and squeezes my shoulder. "You're right. You can't fix our marriage. You can't keep your mother and I together."

"But you and Ma," I say, "you've always come to me with your problems. About each other. The restaurant. Nina and Elio. I thought I could help like I have before. But everything I've tried hasn't worked."

Pop nods slowly. "We do do that, don't we?"

I nod. "Yeah. A lot."

We're real quiet for a while. The light turns green. Pop drives. I watch the white lines on the asphalt pass by. I worry I said the wrong thing. Or too much. I didn't mean to upset him.

But when we turn onto our street—well, *my* street—he clears his throat and says, "Luca, I'm gonna talk to your mother about how we treat you. The more I think about it, the more I realize what a tough spot we've put you in, especially the past few years. We've gotten so caught up in the restaurant and our marriage that we've depended on you for too much." He thumbs his nose. "Watching you dance tonight, seeing you with your friends—I can't remember the last time I saw you just be a kid. That's my fault. Your mom's too. We've put all this pressure on you to be older than you are, but you're only twelve. You shouldn't have to worry about money or businesses or marriages." His voice cracks. "I—I'm really sorry, bud."

"It's okay," I say. I don't want him to be sad, but it feels really good to hear him say all that. I didn't realize how badly I needed that.

But he shakes his head. "It's not okay. You don't have to make me feel better about it. It's okay for your mom and I not to be okay."

I nod. My gut says I should soothe him. (How do I turn off this fixing-people setting?!) But I don't. I hear what he's saying: I don't have to fix this. Pop can take care of himself. And I can let him help me because something *is* wrong with me. He can be my dad, and I can be his son. So I simply say, "Thanks."

"I love you, Luca," he says. "More than air. More than life itself."

"I love you too," I say. My leg slides out from under me. I sit a little easier in the seat.

When we get home, he follows me inside the house. He pulls Ma into the kitchen, and they talk for a long time while I wait in my bedroom. Familiar worries and thoughts gather like storm clouds in my head. They come in an hour later, like they've done so many times before, and my instinct is to seek shelter or, at the very least, grab my umbrella. But instead of pelting me with a hailstorm of their frustrations, they apologize. Over and over and over. They tell me how proud they are of me and how sorry they are for asking too much of me.

"I forgive you," I say at last. "Really."

"Your father and I," Ma says, taking Pop's hand in hers. "We don't know what's going to happen with us, but we can commit to you, Luca, that we'll put a stop to how we treat you. We won't put our baggage on you anymore. We'll do our best to let you be a kid."

"We'll make *sure* you get to be a kid," says Pop.

"Right," says Ma. "See? I'm still having trouble. You're father's right. We'll force you to be a kid, even if you don't like it. Capisce?"

A small laugh escapes me. "Capisce."

Then they kiss me on each cheek and say good night. I cozy into my pillow, breathing deeply through my nose. Maybe I can't fix my parents, but I can do something for myself. I can stop putting everyone first. I can slow down. I can be twelve with twelve-year-old-sized problems.

As my eyes close, I have one final epiphany for the night: I was just part of a healthy, solid triangle. Me, Ma, and Pop. Three people coming together, each one holding their own weight, loving each other into the shape they were always meant to be.

PIZZA PERFECT

Reality • TV-PG • 7 Seasons ★★★★

Join Travis Parker as he visits pizza joints across America in search of the perfect slice.

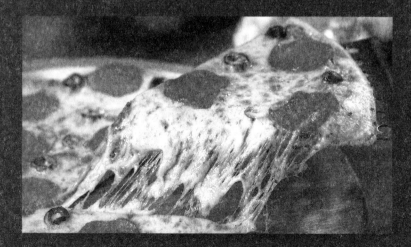

S7 E8 • **Mamma Gianna's**

Dough

No one likes a soggy bottom, especially when it comes to pizza. If the crust is undercooked, the pizza flops like bologna. If it's too crunchy, you'll crack a tooth. And with all the deliciousness a pizza dough's gotta carry, the foundation's gotta be solid.

Mamma Gianna's foundation—heck, the Salvatore foundation—had pretty much disintegrated by the time Travis Parker arrived. I knew things at the restaurant weren't great, but ever since TP awarded us those big bucks in April, I noticed just how rough we were looking. The more we revamp Mamma Gianna's back to her golden days, the more I see just how much our family drama and financial problems got in the way. The restaurant I thought was so awesome was really messed up, but I couldn't see how bad things had gotten because of our giant Salvatore mess. It's like I was so caught up staring at the flames that I missed that the whole freaking house was on fire.

Now we've replaced broken furniture and touched up the mural with fresh paint. The front door's bell finally chimes when people barge in, clamoring for the Luca Specialty Pizza of the Week. We even hired two new employees, Marcus and Trina, to give Ma and Pop more time to expand the business *and* be around for me, Nina, and Elio. And they have been. I don't babysit the twins nearly as much, and I don't *have* to work at Mamma Gianna's the way I used to. In fact, I'm not allowed.

Ma pulled me aside on the first day of summer break. "We know you love the restaurant, Luca, but your father and I've been talking, and before you get too invested in working at the restaurant this summer, we decided something's gotta give if we're gonna commit to letting you be a kid."

Pop scratched under his nose. "Don't get us wrong, this is hard for us to say, but . . ."

"You're fired," said Ma. "With all the love in our hearts, you're canned."

At first, I was gutted. It felt like someone took all my organs and put them in a food processor. I told them they were being unfair. I told them I didn't want to be fired. I told them they were taking everything I am away from me.

And that's when it hit me: maybe I *am* more than pizza. Maybe I've been a one-note dish all this time, and I didn't realize it. Maybe my metaphorical restaurant had lost its luster too, and it was time to remodel myself from the inside out.

Don't be mistaken: I still make pizzas whenever I want, but now it's *only* when I want, which is still a heck of a lot. But I'm realizing more and more each day that who I was before Travis Parker came was an overkneaded dough of a boy. I was overworked and too tough for my own good.

It's the beginning of July now, and business is booming. Ma and Pop's second chance to revitalize our restaurant has paid off, and it's only the beginning. Locals know about us, and in a couple more months, people all over the country—all over the *world*—will hear our story and see what the Salvatores are made of. And if there's a patron saint of pizza, our business will skyrocket even more.

Sauce

The best pizza sauce is robust, savory, not too thick, not too thin—but it can get everywhere if you're not careful. It's also what ties the whole pie together, gluing toppings to the dough. Without that messy splat smeared on the creamy canvas, the pizza wouldn't be complete. And if the foundation is good, it can handle a heavy dose of sauce.

As much as things are looking up for Mamma Gianna's, my family and I are still figuring out how to handle the sauce in our lives. My therapist tells me messy things usually get messier before they get better.

So, yeah, I guess that's another change. I started seeing a therapist in June, right after Ma and Pop fired me. I fought my parents on going to counseling before, but Will helped me understand that seeing a therapist is just another way of caring for myself. (He sees one too.)

Turns out I'm not so good at letting go of control. When Ma and Pop told me my only job this summer was to be a kid, I felt weird. Then I felt lost. It was like my purpose, who I am, was taken from me. Who the heck is Luca Salvatore if he isn't working to keep his family and their business afloat? I didn't know. And that sucked. So I felt sad and more worried than ever. Now I see my therapist Deb once a week, and she's really helped.

It's August now, and I'm gladder than ever that I've got her to talk to. Even though Ma and Pop assured us the separation was temporary, they announced yesterday that they're filing for divorce. I'm angry. I'm sad. I'm confused. And I know I can't change their minds, but that doesn't stop me from feeling awful. Thankfully, Deb's like a journal. I can pour my guts out to her but my hand never cramps. (I've got a lot to say, so she's saving me plenty of pain.) Deb doesn't try to fix me or tell me what to do. She asks questions. She makes me find my own answers. Then, she helps me better understand what I'm feeling and why. It sounds silly, but I never knew people could help each other without taking over.

It's taken me weeks, but now I honestly believe I never could do anything to fix or save my parents' marriage. And I believe they did everything they could to make their marriage work. Our family looks different now, but we're still a family. Don't get me wrong—I'm still sad and hurt, but I don't feel guilty. I don't feel like it's my fault Ma and Pop aren't staying together. Each day gets a little easier as we figure out the new shape our family is taking.

Toppings

People appreciate a crunchy crust or a zesty sauce, but what gets most people pumped are toppings. Endless combinations. Limitless possibilities. Infinite choices. And the best part is that if one topping doesn't work, you can try something else. Toppings keep pizza evolving and exciting. If dough makes me look to the past and sauce is the present, toppings are the future.

Somehow, the future catches up to us, and suddenly it's the first Friday in September. Ever since Travis Parker walked out our door, we've been prepping and planning for this day—the day our lives change forever (. . . again). Tonight is the premiere of the final season of *Pizza Perfect*. All eight episodes, including ours, are available to stream, and we're throwing one heck of a party at Mamma Gianna's to celebrate.

I'm in the kitchen at our new prep station, next to our new oven, making specialty pizzas to commemorate the event. This Luca original is a veggie pie made with red, orange, yellow, and green bell peppers, purple onions, and blue cheese crumbles. Each veggie is chopped up real small, so it looks like rainbow confetti. I'm calling it Luca's Celebration Pizza.

"How's it coming?" Ma adjusts one of her gold hoop earrings. "You ready for us to open in ten?"

I drizzle another handful of blue cheese over my last Celebration Pizza. "Ready as I'll ever be. It's gonna be weird watching *ourselves* on TV!"

Ma grins. "Pretty surreal. Now, why don't you clean up and come out? June and Will just got here. You should grab a spot with them before it gets too busy."

I wipe my hands on my apron, hang it on a hook, and dash into the dining room. Will, June, and I snag a booth with a view of the massive TV Ma and Pop ordered for the restaurant. It's mounted so you can see it from anywhere in the eating area. We usually put on football or baseball, but tonight everything is about pizza. *Our* pizza.

My friends and I grew taller over the summer. A little more meat clings to our bones, but our faces are longer, thinner. More grown-up. Bodies are weird.

"OMG. Are you nervous?" June asks from across the booth. She and Will are in Mamma Gianna's T-shirts as part of our ultimate fan club. Her hair is pulled back in a ponytail, one strand of her bangs dyed purple. She and her theater friends started experimenting with hair colors over the summer. I'm a fan.

"A little," I say. "It was bananas when we filmed—you had front row seats to the chaos—but we haven't seen any of the episode yet. I have no idea what they put together."

"Eek," says Will next to me. His hair is new too—a faded buzz on the sides and long on top. He combs it up and a little off to the right in an ebony wave. He's gotten a lot taller too—taller than me. Faint lines define the newly expanding muscles in his arms. I try not to stare.

"That'd make me super nervous." His hand nuzzles into mine. I squeeze it. I like how his palm feels. Warm and so freaking soft. He smiles. "You're totally gonna rock this."

Will and I officially started going out this summer, and it's been awesome, but it hasn't changed much about how we act around each other. We still play a lot of video games and eat homemade cookies. But now we hold hands too. And we hug. A lot. We still haven't *kissed*, but maybe now that we're in eighth grade . . .

More customers pour in, and I'm forced to stop thinking about what Will White's lips would feel like on mine. Gramma Salvatore arrives with the twins. While she and I might always be crunchy because of how much she still complains about Ma, things between me, Nina, and Elio have gotten a lot better. We've started becoming . . . *friends*? I never thought I'd say that about my little brother and sister, but this summer I didn't have to be their parent. Turns out Nina is really funny, and Elio is a better listener than I ever gave him credit for. It's been nice being on their team, instead of acting like their coach.

I invite Nina and Elio to sit with us. They scoot in beside

June. She and Nina immediately chatter about June's next hair color. Elio pulls out the iPad and flips through his latest photoshoot of his hermit crab, Baxter. (He finally saved up enough allowance in June. Turns out, he's a natural caretaker. Gets it from his older brother.) Will and I *ooo* and *ahh* at each photo. I squeeze Will's hand under the table because it means so much to me that he's kind to the twins and that he's like, *real*, about it. He isn't kind because he thinks he should be or because he thinks he's gotta be. It's just who he is, which is one of my favorite things about him.

The restaurant fills up more and more. June's parents and Will's mom take up another table. Even Mrs. Ochoa, our Culinary Arts teacher, and her family come. Marcus seats patrons. Trina and Ma take orders, making sure everyone knows about my exclusive, limited-time Celebration Pizza. Pop and Cesar fire pies in the kitchen. The restaurant is full within twenty minutes and there's still a line out the door. Good thing the night air is warm and welcoming.

When our final guest of honor arrives, I leap from the booth, with Nina and Elio in my wake. We attack the olive-skinned woman with big, wispy, gray hair, beach clothes, and palm tree sunglasses.

"You're here!" I shout, wrapping my arms around Nonna Zaza. She smells like coconut and sea salt.

She squeezes me, smacking my cheek with a wet kiss. I'm so happy to see her, I don't even get embarrassed that she left a lipstick mark so thick on my cheek that I can feel it. "You think I'd miss this?" she says, taking in the tidy restaurant. "Madone. Look at this place." She dabs her eye. "Your great-grandma Gianna would be so proud. You did good, Luca. Molto bene."

I pull Nina and Elio under my wings. "We *all* did this. Nina and Elio too."

They gaze up at Nonna Zaza bashfully. She kisses the tops of the twins' heads, but she winks at me, like we're in on a secret. "Of course, of course."

She hasn't been around to know that it's not the Luca show anymore. The Salvatores are a team now, even if our captains live in different homes.

But I'll have to explain that to her later. At six o'clock sharp, when everyone has their pizzas and drinks, Ma cues up the Mamma Gianna's episode of *Pizza Perfect*, which just so happens to be the final episode of the season. Our story ends the whole show. My stomach gurgles. That feels big. Important.

Will scoots closer when the opening title appears. His smooth arm sparks invisible static against mine. Travis Parker's voice picks up over footage of Chicago streets and buildings: "For the final course of *Pizza Perfect* we're serving up an extra special order of za delivered straight from Chicago, Illinois, home of the deep-dish pizza but, more important, home of Mamma Gianna's, a family-owned joint run by the incomparable Salvatore family."

Everyone hoots and hollers, myself included, as the B-roll shows the front of our restaurant, panning over the mural, our kitchen, and then Ma, Pop, Nina, Elio, and me waving at the camera. I sink lower into the booth. It's SO weird seeing myself on-screen. I look so much younger than the person I see in the mirror today, and it hasn't even been a year! It's weird that the version of me thousands of people will get to know isn't the Luca I am today.

The episode takes us through that week, starting with the "Dough" segment. Travis Parker tours our restaurant and tries our pizzas. He shops with Ma at the grocery, and they talk about the history of our family. He walks with Pop through a department store as they talk about the merits of different refrigerators. Whoever edited this episode made us seem way more put together than we were, and that makes me worried for the "Sauce" segment when things usually get . . . complicated and Travis Parker airs out the less-flattering side of the business. It starts with footage of Ma and TP discussing finances and how hard it's been to maintain the legacy of Great-Grandma Gianna. That segues into the heart-to-heart I had with Travis Parker when I was rage making that pizza. I didn't even realize they'd filmed any of him talking to me. It's hard not to turn beet red when I hear my voice. *Why do I sound like a mouse?* I sink lower into the booth.

Then the episode gets to the moment I've been dreading: the mega-fail first-date re-creation Nina, Elio, and I concocted for Ma and Pop. I didn't realize I was biting my fingernails. I stop when Will reaches for my hand. He gives me a face that says, "It'll be okay," and I believe him, but I'm still anxious.

I audibly sigh when the scene ends. They edit the whole date debacle into something sweet, completely leaving out the part where Ma bolts and everything was the worst. They make it seem like a success. I feel weird that the scene is a lie, and that makes me wonder about just how much we see on shows—even *Pizza Perfect*—isn't true, which makes me uncomfortable, but I'm also relieved they don't show what really happened to the entire world.

The episode goes on, taking us to the "Toppings." Right after the date scene, there's a close-up of me making that arancini pizza. It's weird how much of the episode is out of order, but the story of it all makes sense. Travis Parker narrates over the footage of my hands kneading the dough, stirring the bowl of saffron rice, grating the Parmesan. I sit up a little taller. *This* is the exact moment I've dreamed of my whole life. TRAVIS PARKER IS TALKING ABOUT ME AND MY PIZZA! AHHHHH!!!!

I'm proud of that pizza, especially since it won us so much money, but I think about how no one will know what I was feeling in that moment. How that pizza took all my rage and frustration and became something beautiful.

On-screen, it looks like I'm having the time of my life—no one would ever know I was upset. Seeing the footage, thinking about everything I've shared with Deb, how many times I said I was "fine" or agreed to help when it was hurting me, watching it back, it hits harder than ever that I can never go back to putting on a show.

Travis Parker's voice-over says, "While Mamma Gianna's has a lot going for it, the secret ingredient that keeps this remarkable pizzeria fresh is this kid here. Meet Luca Salvatore, the twelve-year-old pizza maker who's gonna change the pizza game. Mark my words. Not only is Luca a top-notch chef, he's also got a heart of gold. The moment I met him, I knew I'd encountered greatness. His passion for pizza is infectious. While I was visiting, he came up with some truly ingenious recipes, including this mouthwatering arancini pizza—a za he whipped up out of thin air. And, mamma mia, did it blow me away! I had no idea the Windy City was hiding this kinda talent!"

The voice-over stops. My whole face is a furnace. A title graphic appears with spinning letters: "Pizza Perfect Challenge." The scene cuts to footage of Travis Parker biting into a steaming piece of the arancini pizza, instead of the one Ma fed him. The camera zooms in on his outrageous grin. While he's saying his signature pizza perfect line about *my* pizza, everyone in Mamma Gianna's whoops and cheers for me. My face legit hurts my smile is so big. I've never been this proud of anything. It feels amazing.

Travis Parker's voice-over starts up again over footage of me in the kitchen. "I was personally struck by Luca's talent and heart because he reminded me so much of myself when I was his age. I've never met another young chef like him. He lights up as much as I do when we talk about the trifecta of dough, sauce, and toppings. Keep it up, Luca. Never stop chasing your joy."

My face is wet. Everything is blurry. Mamma mia—I'm crying. *UGH. I wasn't expecting THIS.* But it's happening, and there's no stopping it. I don't want to stop. This is how I really feel. Travis Parker, my food hero, just said all of that about me. ME. Luca Salvatore.

Not because I fixed my family. Not because I saved our restaurant. Not because I helped my friends. But because I was doing what I love.

I wipe my eyes dry with the hand Will isn't holding. I look around the restaurant, at all these people I care about. My teachers, my friends. Will and June. Gramma Salvatore. Nonna Zaza. Nina and Elio. Ma and Pop. I couldn't fix everything, but I've fixed the only thing I can: me.

Pizza Perfect Challenge

It's early fall. The sun is setting earlier, and the wind is getting crisper. Instead of just a T-shirt, I wear a zip-up on my way to the park the second Saturday in October. I kick tangerine, crimson, and goldenrod leaves off the sidewalk, picking up one or two standouts that are too vibrant to be real.

I find Will sitting on a park bench, acoustic guitar in his lap. He's wearing an orange pullover hoodie, black skinny jeans, and neon-green high-top Converse. Cute and cool as ever. And he's so effortless about it. Totally unfair.

"Waiting for someone?" I say.

"Hey there." He scooches to the left, making just enough room for me. "Your mom okay with you not being at Mamma Gianna's? I know it's—"

I pull my sleeves over my hands. "Yep. They'll be fine."

And they will be, and even if they aren't, Ma will figure it out. She's smart. She's capable. And she's got all the help she needs.

"Good," says Will. "I wanna play you a song I've been working on. My first original."

I almost fall off the bench. "I didn't know you *wrote* your own music too! DUDE!"

"It's not that big a deal. I mean, it's not that good, but—"

"Just play it for me!"

He laughs. "All right, all right!" He clears his throat, adjusts his fingers on the strings. Then he strums the start of a bright, upbeat ballad that sounds the way skipping feels. A very different Will White vibe than I'm used to, but I'm here for it. And then he sings, and I melt.

There's a boy at the register
With pizza sauce on his shirt
He doesn't know I'm here
But heck—I'm gonna flirt

I'm dead. I'm dying. My boyfriend—my *boy*friend— wrote a song about *me*. And he's singing it to me. Right now. In public. I'M. DEAD. How is this my life?

He's all caught up in triangles
Slicing and dicing to make that dough
But one glance from me wrangles
That pizza boy to my muscle show

He stops singing to display his right bicep. I bust out laughing. Even when he makes a muscle, it's not big. But I do like his arms. Then he strums again and sings the chorus.

Because pizza boy makes me cheese
With his mozzarella-white teeth
And pizza boy quakes my knees
With his "May I take your order, please?"
Oh, pizza boy—won't you go on a date with me?

He sings the chorus again, and then slowly strums to a stop. "It's not finished yet, but yeah, I just wanted to play that. So, uh, what do you think?"

I think so many things all at once. "One: that was amazing. You are *so* talented."

He shrugs. "You don't have to say that just because, you know, we're a thing."

I shove him. "I'm not! And two: I can't believe you wrote that about me."

"Oh. This is awkward. So, uh, this was actually about a *different* pizza-obsessed boy I know. So . . ."

I shove him harder, laughing. "You're such a dweeb."

He laughs, hugging the guitar. "Watch the gear, man! If I scratch this, Uncle Leon's gonna kill me."

I hold my hands up. "Fine, fine." I sit on my hands to prove he's safe. "But seriously, that was incredible. No one's ever done something like that for me."

He looks me in the eye. "You make me want to do nice things for you."

My tongue goes dry, but I want to say something. Deb

would tell me it's best to be honest, to put myself out there. So I do.

"I've never done this before, but, uh, I kinda want to, uh—well, I don't know if you want to, but I . . ." *Madonna mia.* I drag my hands down my face. "Oh hell. Can I kiss you, Will White?"

His eyes widen. His lips press into a thin, nervous line. I'm afraid he's gonna bolt, but then he says, "I'd like that, Luca Salvatore. But I've never done this either."

"Okay," I say, nodding. *Omgomgomg.*

"Okay," Will echoes.

Then our heads are leaning in. I close my eyes. I hold my breath. I press my lips together and go for it. It's quick, but the phantom zing of his soft lips on mine tingles like buffalo sauce. I can't stop smiling. Neither can Will.

"I just kissed a boy," I say, my thoughts spilling out.

"That's funny," Will laughs. "I just did too. I liked it."

I grab his hand. "Me too."

We sit on the park bench for a while holding hands and brainstorming lyrics to the rest of Will's song. We laugh. We talk. I've never been happier.

This moment, between just me and Will, with the sun sinking behind buildings and trees and swing sets, feels just as good as the moment Travis Parker told us we'd won $50,000. Maybe even better. And for the first time in my life, I feel like I'm getting a taste of a real piece of perfect.

Acknowledgments

This story is a triangle-shaped piece of my heart, and I'm grateful to so many for helping it become a fully realized book. First and foremost, thank you to my fabulous agent, Sara Crowe, and the team at Sara Crowe Literary for championing me and my work.

My deepest appreciation to the crew at HarperCollins for putting this book on the menu for readers. I especially want to thank my two outstanding editors, Stephanie Stein and Elizabeth Agyemang. You both brought such clarity and life to this story. A special thank you to Ariel Vittori for another delicious cover, and Corina Lupp for the gorgeous design.

I owe so much to my writing community for all the care and kindness they've shown me, especially the Turth Machine, the Beverly Shores crew, and the Guardians of Literary Mischief, with a special shout-out to my massively talented critique partners and friends Sarah Willis and Adina King. You're the secret ingredients that make this story a chef's kiss!

Thank you to the educators, librarians, booksellers, and readers who have cheered me and my stories on. I hope Luca's story speaks to you, too. And I especially want to thank my youngest readers—*you* are the reason that I do what I do! Keep reading. Tell your stories. The world needs *you*.

Thank you to all my friends. Your light and goodness fuel me in ways you'll never fully comprehend. I couldn't do this work without you.

Last, and most important, I'm so grateful to my family for always standing by me. And thank you to Tim for being the best partner I could have ever dreamed of. I love you all very much.